SEIZING SHATTERED PROMISES

THE ERASEHER SERIES BOOK FIVE

SARA NICHOL QUINCY

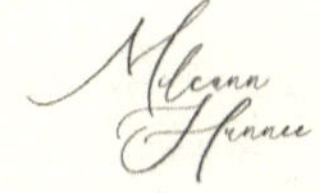

First published by Milcann Hunnee 2022

ISBN: 978-1-957719-08-5 (Epub)

ISBN: 978-1-957719–09-2 (Paperback)

ISBN: 978-1-957719-14-6 (Hardcover)

SaraNicholQuincy.com

Milcann Hunnee

PUBLISHING COMPANY

For Phoenix

The scared little girl that I locked up in a dark place in my mind for so many years because I thought I hated you and that you would never be good enough. I was wrong; you've achieved more than I could have ever imagined and I'm sorry. You are enough; you have always been. This is for you beautiful, be free. I'm proud of you!

CONTENTS

I

HORSEMEN

"Baby, I know it might be tempting, but remember when we get to Mom's, you can't tell anyone about who you really are just yet."

"I know. I heard what Dad said… It's for my safety… yada, yada… whatever." I couldn't help but say it sarcastically as I stared out the car window. I figured everyone at this point could see that I could take care of myself, but apparently both Dad and Jake still thought I needed a protection detail, until something was done about Miller, anyway. "Do you even know if he's still alive? Surely I maimed him at least, right?"

"Who? Miller?" Jake sounded confused, like he was having a hard time following my train of thought.

"Yeah! He's the reason Dad said I had to stay hidden for a while, right?" I assumed he was anyway, but I wasn't technically in on the last conversation Dad and Jake had about me, so I wasn't all that sure.

"Well, Miller's part of it, but no… It's to keep you safe from the Sicari, too. If they can infiltrate your dad's household enough to pretend to be his doctor, then we don't know what else they're capable of. For right now, we just need to do whatever it takes to keep you safe."

"Oh…" I said, thinking about what exactly that meant. "But I told you, the Sicari shouldn't be an issue anymore. With Reagan dead, I don't see a reason Parker would send men after me again now that she has the intel, too." I turned to look at him to see if he would accept that or not.

He took his right hand from the steering wheel and reached over to grab mine as he continued to drive. "Jayde, baby… I know you don't think you're in any danger. I get that, all right? But we just can't be too careful."

I quietly sighed to myself. I didn't want to argue with him and knew even if I tried, it wouldn't get me anywhere. "All right…" I said, then turned to watch out the window again. "By the way, I'd prefer if you went back to calling me Eva."

"Really?" He sounded surprised.

"Yeah… I feel like that's who I really am." I looked back over at him. "Why? What do you want to call me?"

"I'll call you Eva if that's what you want."

"Ok, but what name do *you* want?" He hadn't answered the question, so I thought I would repeat it.

He paused, like he was thinking about it. "I don't know… To be honest, it's kind of hard. I mean, each name seems like it's a different side of you."

"That's fair…" I let my eyes slowly gaze toward the floor as I thought about that. "So which side are you more attracted to, like I mean… am I, uh… which side of me is your *type*?"

"If I had a type that I'd say I'm generally more drawn to, it'd be Eva. Something about your fighting spirit and strong will call to me. In the past, if I think about it, all the women I've been with have been more like that. I never really was much for the sweet, timid kind… that was always Lane's type. Makes sense now… we never really liked the same girls growing up… I really like Kaleah, though. After all, Kaleah is who I fell in love with, but I've always been drawn to Eva. You having both sides I think just makes me love you that much more." He smiled. "With all that being said, Kaleah feels more special. I can't deny there's something about her that feels like she belongs to me."

"Not Eva?" I was intrigued.

"As far as belonging to me, no… not as much," he sounded like he was trying to be honest. "Eva is your independent side. She doesn't need me. You feel like you can protect yourself. That's how you act, anyway. Plus, that side of you is more stubborn…" He paused as he started to grin. "I mean, Eva's way more fun in other ways. I'll give you that." He said, finally looking over at me with an enormous smile.

"Ooh, ok, I get it. Angel by day, vixen at night… is that what you like?" I smirked.

"Something like that…" He said, then took his hand back to the wheel to make a sharp turn.

"Well, what side of me is Jayde then?"

"I don't guess I know yet. We'll just have to wait and see. Maybe she'll be the perfect blend of the other two… Besides, after we see your dad again and you get your Coldier tag, I'll probably have to call you Jayde, anyway. Not to mention once we're married, that'll be your official name… Jayde Miles."

"Jake and Jayde sittin' in a tree, k-i-s-s-s-i-n-g," I giggled, unable to help myself. "Jayde Miles… Hmmm… That does have a nice ring to it, doesn't it?"

Jake didn't respond, he just squinted his eyes like he was looking at something in the road up ahead. "What is that?"

"What is wha—" I turned to see what he was looking at when I suddenly recognized what it was. "Stop! Now!"

He did and quickly slowed the car down to a complete stop.

"They're horses… Sicari! Quick, turn around. We'll have to find a different way." I said, turning around to see how close the vehicles with the other agents in them were behind us.

"How many do you think there are?" Jake asked as he maneuvered the vehicle to turn it around.

"I don't know… They're too far away, I can't tell. Too many, I know that!" I said with a sense of urgency as I leaned forward to see them better. "It doesn't make sense, though. They never travel in groups that big. And why would they be this close to the city… We're almost to New York, right?" I asked, trying to make sense of it.

"Hang on, baby…" Jake said, too focused on turning the car around to address my questions. After a few moments and finally getting turned to drive the opposite way, I could see him breathe a sigh of relief.

"Where are the other agents? Weren't they right behind us?" I asked as I turned to look back to make sure the horses weren't following us.

"They were, but once we got close enough to the city, they split to go to the agency downtown. None of them were following us to my parents'." Jake said like he now regretted whoever made that decision —probably him.

"Oh…" I turned back to face front when I couldn't see the horses anymore.

"That's a problem…" He said, looking down at the gauges, thinking out loud.

"What?"

"That was the best way to get to my parents. I don't have enough gas to go all the way around."

"Okay?"

"It's not the plan I discussed with your father but now we'll either have to go to the agency or to Lane's." He said then paused. "Never mind, we're going to Lane's. Until you have your tag, I don't want you anywhere near the agency."

"All right." I understood where he was coming from, so I agreed. I also liked the idea of finally seeing Lane again, not Jake's mother, so no part of me was upset about this recent development.

"Why would that many Sicari be this far east?" Jake asked, assuming I knew.

"Uh…" I really wasn't sure, but I didn't want to tell him that. I didn't want him to assume it was because they were after me, so I intended to make something up. "Maybe they want to talk to Dad… you know, like to make some kind of agreement since they know both sides have the intel. Maybe they don't want another battle, like we don't want one."

Jake briefly took his eyes off the road to give me a look like he knew I was making shit up. "Eva…" He said, ready to call me on it. "The Sicari would never do that. You, of all people, should know that."

"Okay?" I said, stalling, trying to think of another reason without denying what he said.

"They're here for you…" He didn't give me a chance to come up with another alternative before he gave me his conclusion.

"No… that wouldn't even make sense. I told you, they—"

"We're gonna assume that's the reason for now." He said, cutting me off. "If one agent can take you from me in the middle of the city and one agent can infiltrate all the security perimeters of your father's, then I don't even wanna think about what a horde of agents could do."

"Well, would it still be safe at Lane's for me, then? I mean… that's how Reagan found me. Lane put my exfil name and his address on the new papers he made for me."

"Your exfil name?" Jake asked, turning briefly to give me a pointed look.

"Yeah, *Elliceva*… It was my exfil name for the Sicari. The name I'm supposed to use when I'm in danger and I need their help." I hoped I didn't get Lane in trouble telling him that since neither of us knew any better when he did it.

Jake didn't say anything for a second, he just went silent like he was thinking. "Eva?" He said finally.

"Yeah… what?"

"While we were at the cabin before we left for the grotto lands, you told me you wanted to be called Elliceva." His voice had hardened and tension now covered his face.

"Okay?" *Shit, why's he so upset?*

"Why would you do that… if you knew what that name meant?"

Ohhh… I suddenly realized what he was saying. "Um… I'm sorry." I thought I would start with that first. "To be honest, I didn't trust you yet. I thought you were probably working with Miller and just lying to me about it. It was like a backup plan for me."

"So you lied…" He said it solemnly, like my apology hadn't made him feel any better.

"Well, that was almost a year ago now, Jake… A lot has happened since then. I mean—"

"What else have you lied to me about?" He interrupted me.

"What?" I wasn't sure why he would still be so upset even after I just tried to explain it. "I don't know." I said, looking around like I was surprised by how he was acting. "Here recently, nothing! At the cabin though, yeah… I lied, but like I said, I'm sorry! I was Eva, a Sicari! You were a Coldier. One that I didn't know if I could trust because I had intel that I knew Miller wanted, and you just so happened to be working for him…" I paused to look at him to see how he was reacting but saw nothing, his face was stone cold. "Okay, fine, I didn't tell you I was Jayde, who my father was, or that I had a sister, but that's all. Happy?"

"That's not what I'm upset about. I understand why you wouldn't tell me about those things at first. But if you gave me that name, then you intended to go back to the Sicari."

"That's not true!" I thought I would set him straight before he took it and ran with it. "I never intended to go back to them after we left the cabin."

"Then why did you tell me to call you that name?" He asked with hints of anger still in his voice.

"Why are you so upset?" I could tell there was something deeper that was bothering him, and it wasn't that I gave him that name.

"How do I know what was real versus what wasn't? How much were you pretending?"

"You think I was pretending?" My voice cracked. It hurt to hear him say that.

"Yeah, I do." He said matter-of-factly, confident in his statement.

"Then you don't know me at all, Jacob." I said softly, then turned my head to watch out the window again, done with the conversation. We drove the rest of the way to Lane's in silence.

. . .

"I'm sorry." Jake finally broke the silence between us after he parked the car in the garage below Lane's apartment building.

"For what?" I could have assumed what, but I wanted to hear him say it.

"I just love you, baby, and the thought that there was a time that you might not have been genuine about loving me back…" He paused to roll his eyes up like he was feeling vulnerable and having a hard time thinking about what to say. "It's just… I can't handle that. I don't want a relationship like that."

I furrowed my brow, confused, not understanding where he was going with it. "Are you breaking up with me?"

His face quickly contorted to sheer shock at my response. "What? Hell no! I'm just trying to say sorry for… I don't know, whatever that was between us back there. I just didn't want you upset with me anymore so I was letting you know I'm not upset with you… that's all." He said it almost frantically, like wanting to break up was the last thing he had wanted me to take from what he'd said.

"Oh…"

He turned and rested his head back against the headrest and let out a deep breath as he let the tension release from his shoulders, probably happy to be done with that very intense moment. "Oh my gosh, baby," he said, closing his eyes for a second. "Don't do that to me…" He paused again. "I can't handle it."

I didn't say anything. I just reached over, grabbed his hand, and gave it a squeeze so he knew he was okay. He looked over and slowly smiled, then brought it up to his mouth to kiss the back of it.

"I never pretended to love you, Jake. If I said I did, then I did."

He nodded before kissing the back of my hand again. "Good…" He let out another long breath. "Are you ready to see Lane now?"

I smiled, then tilted my head like he was silly for even asking, "Yes!"

"All right, I'm sure he'll be happy to see that I have you back, too. He was pretty upset when I wouldn't let him come with me to help look for you. We've been gone long enough that his leg should be all healed up now."

"He's not expecting us is he?" I asked realizing he couldn't make phone calls from Nashville to New York so Jake wouldn't have been able to give him a heads up that we were on our way back, or that he'd even found me, for that matter.

"No… To be honest, now that you told me about your name and Lane's address being in the system like it is, I don't really like you being here either but I don't have anywhere else to take you for right now. This place is safer than Mom's or the agency, so it'll have to do. Until I can call your father and make better arrangements, that is." He said, as he opened his door to get out.

"I'm so excited." I smiled, thinking about seeing Lane. "I can't wait to tell him I have a sister. He's gonna be so happy!" I thought back to one of the last conversations we'd had when we were at the agency together.

"Eva, baby, you can't tell him… remember?" Jake said as he took his bags out of the backseat and walked around to me.

"What? Why not?" I asked, disappointed. "He's an agent… He needs to know. That way, he can help you protect me." I hoped saying those things would convince Jake it was a good idea. "Besides, he already knows about Reagan and that I'm a… you know…" I winked, so Jake got the idea.

"Believe me, I would like nothing better than to tell him everything. But your father gave me specific orders. *No one* is supposed to know yet. Not until we have a safe place for you to stay with adequate safety measures in place and plenty of agents to guard you."

"Geez, that sounds excessive." I said. All I could think about, though, was that I didn't have to follow orders that Dad gave Jake. He never ordered me to stay quiet. Besides, what was Dad really gonna do if I was the one who told Lane, rather than Jake? *Ground me?*

"It's not excessive when you consider how valuable you are. If you got taken again—" He stopped like it bothered him to say it. "I don't want to even think about it, baby."

I didn't say anything. I just nodded, showing I understood. He didn't have to continue; I got the idea and the more I thought about it, it actually did make sense. With what happened to Mom and how Miller treated me when he knew who I was, plus all the other reasons the Sicari might want me, I knew he was right. It was hard to accept, but the idea that I was wanted by everyone for all the wrong reasons was a good reason to have extra protection, even if I wasn't in love with the idea.

When we got into the elevator, I stepped forward and pushed the button for the 22nd floor, then stepped back and stood by Jake.

"I agreed not to tell anybody who you were, but that doesn't mean you can't." Jake said softly like he'd read my mind.

I smiled really big when I heard it. "Good, because I already thought that."

He chuckled, "I figured."

After a few moments, the elevator stopped, and Jake pushed a button to speak into the speaker. "Lane… It's Miles. You there?"

We didn't hear anything back but after a minute or so, the clicking sound of the elevator stopped and the doors opened. I was anxiously waiting to see Lane standing on the other side and see his expression when he saw I was back.

When the doors opened, there was no one standing there ready to greet us. Jake must have thought that was odd as well. He looked over at me with a perplexed look, then made a motion, wanting me to wait where I was while he went in to check it out.

"Lane?" He yelled out, when suddenly I heard Lane from the kitchen.

"Yeah, man… Sorry, I'm in here. Come on in. We're just having dinner."

Jake walked over and looked in, confirming it was all clear before he looked back at me and motioned for me to enter. Then suddenly he froze like he saw something he hadn't that he didn't like. "Lane, why is she here?" Jake scowled, then put his hand up, suggesting I didn't get closer to see who he was talking about.

"Miles. Man, it's good to see—"

"No, stay where you are… answer me." Jake interrupted him. His tone was nearly seething, making me definitely want to walk over and see who Lane was with.

"Miles…" Lane spoke again, wanting a chance to explain himself.

When Jake wasn't looking, I quickly walked over to stand next to him to see what he was seeing.

"Kaleah!" Lane's face froze. There were too many emotions suddenly blazing through his eyes for me to catch them all. It was obvious he hadn't expected to see me whatsoever. "Oh my God, Kaleah!" He said as he quickly set things down and turned to walk toward me like he was going to give me a hug, when suddenly sitting behind him I saw who Jake saw.

"What?" I felt my face harden. "Lane… why?"

Lane hadn't made it to me yet when he saw I was just as disapproving of his dinner guest as Jake was. "Kaleah… I can explain."

I didn't want him to explain. I didn't say anything else. I slowly shook my head, then turned to go back to the elevator when I felt him reach out for my hand. "Kaleah, please!"

I pulled it away as I turned back to address him. "No… I'm sorry we interrupted. Please… finish your dinner… pretend like I was never gone."

2

FOREIGN RELATIONS

"Eva… we gotta stay here." Jake whispered, reminding me we had no other choice. There wasn't a get back on the elevator and leave option. "If you want to sit on the couch, or go to his study, I'll talk to him."

I nodded, then looked over at Lane one more time before walking away toward the living room. He looked like a whipped puppy that was now ashamed of himself and what he'd done. I intentionally went to sit on a couch where I didn't have to see her, but could still hear the conversation.

"Lane, why's Katherine here?" Jake said loudly. It sounded like he had pulled Lane over toward the elevator to speak with him.

"Look man, I swear I didn't know you both were gonna be back—"

Jake didn't let him continue before he interrupted him. "But why is she here? Are you guys together now? Is that it?"

"No… ah… Miles, shit… it's complicated… After you left she came over here looking for you and… well… no, we're not seeing each other. I mean… like, we're not dating but… it's just… you guys were gone, and I was lonely, and worried sick and—"

"Lane…" Jake didn't sound like he wanted to hear any more.

"I'm sorry, man. I mean, I know how this looks. Shit… especially to Kaleah… Ugh…"

"We can come back if you want to finish your dinner with her, but either she needs to leave or Eva will have to. I can't have her and Eva in the same room." Jake started to give him an ultimatum, but before Lane had a chance to answer, I heard Kat speak like she'd walked in on them.

"Jacob, it's good to see you too…" She said sarcastically. "Don't worry about it Henry, I can go. I know when I'm not wanted somewhere."

"Kat… I'm sorry," Lane sounded conflicted.

"Lane, it's your house. I'm not asking you to kick her out, it's just… we won't be able to stay then."

"Why don't you just order your Gypsyin to leave? It's a shame you boys treat her like she's more than she is."

"Seriously, Katherine? Forget what I said. Get the hell out!" Jake growled. It didn't sound like he was willing to keep going with the—Lane's house, Lane's rules—game anymore after that comment of hers. I'm sure he was hoping I couldn't hear her, and probably scared of what I would do if I could.

"Yeah, Kat, you need to leave." Lane said suddenly, agreeing.

"Fine, but when you change your mind, Henry, you have my number. Maybe one of you will learn to value a *real* woman…" After a minute, I heard the elevator doors opening and then closing like she had left.

"Is this just something physical between you two or is it more than that?" Jake asked, probably still assuming I wasn't listening to their conversation.

"Miles, man… I… I know how this looks—"

"Look, I don't care what you're doing with her. That's your business. She's not my fiancée anymore. Hell, it's your house, your life, do whatever you want. It's a horrible idea… I wouldn't recommend it, but whatever. For right now, I have a different issue… the reason we're here in the first place."

"Kaleah?" Lane quickly guessed what Jake's issue might pertain to.

"Yeah, I can't explain it all to you right now. There's a lot going on, but she's in more danger than she was before, so we need to stay here. Just for the night should be enough. Then tomorrow, we'll leave—"

"Wait, you don't wanna stay longer than that? Why just for the night?" Lane interrupted. "Serious man, I want you both to stay here as long as you need. I can help keep her safe. I mean, I know last time we had a minor hiccup but, I know what not to do now."

"Look man, I appreciate it but…" Jake started then paused like he was thinking about how to tell Lane why only one night without telling him things he wasn't allowed to say.

"Do you think she's mad at me now? I mean, since she saw Kat was here with me?"

"Well, yeah! If I'm being honest, her being pissed is probably an understatement. She was really excited to see you, stupid! She's been talking about it ever since we left Nashville."

"Oh… she has?" Lane sounded upset with himself at the thought that I was upset with him. "Wait… Nashville?"

"Yeah, I know… A lot has happened the last month we've been gone. I've got a lot I need to tell you, too. I just gotta make sure she's somewhere safe first."

"Ok, I understand. You think she'd be willing to talk to me or…"

"You can go and see. Just don't get your feelings hurt if she's not in the mood right now."

"Okay," It sounded like Lane had started to walk closer. He began to pass the living room, walking toward his study, when he looked over and saw me on the couch. "Oh, uh, hey… I didn't realize you were in here…" I think he also just realized I had probably heard their entire conversation as well. Jake walked around and came into the living room with him when he heard where I was.

"Do you love her?" For whatever reason, I needed to know. If the answer was no, it would be easier for me to forgive him. The idea of him actually *loving* her and it being more than just something physical between them bothered me.

"What?" He inhaled sharply, taken aback by my assertive demeanor.

"Ugh…" Jake sighed, then scratched his head. "Lane, meet Eva… The *real* Eva."

Lane still looked shocked, but nodded toward Jake like he was trying to understand, even though he was obviously confused.

"You said you would explain it, so please, here I am… I would like for you to explain it now." I said as I leaned back, willing to listen.

"Um… well…" He started like he was thinking about the best way to say it, then he closed his eyes and nodded, willing to answer even if it would be hard. "Okay, no… I don't love her. It was all purely physical between us. Kaleah, that's honestly all it is, all it's been… I—"

"So you two *aren't* together, then?" I interrupted, hoping to make it easier on him.

"No!" He furrowed his brow, jerking back suddenly like he was offended at even the idea. "Of course not…"

"Then why are you even messing around with her?" I suspected the answer, but I wanted to hear it from him.

He squinted his eyes, trying to read me, with no luck. "Um, I… I don't know… She was here and after you were taken I was alone and upset… To be honest with you, it started when I got drunk and… I just didn't stop it, I guess." He sat down across from me as he said it. His shoulders relaxed and slumped forward a little. I could see he felt ashamed of himself and was remorseful.

"She tried to get me taken from Jake…" I knew he was already feeling guilty, but I still needed to vent. "You were there, Lane… I could have been erased, sterilized… I might not have ever seen Jake again, or you! And that's if they didn't realize the papers were counterfeit…" I paused and lowered my voice. "I'd have been hung, Lane… I didn't even do anything wrong and she…" I blinked back emotion I didn't even realize was beginning to boil up.

The way he looked at me suddenly was like he'd just woken up from a daze that had blinded him to how evil she was. "Kaleah… I'm so sorry… I really am. I was upset and desperate. I mean, I didn't know if I'd ever see you again. I didn't know what to do. I hadn't thought about any of that, I just—"

"Needed attention?"

He shrugged slightly like he knew that wasn't a good excuse, but it was the reason, nonetheless.

"Then go make friends, Lane!" As soon as the words came out of my mouth, Jake burst out laughing.

Lane, on the other hand, didn't seem to think it was as funny. "Dude… really?" He gave Jake a dirty look and waited for his laughter to subside. "Do you mind if I just talk to her alone? Please…"

Jake continued to grin, then looked over at me to make sure I was good with it. I nodded that I would be fine. "All right," he said, looking back at Lane. "I'll go to the kitchen for a minute. Maybe you got something in there I can eat that the cat hasn't contaminated."

After Jake slowly meandered off, Lane leaned forward again, avoiding eye contact with me. He stared off into space for a moment, like he was gathering his words, then finally looked back at me, ready to continue. "Kaleah… I know how this must look to you… and I… I just…" He didn't continue. He just leaned forward, rested his elbows on his knees, and put his head into his palms.

"If it was just physical, then why were you having dinner with her?" I asked softly. I didn't think he was lying, but I couldn't help but wonder about that part.

He looked up, then leaned back to rest against the couch. "I felt guilty…"

"About what?"

"Using her…" The way he said it, I could see he was being genuine, just as I had always known him to be. "I don't want you to think I've forgotten about you, though… that's what started this whole mess… I felt awful when Miles had to leave to go get you. You shouldn't have ever been taken, Kaleah! It was my fault. I let you both down, and it shouldn't have ever happened… I'm sorry! Honestly, I don't know what this whole thing with Kat has been… Deep down I think since she tried to hurt you I wanted to hurt her back. So when she came over, I used her for my own selfish needs… Then…" he shrugged, "then I felt guilty 'cause that's not me."

I didn't say anything for a moment as I thought about what he was saying, then I nodded. "I forgive you."

The look on his face when he heard me say it was a mix of relief and abatement of the guilt he'd been carrying. "Oh my gosh, thank you!" He said quickly as he got up to come sit on the couch next to me. "Come here," he leaned in for a hug. "I'm so glad you're back." He wrapped one arm around my waist and used the other to cradle my head and pull me toward him. "I really did miss you. I promise I won't let anything like that ever happen again."

"Ehh," I couldn't help but tense up when his hand at my waist squeezed a little too tight where the area I had been shot was still tender.

"What's wrong?" He leaned back to look at me like he could tell I wasn't acting normal.

"Nothing," I said, then looked over toward the kitchen to see if Jake was on his way back yet. "I just—"

"Are you hurt? What happened?" He looked down at my side, making a face like he had just realized we hadn't gotten a chance to tell him anything about what had happened while we were gone.

"Oh, it's… it's nothing, really…" I said, scooting back a little.

"She was shot!" Jake said suddenly, like he'd decided it was finally a good time to walk back in and rejoin the conversation.

Lane sucked in a sharp breath, with widened eyes as he looked from Jake back to me. "What? By who… Where?"

"It's a long story," I started to dismiss it again before Jake interrupted.

"By another Coldier agent… That's what I mean when I tell you she's in more danger than she was before, Lane. I'm not even sure I'm comfortable staying with her here for the night, but it's our only option right now, so it'll have to do."

Lane looked back at me, confused like he was hoping one of us would clear it up for him.

"Ugh, Jake… You're just confusing him… Lane," I said, gently putting my hand on his shoulder. "I'm not who you think I am… I'm—"

"Oh, right…" he interrupted. I was about to tell him I was Jayde when he acted like he already knew that I wasn't who I said I was. "I know, you're a Sicari… Or well… that's what that guy said you were, but I didn't believe him, Kaleah."

When he said that, I looked over at Jake. "Before you came to get me, did you not tell Lane who I was, or why I was taken?"

Jake was in the middle of taking a big bite of sandwich when I asked. He quickly choked it down to respond. "Uh, no! If I'm honest, I was a little pissed with him about the whole thing and how it happened. I made sure he was gonna be okay and got him to a hospital, then I came after you as soon as I could."

Lane looked away from Jake then kind of nodded to himself like he remembered that was pretty well the way it went.

"Ugh…" I rolled my eyes a little, seeing we had a lot more to clear up than I thought we did. "Lane," I said, getting his attention again. "What do you know about Jayde Prescott?"

He squinted his eyes, then quickly glanced over at Jake, curious where I was going with it. Jake, with another mouthful of food, just grunted as he gestured with his sandwich for Lane to answer me. "Um… I don't know anything other than that's the same last name as the First Rank… Is that like his wife or something?"

"It's his daughter…" I said cautiously, seeing how he'd react.

He didn't say anything, he just continued to stare at me blankly, waiting for me to go on.

"It's me… I'm his daughter."

Lane's face froze with complete shock, then he let it relax as he slowly grinned and looked over at Jake. "Oh, you guys are funny. I see what you're doing here… Ha ha, you got me."

Jake didn't smile, he just shook his head, still looking at Lane with a serious face.

"What?" Lane lost his grin as he turned to look back at me. "You're serious?"

I didn't say anything either. I just nodded.

"Holy shit!" Lane's eyes widened. "Ho-ly shit…" He said slower, then looked back at Jake. "Dude… how the hell did you accomplish that! You're with the First Rank's daughter? Lucky bastard…" Then Lane looked back at me briefly, like he was thinking about what it all meant. "Did… but… wait… then Kaleah… I thought—"

"I was erased with the Sicari serum. I didn't remember who I was when I was here in New York with Jake. So, no, I didn't know who I was then…" I interrupted him, hoping to clear it up a little more.

"But… did Miles know?" He looked over at Jake as he asked.

"No…" Jake said, clearly getting uncomfortable with where the conversation was going. "You already know more right now than you should, too. Mr. Prescott didn't want me to tell anyone. We're supposed to keep it a secret until we know Eva is safe within the agency. As of right now, he's not certain who he can trust. There might be a mole or a Sicari spy, so she's supposed to stay with me and keep pretending to be Kaleah Eva, my Gypsyin, until he has more safety measures in place."

"I knew we could trust you, though." I reached out to pat Lane's hand. "So I convinced Jake to let me tell you."

"Of course," Lane said, like he understood the gravity of the situation. "You can! I'll help you protect her now… Well, I would have anyway, but definitely now!" He said, looking at Jake like he was hoping he wasn't still upset about what happened last time he was entrusted with watching me.

"Great," Jake said sarcastically like he probably wasn't over it. "Well, first we should decide what we'll do if Kat tries to report us again, since she knows we're back, and acted like Eva being a Gypsyin wasn't still a secret!"

"Dude," Lane suddenly acted really defensive, "I didn't tell her! I swear, man, we didn't really ever talk about Kaleah when she was here."

"No? Okay, then what did you talk about?" Jake still sounded sour, like he hadn't forgiven Lane like I had.

"Um," Lane let his eyes roll a little, like he wasn't sure or couldn't quite remember. "Well, we talked about you initially. Like I mean, I told her you and Kaleah both left to go on vacation, ya know…" Lane smiled, apparently proud of himself and thought that was an excellent cover. "And when she asked why I was shot, I just told her it was an accident, you know, while on duty…"

"Okay, well, if I was gone and you're obviously incompetent, then why did she keep coming back?"

"Jake!" I huffed. He apparently hadn't gotten over what happened and now he felt more free to take it out on Lane, even though Lane was sorry and had already apologized.

"No, it's okay, Kaleah…" Lane dismissed my disapproval of Jake's remarks. "I knew he was mad at me. We're brothers. This is how we deal with these kinds of things." He said, then looked back at Jake. "Go ahead, don't hold back. I can take it!"

Jake nodded, then gave him a look like he didn't actually think he could take what he wanted to dish, but was willing to dish it, anyway. He leaned forward, resting his hands on the back of the couch across from us, when I saw his shoulders tense as he prepared to let Lane have it. "I had her here. She was safe! Next thing I know, you got yourself shot and she's who knows where with God knows who, ready to do who knows what to her! She was taken by a freakin' Sicari, for goodness sake! Do you know what kind of shit could have happened to her? Not to mention the things that actually did happen to her while she was gone." Jake took in a large breath as he leaned back, now red in the face.

"Lane, I can't even tell you everything that she went through! If you had ever loved someone before, you'd know what that felt like… The moment I sat there tied up watching as another Coldier intended to rape her *after* he thought he'd successfully erased her again… You don't even freakin' get it, you don't!" The longer he talked, the more Jake was getting worked up. "She was shot while we were trying to escape. We're lucky it wasn't anywhere vital, or I'd have lost her! Then we come back here and find out you've been sleeping with Katherine. I just… I don't even know what to say to you! Yeah, I'm freakin' mad…"

Lane nodded, accepting the blame as he slowly stood up. "You're right Jacob, I screwed up… and I'm sorry. You're also right when you say I'll never know what you went through, what she went through…

but you're wrong when you say I've never loved anyone… I love Kaleah. Maybe not as much or in the same way as you do, but I do love her, and I never wanted anything like that to happen to her, nor do I ever again. I promise you, man, I'm gonna help you watch after her. Nothing's ever gonna happen to her like that again!" He walked over to Jake and motioned, wanting to give him a hug if he'd allow it.

Jake slowly relaxed and nodded, then opened his arms to hug him back like he was accepting his apology and willing to fully forgive him.

"I won't see Kat anymore either," Lane said after a moment, when he stepped back to look at Jake.

Jake let out a large breath like he was releasing his anger and willing to relax again then nodded as he reached over to pat Lane on the shoulder. "That's probably for the best, man. She was likely just using you anyway… Not to mention you probably don't want to be with someone else when you meet Jayde's sister. I mean, who know's, maybe she's still single too…" Jake grinned, then looked over at me.

"What? Kaleah said she didn't have a sister…" Lane turned to look at me to see if Jake was messing with him.

I innocently smiled, then shrugged. "Kaleah didn't know she did." I said, now grinning as well.

"No freaking way!" Lane said with an enormous smile. "Holy shit! Are you serious? That's freakin' awesome!"

3

LOST SECRETS

"Eva... wake up, we gotta go. Hurry..." Jake whispered as he vigorously rubbed his hand up and down my side to wake me up.

"What?" my body wasn't ready to wake up yet and didn't want to cooperate.

"There are agents here... Lane's talking to them. Stay quiet, I'm gonna take you out the back way..."

"What?" I whispered back as quietly as I could. My body wasn't fighting me so much once the realization of what Jake was saying had registered in my brain.

"I wondered if this was gonna happen. I'm glad we stayed in Lane's room last night... Here, let me help you up." He whispered as he put his hand under my side to push me to a sitting position. "I don't know how much time we have. He's gonna try to convince them we didn't stay here last night, but I don't know how successful he'll be."

I nodded as I looked around at the floor, looking for my shoes. At that moment, I was happy that we had slept with our clothes on as well.

"Are you awake enough? You think you can walk quietly? I mean, I can probably carry you if—"

"No, I'm good, baby." I stopped him and leaned down to pick up my shoes and slip them on my feet. "When did they get here?"

"Just a couple of minutes ago. We were in the kitchen making breakfast when I heard them over the intercom."

"Okay… Well, where are we gonna go now, then?" I finished with my second shoe and stood up.

"Nowhere… we're just gonna take the back stairs down a couple levels and hide there. Then once they're gone, Lane said he'll come get us."

"Are we not safe just hiding here in his room?" I wasn't trying to argue with him. I just wasn't sure if I was awake enough to walk around quietly yet.

"No, baby… if they don't believe him, then they might sweep his apartment…"

"Okay," I said as I tried to softly tippy-toe toward the door, but before I got there, I saw a shadow of feet walk over in front of the crack at the bottom. I turned to look at Jake, who apparently saw them at the same time as I did. He suddenly stood, reached over and wrapped his hand around my mouth, then pulled me with him back against the wall behind where the door would swing open.

"Shh," he whispered softly in my ear as he released his hand.

A couple seconds later, the door opened toward us and whoever it was on the other side flipped the switch to turn the lights on. "Miles?" It was Lane.

Jake didn't say anything, he just stayed quiet as he reached up with his hand to slowly push the door toward Lane.

When Lane felt it touch him, he turned to look at us behind it. "Oh, hey!" He said smiling. "They're gone now. So it's all clear."

"You positive?" Jake asked, not ready to jump back into his normal morning just yet.

"Yeah, man… I told them you both left last night and that you just came by to say hi since I hadn't seen you in a while and that was it. I didn't know where you went." Then he shrugged. "Are you all right?" Lane asked, looking at me.

"Yeah… I'm fine." I said, taking a couple of steps back out into the room. "What was the reason they said they were here?"

"Uh," Lane started like he knew, but didn't want to say. "Well… Katherine reported you," he mumbled, probably hoping we couldn't hear him.

"I freakin' knew it!" Jake pipped up, now giving Lane the side-eye before walking toward me to sit on the bed. "Eva, baby, we can't stay here. If you'll get the bags together, I'll go call the agency and see if I can speak to your father. Maybe he'll have a better idea of where we can go that's safe for you."

"Miles, they're gone now. I really don't think you should have any more issues. I'm sure she's still safe here." Lane clearly wasn't ready for us to leave so soon.

"And what if you're wrong? What then, Lane?" Jake leaned down to lace up his boots after slipping them back on.

"I… well—"

"Exactly!" Jake cut him off before he had a chance to even answer.

"It's okay, Lane. We won't have to be in hiding too terribly long, I wouldn't think. We'll probably get a chance to see you again here in another month or so." I said, hoping it helped him feel better. However, after I said it, I realized it likely did the opposite when I saw his face.

"A month or so?" He furrowed his brow like that wasn't acceptable. "Wait, no… seriously, Miles… Let me help you! We can talk about it… I'll help hide her, watch her… really! She can be safe here, I know it!" I don't know if he wanted a chance to redeem himself to Jake or if he just really missed both of us that much, but he sounded desperate for us to stay.

Jake didn't respond, he just kept tying his laces.

"Lane," I sat down on the bed next to Jake, "we appreciate it, we really do… But maybe it's for the best, you know?" I said as I reached over to rub Jake's back. I knew he was probably irritated with Lane again, since the only reason Kat even knew we were here to report us was because he'd had her in his apartment.

Lane's face quickly grew solemn as he looked from me over to Jake, who still refused to sit up and look at him. Then Lane looked back at me and nodded. "All right…" he said quietly, then turned to walk out of the room, shutting the door behind him.

"Jake, I know you're not happy with him, but you shouldn't treat him like that." I said as I stood up and walked around the bed to gather our bags.

Jake sat up quickly and reached for my wrist to stop me. "Come here…" He said as he pulled me toward him to sit in his lap.

"What?" I asked, searching his eyes to see if I could tell what he might have been thinking.

"What do you want to do?" He asked softly, like he really wanted my opinion.

I looked at him, a bit puzzled and surprised. I wasn't sure, but from what I could remember, that was the first time he'd actually been willing to consult with me instead of just deciding our fate all by himself. "Really?" I asked, making sure this wasn't a trick. "You… you're really asking?"

He looked away as he took in a deep breath, like he was also wondering why before returning his gaze to mine. "Yes, baby… I'm really asking."

"Oh… well…" I sat there and stared off for a second while I thought about it. "Um… Well, I kinda agree with him. Now that the agents have left, I don't see why they would come back. And he's not gonna have Kat over again so I don't see where she could cause any more damage, I don't guess. Not to mention, he's right… with both you and him watching me, I should be safer. He can come and go just like if we weren't here… No one has to know, really!"

Jake was quiet like he was listening and trying to take every point I made seriously, then nodded. "Okay!" He said, leaning in to kiss me. "We'll do what you want this time. I'll go talk to him."

I smiled, "Thank you." I said softly, still gazing into his eyes.

He smiled back, then looked up at my hair as he raised his hand to sweep it out of my face. "You still tired?" He asked as he looked down at my lips, then back at my eyes.

I half-smiled, assuming I knew why he was asking. "Yes, very…"

He nodded, "Okay." He said, then leaned his forehead in to rest against mine. "Lie back down then, baby. I'll go talk to Lane, make sure we have a good game plan and see where he wants us to stay—in here or in the guest room again."

"Sounds good." I leaned in to kiss him again, then turned to crawl across his knee to lie back down.

I doubt I was asleep long, if at all, when I heard the door open then shut like Jake had come back. I didn't open my eyes, I just lay there pretending to be asleep just in case him seeing me awake gave him any ideas. After a couple minutes, I felt him crawl under the covers and lay down behind me, pressing his warm body against my back, resting his hand against my waist.

After a few moments of him lightly rubbing from my waist to my thigh and back, I felt his breath on my neck like he'd leaned in preparing to kiss it. "Eva..." He whispered into my ear.

"What?"

"I need to tell you something..." He said, hesitantly.

"What?" I wasn't so quiet anymore.

"I have some bad news... but I hoped this would relax you enough that you wouldn't be as mad when you heard it?"

I furrowed my brow. "What the hell, Jake... If you had something to tell me, I wish you hadn't waited!" I said, instantly feeling anxious. Whatever it was, I wanted for him to just come out with it already. "Ugh... What is it?"

"Okay... Well I talked to Lane and we can stay in the guest room for as long as we need, so that's good..." He said still hesitating to tell me what exactly the bad news was.

"And..."

"Ok, well..." He paused, then reached up to tuck the hair from my face behind my ear. "I also called and spoke with your father... He knows about where we are now and he's good with it. I didn't have time to talk to him long, but he said he'd heard from the men he sent to look for Miller..."

"Okay?"

"They searched for him in Nashville and Knoxville but they couldn't find him, baby. I'm sorry."

I didn't say anything for a moment. I didn't know what to say. I just stared at him, uncertain how to even feel about that. "Well, where would he be then? If he wasn't in Nashville when they looked for him and he didn't go down to Knoxville to the vault... I mean... doesn't he have a tracker like all the rest of you?"

Jake nodded slightly as he let his eyes dart to the side like he was thinking of how to answer me. "Uh, yeah, he does... or well, did... It showed he was in Knoxville, just not anymore..."

"All right?" I couldn't help but think Jake was acting weird. "Do they know where he went?"

"I need to ask you about something first," he said, looking straight at me. "By any chance, were you holding back some of the intel?"

I crinkled my face again in confusion. "Jake, I don't understand... What aren't you telling me?"

"Just answer me first..."

I looked away for a second to think. "No," I said, suddenly looking back at him. "I told you everything already. I'm not keeping any more secrets!"

"Okay..." he sighed as he nodded to himself, like he was thinking about what that meant. "Ahh, hell... then we have a problem, baby."

"What?" I didn't understand.

"Get up." He rolled out of the bed. "We need to go talk to Lane. I'm not sure we're still safe here."

I refused to move. I just sat up and stared at him instead. "I'm not getting up until you tell me what's going on, Jacob!" It was clear that he had information that I didn't that he wasn't wanting to tell me yet. For what reason, I had no idea.

He stopped and looked at me, then softly sighed, knowing he wouldn't win even if he tried. "I think Miller's in New York..." He said reluctantly under his breath like maybe it wouldn't bother me as much that way.

"What? Why?" I started to ask until I realized that might not be such a bad thing after all. Maybe this way I could get another chance at killing him.

Jake started to pace as he answered me. "I wasn't sure at first, but now I think it's for the same reason we saw all those Sicari yesterday… Your father told me when the men were looking for Miller they tried to get into the vault with the code you gave him and it wouldn't work. The number wasn't right."

"What?" I was perplexed. Of course, the number I gave him was right… it had to be right. There was no other number I'd memorized.

"I told you what you wanted to know. Now please do what I asked and get up." Jake said firmly.

"All right…" I said, still thinking about what it all meant as I scooted myself over to the edge of the bed to stand. "The intel was good, Jake. I swear I didn't lie about any of it."

"I know, baby. That's honestly what I was afraid of. Now that everyone thinks you have the missing piece of the puzzle, they'll do whatever they can to find you to get it."

"How do you know Miller's in New York?" It was probably foolish, but I wasn't as concerned about the Sicari as I was about Miller.

"I don't. It's a reasonable assumption, since he knows who you are and where you'll probably be." He walked over to the door and reached for the knob, then turned to wait on me. "Ready?"

I finished slipping my shoes back on, then nodded.

He turned and opened the door. "Lane," he yelled out as he started down the hall toward the kitchen, "family meeting time!"

"Okay, well what do we do then?" Lane asked like he was as dumbfounded as Jake and I both were. It felt like we'd been sitting there discussing every option under the sun for the last hour and a half with no one coming up with a perfect solution yet.

I knew of one, but I hadn't mentioned it yet, just for the sheer fact that I knew Jake wouldn't accept it as well as I didn't really like it, either.

"What if I took the serum again?" I couldn't help but put it out there, despite my misgivings. I knew we'd all thought about it already anyway, just no one was comfortable enough mentioning it yet.

I was waiting for Jake to have his usual reaction, expecting a stern 'hell no,' but surprisingly, Lane beat him to it. "What the hell are you thinking?" He blurted out with a furrow to his brow, then quickly relaxed as he glanced at Jake, "I mean... sorry... I just don't think that's a good idea." He said, softening his tone.

Jake nodded, excusing his reaction, probably since he felt the same way. Then he reached over to take my hand. "Baby, I appreciate the sacrifice you're willing to make, but I'm with Lane on this. I really don't think that's a good idea. As a last resort, okay... we might consider it then, but right now we can do better than that."

"I know... I don't want to do it either, believe me, this time I really don't. It just seemed like it would solve all the problems and make it easier to hide me."

"It might solve some, yeah, but it would cause more. More that I don't want to deal with, so let's just assume it's not an option, all right?" Jake said it kindly but still assertively.

"All right... Well, what if you just take me to my dad's then?" It was an option one of them briefly mentioned when we first started talking, but it was passed over, hoping a better option would present itself.

Jake just looked at me showing he was listening, then slowly nodded as he looked down, like he was thinking about it. "I hate it, because I don't know who I can trust there, but... that might be the best we can do."

"It *is* the most fortified place in the city." Lane chimed in, like maybe he was trying to suggest that it wasn't that bad of an idea after all.

"It is... but that doesn't mean it's the safest. I mean, if that's the case then—" Jake stopped mid-sentence, probably knowing what he was about to say might not be taken well.

"He wouldn't have lost my mom?" I sighed.

He nodded, then looked down.

"Jake, that was years ago. I know you don't feel like it's safe because of that and what happened with the doctor in Nashville. But if it really wasn't that safe, then Ellie would have been taken by now, too. If Miller or the Sicari came here with enough men, there would be nothing you or Lane could do to protect me. At least at Dad's, there would be enough manpower to defend against a major attack."

Jake looked back up at me and took in a deep breath. "Fine…" He didn't sound thrilled, but still willing. "I'll call him back then."

4
USURPER

"You nervous, baby?" Jake asked, like he could sense it on me somehow. We'd made it through the gates, past all the guards, the sentries, and who knows what else, and now we were at the front door. For whatever reason, though, yes, I was nervous. I didn't say anything. I just shook my head slightly, denying it.

"We're both here with you; nothing's gonna happen…" Lane said softly, standing beside me—the opposite side of Jake. I knew he was probably just trying to make me feel better, but it didn't really help much.

I wasn't sure what I was expecting when the doors opened, but it wasn't what I saw. Ten or more armed guards were standing just inside, like they were waiting to receive me and take me to my father. I looked around at each of their faces, wondering if there were any I recognized or if any were Jake's men, but none were familiar to me.

As soon as they saw me, the man standing near the front stepped forward to greet me. "Miss Prescott, my name is Xavier. It's a pleasure to meet you." Then he looked over at Jake to address him. "Thank you, Agent Miles. We'll take her from here. I'll make sure she gets to her father safely." He said as he gently rested his hand behind my arm, ready to guide me inside.

"I'll take her to her father, Hernandez. You and your men may escort us, but I won't be leaving her side." I assumed Jake must have met Xavier before, since he knew his last name.

"That's not what my orders were." Xavier said quickly, ready to argue with Jake.

"What's your rank now, Hernandez?" Jake asked as he reached forward to gently grab my other arm.

Xavier scowled, apparently not in the mood for games. "Forth! Now let her go and I won't mention this to Mr. Prescott."

I turned back toward Jake to see how he was going to respond since they were the same rank, when he quickly dropped the glower on his face as he looked past me then let go of my arm. "Mr. Prescott!"

I turned back around to see my dad quickly making his way through all the men. "Jayde!" He said like he hadn't seen me in forever, even though it'd barely been more than a few days. He walked over and gave me a hug. "I'm glad to finally have you home, where you belong. You'll be safe here. No one's going to get you now, sweetheart." He said with a warm smile. "Hernandez, Miles… men," he said, motioning for them to follow. Then he turned to walk back inside.

"Agent Hernandez and I have spoken extensively this morning, Agent Miles, and we believe we have the best security measures in place." He said loudly, as the two walked close to us. "I have assigned Agent Hernandez to be Jayde's personal bodyguard. He's agreed to stay with her night and day. He's one of my best men." Dad said with a smile as he continued to lead us farther into the massive house. "Now, Agent Miles, I know how deeply you care for Jayde, and she for you, so I was going to converse with you as well about what measures you'd like to see for her safety and such. Here, have a seat." We'd walked into a large room with six upholstered armchairs arranged in a circle. Dad gestured for me to take a seat as he turned to sit in one himself.

"I appreciate that, Mr. Prescott, I do, but I would prefer to be Jayde's bodyguard myself. As it is, I'm already with her night and day. I also know more about the dangers she faces." I could tell the suggestion Dad had made wasn't sitting well with Jake, but he was doing his best to remain respectful.

"Mm-hmm," Dad thoughtfully leaned back in his chair, rested his elbow on his armrest, and his chin lightly on his fist. "Miles, I do believe you have my daughter's best interests at heart. I am just not entirely sure with you having worked under Agent Miller in the past, if it's a great idea for you to be her main protection right now. Just like we spoke over the phone earlier, if Miller is in the city, then I don't want him to have any advantage in finding her. You yourself even told me that your men were previously his men. I don't know who all I can trust, so I'd prefer to rely on men that I know have had no connection with him in the past."

Jake reluctantly nodded his head. "Yes, Sir, I understand, Sir."

"Now," Dad continued, "that doesn't mean, of course, that you can't see her or that I am intending to split you up in any way. On the contrary, you are free to see her as often as you wish. I do believe that you being around her as well as Agent Hernandez will help make sure that absolutely nothing happens to her."

"And my men?" Jake asked. I assumed he was referring to Lane since he'd not mentioned anything to me about Andry, Lawson, or any of the others since we'd left Nashville without most of them.

"Agent Hernandez has twelve men under him, all assigned to her guard detail. I believe that is sufficient. Like I said Agent Miles, it's not that I don't trust you, it's your men and their loyalties that concern me."

"I understand, Sir." Jake said as he looked around the room at all the men standing around. "May I have just one, then? He's family and has never worked for Miller." Jake said as he caught eyes with Lane. Then he nodded at him, prompting Lane to step forward.

Dad glanced over at Lane, then looked at me. "Jayde?" I assumed he was asking for my approval as well.

"I trust him as much as I trust Jake, Dad. He's like a brother to me. He's taken a bullet trying to protect me already."

Dad closed his eyes for a moment, then nodded slowly before opening them as he quickly stood up. "Okay then!" He said as he spun around. "Hernandez, show Jayde where her room is. Jayde, we'll talk more over supper tonight, my dear." He said as he walked quickly out of the room as though he had other pressing matters to attend to.

Xavier quickly stood up and turned toward me, reaching out his hand to help me up.

"Don't!" Jake growled, eyeing Xavier, then stood up.

Xavier slowly pulled it back as he stared at Jake. "Are we going to have a problem, Miles?"

"I'm not an idiot, Hernandez! When I spoke to Mr. Prescott earlier this morning over the phone, he acted like he knew I was to be her lead guard. Now, after you spoke with him, he's changed his mind and doesn't trust me or my men like he did." Jake said, his voice low and gravely, clearly not happy.

Xavier didn't change his expression much as he shrugged. "I don't know what you're talking about, Miles."

"Bullshit," Jake said, taking a step closer to him. "When did you get to be fourth rank anyway? When I left to go to Nashville, you were still only seventh."

"Things change, Miles. Track and Capture was fun and all… for a while… But when I got a chance to advance and guard Mr. Prescott, I took it. There's no shame in that, not like there would be in running off to another city when you don't like what you see is happening here at home." Xavier smirked.

"You son of a bitch!" Jake said under his breath as he took another step toward him.

I stood up as quickly as I could and rested my palm on Jake's chest to stop him. I'd heard enough. I got the idea they had definitely known each other before and, for whatever reason, weren't the best of pals. "Jake, baby…"

I didn't get to finish what I was saying when he looked down at me and rested his hand on top of mine. "I'm fine." He said as he relaxed his shoulders, reassuring me he wouldn't take it any further.

I looked over at Xavier, who didn't appear to be dazed what so ever. "Follow me, Ms. Prescott." He said, looking down at me with a quaint smile like none of that had just happened.

I looked up at Jake, who quickly nodded, reassuring me he was okay, then turned to follow Xavier. We walked back past a few larger gathering rooms until we came to an enormous staircase that appeared to be near the back of another expansive room. When we had ascended those stairs, we continued down a long balcony overlooking the great room until we came to a wide hallway. To the right was a tall wooden door. Xavier pushed it open and led us into my new room.

It was decorated almost exactly like my room in Nashville was. It had pale pink and white walls with a grand four post bed. Each post had strips of pink and white silk ribbons draped from them. Again, just like in Nashville, I couldn't get over the idea that I had my own room. I hadn't seen my family in over seven years. For all my father knew, I was dead and never coming back. But even so, he took the time to make a place for me—like he'd never lost hope that someday he'd find me again… someday I would come home.

I walked over to the bed and turned to see who'd entered the room with me. All I saw were Jake and Xavier both standing each on their own side of the door, just staring at me. "Where's Lane and the other men?" I asked, looking at Jake, wondering why he'd stopped next to the door and why I didn't see Lane.

"We're not allowed to enter farther into your room without your permission, Miss Prescott." Xavier answered me before Jake had a chance to.

"Oh, okay…" I said, not knowing exactly what new rules were going to be in place for everyone and just how I was going to navigate them. "Well, I would like to allow Jake… I mean Agent Miles, and Agent Lane both in… I guess all the other men can just keep watch out there."

Xavier hesitantly nodded, then glanced at Jake before leaning out into the hall and calling for Lane.

As soon as Lane walked through the doors, Jake walked with him over to my bed and stood at the end, neither saying anything, just standing there, staring at me as I sat on the edge. "Uh… well, this is weird." I said, seeing that no one was acting normal. "At ease, gentlemen!" I said playfully. "So… who, ah, gets to babysit me when I have to go use the bathroom?" I grinned.

"That'll be me!" Jake spoke up quickly before Xavier had time to. I looked over at Lane, who I could tell was stopping himself from laughing.

I smiled at him. "Do you like my room, Lane?"

"Yes, Ma'am," he said, all formal and polite.

"You can call me, Miss. Prescott." I said with a smirk, knowing it was longer so it'd be harder for him.

He gave me a knowing look, seeing I was being ornery, then nodded, "Okay, *Miss Prescott.*"

I was about to go on with teasing him more when I realized I still hadn't seen my sister. I turned to address Xavier, "Can I see Ellie now?"

He quickly nodded, "Yes Ma… I mean, Miss Prescott. I'll send someone to go get her." He said, then turned to speak with someone just outside the door.

"Are you hungry, baby? It's been a while since you've eaten… You can send Hernandez away anytime you want, you should know that." Jake whispered, where only Lane and I were likely to hear him.

"Not really, sorry," I said, trying to be honest. I figured that was Jake's way of getting rid of him for a minute, but I didn't want to lie to Xavier if I didn't have to. "Why don't you like him?" I asked softly, looking at the door to make sure he couldn't hear me, then back at Jake.

"It's a long story. I'll tell you later in private. If we get any privacy that is…" Jake said like he was regretting bringing me to my father's.

"Well, is he safe?" I asked, wondering if that's what Jake's problem was.

Jake sighed, "He's safe. It's just—"

"They were rivals," Lane whispered, bending forward a little.

I tilted my head, wanting to hear more but caught movement from the corner of my eye, where Xavier had come back in to stand where he had been. I looked over at him and stared for a moment, trying to size him up and see just what was so threatening about him—to Jake, anyway. He was tall, but not as tall as Jake. He was muscular as well, but again, not nearly as much as Jake or even Lane, for that matter. He was handsome, with a nice smile. He had rich, dark mahogany colored skin with shiny jet black hair, stylishly combed to the side. From what I could tell, he looked like he was a good guard, but that was just going off of looks alone and nothing else. I knew it would take time and being around him longer before I really could judge his character.

"Is she coming?" I asked when he made a face probably wondering why I was staring at him.

"Yes, Ma—"

"You can call me Jayde," I smiled, then looked back at Jake and Lane, "You can all call me Jayde."

"Thank you, Jayde." Xavier said with a slight accent.

I smiled again. "Are you originally from around here?" I asked curious about his accent.

He narrowed his eyes, briefly shot them over to Jake then back to me before answering. "Yes, Ma'am, I was born and raised in Brooklyn."

I gave him another warm smile. *That must be the accent then.*

Before I could respond, I heard a noise down the hall. As Xavier turned to look, Jake walked over toward the door to investigate as well, motioning for Lane to stay close to me.

"I walk… I can walk, let go me, you… I told… you freaking… where is she? I want to see her…" The voice sounded like my sisters. Surely it was. The stuff she was saying though, was making no sense what so ever.

Jake turned around to look at me when he saw who was coming. "I think she's drunk, Jayde." He said as he took his position back on the other side of the door where he had initially stood.

Xavier, having stepped out, quickly walked back into the room and took his place beside the door as well. He too had a look on his face like he didn't know if I would like what I was about to see.

"Jayde!" Ellie yelled as she stumbled into the room facing the rear wall like she was expecting me to be in that direction. "Jayde?"

I didn't say anything for a moment. I was taking in what she looked like, since I hadn't seen her in over seven years. She looked nothing like what she had when I left. Now she was all grown up, and oddly enough, looked a lot like me.

"Ellie..." I stood up slowly and began to walk toward her.

She turned when she heard me. "Jayde..." Her face went from blank to scowling when she saw me. She didn't look all that thrilled, but rather upset that I was back. I wasn't sure what it was that I saw in her eyes or the way she said my name, but I took a step back as she quickly took a few steps forward and raised her arm like she intended to hit me. "You left me, you little—" she screamed as she got closer when suddenly Lane moved over to stand between us.

"Clark," Xavier called outside the door.

Lane didn't touch her but moved to the left as she moved, then moved to the right as she did, trying to get past him. My heart sank at the sight of what I was seeing. I took a few more steps back toward the bed and sat back down.

Jake didn't hesitate, but walked around Lane and Ellie and stood by the bed next to me.

An older man stepped inside the doorway to speak to Xavier. "Yes, Sir?"

"How much has she drank today?" Xavier asked, like this was a normal occurrence for her.

"Uh... just a few glasses this afternoon, Sir," the man said like he didn't think it was a lot, but I knew better.

"Let me past, you... you... stupid li'l..." Ellie kept verbally attacking Lane as he continued to gently block her swings every time she tried to hit him.

"You all right, baby?" Jake asked, resting a hand on my shoulder, knowing this wasn't what I had expected when I asked to see her.

"Yeah..." I said, feeling disappointed. "Lane, let her go. She can't hurt me."

Lane turned to look at me, then Jake, and finally moved once Jake nodded like he'd allow it.

"What do you... you think you're doing just coming back like this?" Ellie stood there yelling at me. "You don't deserve to be here… you filthy Sicari…"

"Lane, shut the door." Jake took a step forward. "Hernandez, we need to talk." He said as he moved to stand between Ellie and me.

"I know what she is… uh, was… All the men here do, Miles. We've all been debriefed. You don't have to worry." Xavier said calmly as he motioned to stop Lane from shutting the door.

"I hate you, Jayde. I do… you… you're not my sister of mine no more…" Ellie yelled as she began to cry, then slowly lowered herself to her knees on the floor.

I stood up and walked around Jake, then kneeled down next to her on the floor. "Ellie…" I said as I wrapped my arms around her.

"I don't want you, you'rrre not my sister no more…" she slurred as she cried harder, burying her head in her palms.

"I'm sorry, Ellie. I'm sorry I left you…" I laid my head on the top of her back. "I'm sorry I wasn't there when you needed me…"

"Mom needed you… but you weren't there, Jayde!" Her cry broke into a sob, then after a minute she relaxed like she was losing momentum. "You weren't there, I lost you both… I needed you."

"Shhh… I know, Ellie… Just relax," I said, trying to cradle her in my arms.

"But you weren't…" she sobbed.

"I know… Shhh, it's okay… I know…" I whispered as I rocked with her back and forth for a moment, then before long, she passed out, resting against me.

"Lane?" I said, looking up, trying to see where he was.

Jake bent down, seeing that I needed something. "What, baby?"

"Have Lane pick her up and lay her in my bed to rest, please."

Jake nodded, then stood up and motioned for Lane to come over to us. "Will you help me get her and lay her in the bed?"

"No, Jake," I said, looking up at him, "just Lane."

Jake looked at me puzzled, then nodded suddenly like he understood.

Lane must have gotten the idea quicker than Jake when, without hesitation, he quickly moved down and put his arm under her legs and back and picked her up, then gently walked over and lowered her onto the bed just like I'd asked.

"Playing matchmaker when she's drunk might not be very productive," Jake whispered as he reached down to help me up.

"His standards, thus far, seem pretty shitty." I whispered back as I took his hand to stand. "Besides, even drunk, she's a hell of a step up from Kat, so I'd say we're good."

"Fair point," Jake said, as he nodded with a small shrug. "I don't guess it'll hurt anything."

5

A BEAUTIFUL MESS

"**S**he's beautiful!" Apparently, Lane felt free to speak his mind now that I had asked Xavier to step out into the hall so we could have a few minutes of privacy without him.

"She's a mess…" I said as I walked around the bed to stand at the end of it next to Lane.

"A beautiful mess…" He said, staring like he knew he might not get another chance to get as good of a look once she woke up.

"Are you all right, baby?" Jake asked after he walked to the end of the room and sat in one of the two armchairs that were next to a fireplace centered between two tall windows.

"How do you mean?" I walked over by him and sat in the other one. "Like about what she was saying?"

"Yeah," he said as he patted his thigh, motioning for me to sit in his lap instead.

"I guess it would have been unrealistic to think she was still the same little girl that I left." I didn't elaborate, but it did bother me. The thought that I had hurt her so much tore me up inside and I was doing everything I could to not show it.

"You can tell that you're sisters," Lane said loudly without turning toward us.

"Why? Because I'm as awful of a drunk as she is?" I hoped turning the conversation more light-hearted would help me not feel as bad as I did.

Lane broke his trance long enough to turn toward us finally and smirk, "Good point, but no... you look so much alike."

I tried to smile, "Yeah..." I wanted to say more, but I could feel myself tearing up, so I stopped.

"Eva, baby?" Jake reached up for my shoulder so I would turn to look at him. "Do you want us to step out for a minute too?"

I nodded, trying to contain my emotions. "If you would... yes." I said quickly.

He smiled, then leaned forward to kiss me on the forehead. "All right... We'll be just outside the door if you need anything, hear me?"

"Okay," I smiled as I got up and walked back over to the bed.

"Lane, let's give her a minute."

Lane barely turned to acknowledge him when he looked over at me instead. "Don't be upset with yourself. You did what you thought you had to do." He whispered, then walked over and gave me a hug.

I shook my head against his chest, trying not to break down right there in his arms. "Thank you," I said, then pulled away. "You're too kind, Lane. I don't feel like I deserve it."

"Quit it," he scolded, giving me a stern look. "You deserve everything and more... Yell if you need us." He said, then turned to follow Jake out of the room, shutting the door behind them.

"Ellie?" I knew she probably couldn't hear me, but I wanted to talk to her, anyway. I crawled onto the bed and lay down beside her. "Ellie?" I tried again as I brushed her cheek slowly with my hand. "I'm sorry, Ellie... I shouldn't have left you. I regret it. Every day I regret it. I missed you so much..." Tears freely began to roll down my face.

"You were all I had, and I didn't appreciate it. No one ever loved me like you did. You believed in me when I didn't believe in myself... And I left you... all alone... You needed me and I wasn't there..." My light tears turned heavy. "I'm sorry, Ellie... I'm so sorry... I didn't mean for you to end up like this. I don't want you to hate me. I love you. I want you to love me again. Please, Ellie, forgive me for what

I've done… Please…" I pulled the blanket to my face to wipe my tears away, then laid my head against the pillow and grabbed a hold of her hand before closing my eyes to rest beside her.

"It's Latin." I could tell she seemed confused, so I thought I would help. I'd never seen another girl in the espionage program. She seemed so shy and innocent, I wondered what had made her sign up.

"Thanks," she said timidly as she went back to studying the pages.

"We don't have to learn the entire language, just what certain words mean."

"Oh, okay." She smiled like she appreciated it.

"Why are you here?" I couldn't help but ask, seeing she didn't really fit in all that well.

"I… I uh…" she stammered then looked around quickly, like she wasn't sure we were allowed to speak to each other. "Would you believe me if I told you I didn't remember?" She said softly under her breath.

"Umm…" That was odd, I thought. I didn't know how to respond to her. *Why wouldn't she remember how she'd gotten here?* "Well, sure… I guess. You wouldn't have a reason to lie about it. I mean, unless you're practicing lying, since that's kinda what our job is gonna be." I smiled.

"N… no…" she shook her head like that wasn't what she was doing at all.

"What do you remember, then?" I was curious now.

"Not a lot…" She looked around again like she was making sure no one else was listening to her. "But I have dreams… and things happen in them that feel like memories… you know?"

I furrowed my brow a little. That was interesting. "Yeah… I have them too, but they're just dreams, that's all… nothing more."

"No… you don't get it. They're real to me." She wasn't acting as shy anymore now that she felt like she finally had someone who would listen to her. "Especially one of them… I have it over and over."

"What is it?"

"I... I uh... Okay..." She took a deep breath, and continued to whisper, "I'm in school. Kinda like this but it's just me siting there, watching a projector screen, and the teacher keeps asking me to repeat my name and how I got there. I couldn't really remember but I thought it was Paige Cortez, so that's what I told him. He didn't like that, so he hit me across the back with this long thing stick he carried around and said that that wasn't my name and that he'd send me to see the doctor for another shot if I ever mentioned it again. Then he told me my name was Isabella Rain. He made me repeat it over and over. I know it's just a dream, but..." She shrugged like she didn't know what else to say.

"Really?" I asked, wondering why she felt comfortable enough to tell me that when we'd just met.

"Yes... what are your dreams about?" She looked around again as she asked.

I looked at her while I tried to think about the different ones that I'd had and which one was most prominent in my mind. "Well... the main one is just... I'm in a white room. Everything is white, and this lady looks down at me and says, do you know why you're here? I said no. Then she pulls up my sleeve and asks me if I remember my parents. I said, yes, but then she got all quiet and gave me a shot of something... After that she asked me again if I remembered my parents and I said no that time because I didn't want another shot. But I lied. I really did still remember them. Nothing ever happens after that in the dream. I just wake up. My name is Eva, by the way. It's nice to meet you, Isabella."

She smiled softly like she was happy to make a new friend.

I was about to ask her another question when I heard two feet quickly coming up behind us. "Ladies!"

I spun to see, "Yes, Sir?" It was who I was afraid it was, the class's training instructor, Mr. Wilner.

"Eva, this is the third time I've had to get on you about speaking with other classmates during class. Get up!"

"But, Sir... I'm sorry, I was—"

"You know what the punishment is, go to the icebox!" He wouldn't allow me to explain myself.

"No!" I didn't mean to say it, it just slipped out.

His face suddenly looked shocked and puzzled, like along with myself, he couldn't believe I'd do such a thing as to say no to an instructor. "The icebox, NOW!" He pointed toward the door as he screamed at me, making Isabella quickly cover her ears from the high-pitched screech.

I nodded, then walked toward the door and out into the yard, where he promptly followed.

"Your time is doubled… maybe this way it'll be your last offense." He pointed at it, ready for me to get inside.

"You can't do that… I'll freeze to death!" I hesitated to step inside. I was afraid he'd taken it too far in his anger with me.

"Look, you little shit… I don't care who you are or how much Parker thinks you're worth to her… you're gonna do what I say or this ice box won't be what kills you, I will!" He pointed again at it more violently this time.

"No! I'm not getting in it!" I screamed back as I turned around to walk away.

"Oh, yes, you are!" I didn't get far when he pulled me from behind down to the ground, then grabbed my arms at the wrist dragged me backwards toward it.

"No… I won't… Let go of me!"

"Jayde!" I was being shaken. I opened my eyes to see Jake sitting in front of me. "It's just a bad dream, baby."

"Ugh… I freaking hate those." I sat up to look around. Lane, Xavier and four other agents were standing at the end of the bed watching me, but thankfully Ellie was still sound asleep.

"Is this a common problem?" Xavier asked with a straight face.

"Yes, almost nightly… I handle it when she has one, and she's fine." Jake said, turning to address Xavier's question.

"Does Mr. Prescott know you intend to spend the night with his daughter, here… every night?" Xavier asked, still with a straight face. I couldn't help but wonder if he was just good at stirring shit up, though, because the question didn't seem relevant.

Jake stood up slowly and turned to look at him. "She's going to be my wife. I plan on sleeping in her bed *every* freaking night, so if you have a problem with that, Hernandez, you can discuss it with me instead of running your mouth to her father." I'd never heard Jake speak to another agent, except Miller obviously, as flippantly as he did when he spoke to Xavier. I hadn't had a chance to ask what the tension between them was about, but now I was more curious than ever.

Hernandez didn't say anything to Jake. He just ignored him and looked at me. "Are you all right, Jayde? Is there anything you need?"

I looked from him over to Jake, then back with a bit of confusion at how they were acting. "Uh… no, I'm fine."

"Good. You haven't eaten since you arrived. I believe your father was planning on having supper with you and… Ellice." He said as he looked over at her, still sleeping peacefully next to me. "Would you like for me to send someone to tell him you plan on coming to eat with him?"

I looked over at her. I hated to wake her up, not to mention I was slightly concerned when she wasn't drunk if she still hated me and I wasn't prepared to see that. "Um, no… but thank you, Xavier."

He nodded, then made a hand signal to his other men in the room for them to return to the hall.

"When do you eat?" The question shot out of my mouth as I thought about him and Jake and Lane. Surely they were all hungry.

He smiled, which was probably the first time I'd seen his genuine smile, not a smirk or a grin since I'd met him. "You don't need to worry about us, Jayde. My men and I have a schedule we stick to for when we eat, sleep, and take breaks. I will sleep when you do, so I'm awake when you are, but I will always have eight or more men on watch when I am not. And of course, if you ever need anything at night, I'm in the room right next door. I'm a light sleeper as well, so if you or my men need me, I'm available." He said it, then looked over at Lane with an odd look. I'm sure he was wondering if Jake and he already had a routine, which, if so, I wasn't aware of.

"Oh, okay…" Hearing all of that did actually make me feel better. "Who is Ellie's bodyguard? Was that you before I came?" I was curious if me being there was making him pull double duty and if she was in more danger now because of me.

"No, Ma'am… I… well… I used to be, yes. But within the last month, she's refused to be guarded. So your father reassigned me to you."

"Refused?" I glanced at her, then back at him. "Why?"

He stiffened a little then looked away, "She's not been herself since she'd received your father's letter from Nashville when she leaned you'd been found."

"Really?" I asked, hoping for more insight.

"Yes, Ma'am, she thought you were dead, Jayde." He finally looked back at me again.

"How do you know that?" I asked, seeing he felt uncomfortable talking about her, and I wondered why.

He didn't respond right away. He just looked at her, then back at me. "We were in a relationship… but we ended it… mutually." I couldn't help but wonder if he was being vague, because Jake and Lane were both standing there listening.

"Oh… okay," I nodded like I understood. "Jake, baby… you and Lane haven't eaten at all since we've gotten here either, and barely had a break. You should both go get yourself something." I felt safe with Xavier and I wanted an excuse to talk to him more in private, where he would feel comfortable opening up.

"Jayde?" Jake furrowed his brow and tensed up, clearly not okay with leaving me with just Xavier.

"I'll be all right, baby… he's safe. Besides, you really need to eat. You can't protect me if you have no energy."

"She gave you an order. You have to do what she asks." Xavier thought he'd remind Jake how the orders were supposed to go, but I'm sure he was only using it as an excuse to get even deeper under his skin.

Jake didn't respond to him, he just looked back at me. "Jayde… you don't want either of us to stay?" I could tell by the way he asked, he wasn't happy with my suggestion, but I couldn't really explain to him in front of Xavier why I suggested it.

"Um… well, you both really do need to eat." I said, hoping maybe Lane would at least pick up on what I was doing. He generally wasn't as dense as Jake was.

Jake didn't say anything else, he just gave me a look showing he was disappointed in my decision, then nodded before he walked around the bed and joined Lane.

"Good thing we eat fast," Lane said with a grin as he looked at Xavier. "Really fast!" Then he turned to follow Jake out, leaving the door open behind them.

"You look just like her," Xavier said as soon as he saw they'd left.

"Why did you break up?" I asked, looking down at Ellie again, making sure she was still sound asleep.

"I couldn't handle her drinking. When she's sober, she's an amazing woman… she really is but, it just got to be too much."

"So it wasn't really mutual, was it?"

He looked down like he felt bad that he'd said it was. "No, Ma'am, not exactly."

"What do you and Jake have against each other? Why do you antagonize him like you do?"

He looked taken aback by my up front questioning. Maybe he thought since I looked like her, I would be more passive like she was. "Um… I don't mean to antagonize him, Jayde. It's just… we haven't really ever enjoyed each other's company."

"Why?"

"Nothing major, he's just used to getting his way, and I'm used to getting mine. That's really all it is."

"Oh… okay." That was fair enough. I'd actually expected more, but I was happy that's all it was.

"You don't want to marry him, though. I'll warn you."

I didn't have time to ask why, when I must have made a face to prompt him to explain that statement.

"He'll do anything to get to the top. I'm sure that's the only reason he's with you… so he can be with an Elite's daughter."

"So you don't think it has anything to do with how amazing of a woman I am?" I said sarcastically, showing him I didn't appreciate his comment.

He quickly backtracked. "That's not what I meant, I—"

"Sure it is! Is that why you were dating my sister, so you could be with an Elite's daughter?"

I could tell by his face he knew he'd stuck his foot in his mouth. "I'm sorry what I said bothered you, Jayde. That's not how I intended for it to come across. I'm sure you have amazing qualities other than your beauty and your status that would draw a man to want to be with you. I just know how Agent Miles was when I worked with him in the T&C unit. He was zealous… ambitious to a fault, really."

"And you… were you not the same way?"

He paused like he was thinking about it, but didn't get a chance to answer when I heard a voice calling for him, prompting him to turn and walk over to the open doorway. He talked to someone outside for a moment, then closed the door and walked back over to stand at the foot of the bed where he had been.

I knew he didn't intend to answer the last question, so I figured I'd go on with others. "What did my father tell you about me being a Sicari?"

"Not much, to be honest with you. I see you don't have one of their tags, so you can't technically be too much of one, I wouldn't think. He just told me enough to give me the idea that they're after you for intel that will give them weapons."

"Did he say why I was with them?"

"No, Ma'am, our briefing was solely to know how dangerous the enemy is, how likely they are to find you and what measures they'd take to do so."

"Okay… what did he tell you about Miller?" I knew Jake would be tempted to withhold info he had on Miller that he'd received from my father, but maybe Xavier wouldn't.

"A lot… what would you like to know?" Xavier looked surprised that he'd know things that I wouldn't.

"Where is he?" I figured I'd ask that first to see just how much Jake wasn't telling me.

"We don't know exactly where, but we believe he's already in New York."

"Okay… does Dad have units out looking for him or is he waiting for him to come find me?"

"You think he'd use you as bait?" Xavier acted surprised that I'd even suggest it.

"Well… no…" I looked away. I hadn't thought of it like that. It did sound bad when I thought about it, though.

"Jayde… He told me about the things Miller's done to you… what you've told him, anyway. I assume you didn't tell him everything. You have my word, as long as you're in my protection, I won't let that man anywhere near you or Ellice… I promise."

He looked like he meant it, but I had a hard time with promises. Especially since I remember thinking Jake had made the same promise and even though he tried—probably with everything he had in him—he wasn't able to keep it, either. "Thank you, Xavier… you may go now."

He initially looked a bit puzzled at my response, then quickly cleared his expression and nodded. "Yes, Ma'am."

6

PECKING ORDER

"You and Lane can come back in now, Jake," I noticed that he'd stopped just inside the door again to stand across from Xavier.

He nodded like he heard me, but didn't turn to the hall to tell Lane. He just walked over to where I was still sitting on the bed and stood there. "Ask Hernandez to leave. I want to talk to you in private." He didn't whisper. He said it loud enough Xavier could probably hear him. He didn't look all that thrilled with me either, which, to an extent, I could understand.

"Xavier, would you mind giving us some privacy, please?" I asked.

"Yes, Ma'am, would you like for me to carry Ellice to her room? She'd probably be more comfortable waking up in a familiar place when she does."

I looked over at her. She still looked so peaceful, but I didn't know how long she'd be asleep. I figured it wouldn't work out for her to stay there for the night either, so I nodded. "Yes, please."

He walked over and gently picked her up, then turned around to take her away. I could tell by the way he carried her, he cared for her. He didn't look at her the same as I'd seen Jake look at me, though.

Jake walked behind Xavier until he carried her through the door, then Jake shut it and locked it before turning around and walking back to the bed to sit at the foot of it. "What was that all about?" He didn't seem mad, but I could tell he wasn't happy with me either.

"What?" I suspected what he was referring to, but I wanted to know for sure before I answered.

"Why would you send me away?" He asked as he crossed his arms and leaned against the bedpost.

"I wanted to talk to him in private." I didn't think that needed an explanation, so that's all I said.

Jake looked down and nodded, like he was thinking. "Is there anything else you need your privacy for, 'cause I can leave and go home?" He said sarcastically as he looked back up at me.

I wasn't sure how to respond. Him being sarcastic like that with me was unusual, and I didn't appreciate it. The Eva in me wanted to tell him he could go right ahead if he was going to have that kind of attitude. Kaleah wanted to sit there and explain herself so he wouldn't be so upset with her. Then there was Jayde, the one I believed was probably the most level-headed. The one this time I would let decide how to respond. "Why are you angry, Jacob? Am I not allowed to speak to someone without you?" I asked calmly.

He must not have expected my response, either. He uncrossed his arms and relaxed a little. "What'd you feel you needed to discuss with him in private that you couldn't with me in the room?"

"Ellie..." I said unapologetically. "I wanted to know what he knew. I wanted to know what they had together... I wanted to read him, to see if I could trust him. And I'm sorry to tell you, but I knew none of that would be possible with you breathing down his neck... Now, are you satisfied?" I was now irritated that I had to explain myself. I had hoped Lane would have gotten the idea and explained it to him while they ate, but apparently that hadn't happened.

Jake didn't say anything, he just made a face like he was thinking about what I said.

"What's really your problem, Jake? Is it you have to take orders from me now? Is that what's bugging you? You're no longer in charge?"

"No, it's that you don't know how to keep yourself out of trouble, despite whatever I try to do to protect you. You have no idea who Hernandez is or who his men are, yet you think it's a good idea to send away the only two men that care about you, that love you… and are willing to protect you with our lives." He didn't raise his voice, but I could tell he was irritated by the tone he used.

"Are you serious? You're gonna blame me for the things that have happened to me?"

"That's not what I said, Eva, and you know it!"

"No, it sounds a lot like what you said… Despite whatever you do to protect me, I don't know how to keep myself out of trouble. Is there anything else you want to blame me for before you leave?"

"Eva…" He said with a look like I'd taken it too far.

"No, Jake, I'm not doing this with you… If you want to go home so bad, then fine, go home. I'm sorry I'm so much work for you and I keep getting myself in trouble or whatever the hell you said!" I motioned to the door as I said it.

He shook his head as he stood up. "No! I'm not leaving unless you order me to, and even then I won't listen."

"So you just plan on standing here, arguing with me?" I asked as I got out of the bed to stand in front of him.

"You don't know Hernandez, Eva. You don't know what his intentions are, what his motivations are… why he does the things he does. You don't know if he'll protect you the way you need protecting!" He must not have been over that part of our argument and felt the need to go back.

"Maybe I don't, but I know what he thinks of you now, and I wouldn't have if I hadn't been able to talk to him alone."

"What? What did he say?"

"He said I shouldn't marry you, that you were zealous and too ambitious, and you were only with me because of my father."

Jake instantly looked baffled. "See, that's the shit I'm talking about. He's an idiot that has no clue about who you really are, or what's the best way to protect you."

"Is that why you're upset with me? Are you afraid he's gonna win, like a 'who can protect me the best'—kind of thing?"

"It's because I'm not in control anymore, okay?" He said, taking a hold of both of my arms and making me sit back down on the bed. "You're mine, Eva! Hear me? Mine! And I love you more than anyone else ever will, and I want to protect you more than anyone else ever will, and that was taken from me. He took that!"

I didn't say anything. I just looked up at him and nodded like I understood because I did. He let his guard down and in his vulnerability told me the truth. He was upset because his world was now out of control—his control.

"I only have one job now, and it's the only job I want—protecting you! You're my life, baby. And the thought that I'm not in charge… yeah, it bugs me. It bugs the freakin' hell out of me."

I could see he felt overwhelmed, so I stood up and kissed him. Which, by the way he jerked, probably took him by surprise. "I'm sorry!" I said, pulling back for a second. "You're still in charge, baby." I wrapped my hands around his back and pulled back to lie against the bed, bringing him with me. "You can be in charge of me, since I'm in charge of him… Then you're in charge of him… okay?"

He nodded. "You're mine, Eva!" He whispered pushing the hair back out of my face, "Hear me?" He said softly.

I smiled.

"Say it," he whispered.

"I'm yours. You're in charge…" I said, smiling bigger.

"That's my girl," He said resting his forehead against mine.

"I'm sorry I threatened to leave you and go home," Jake whispered as he gently caressed my side. I was almost asleep, and it'd been hours since then, but he must have still been thinking about it.

I smiled, then opened my eyes to look at him. "What would you have done if I ordered you to?"

"Pretend to not hear you, just long enough to make you change your mind." He said with a large grin.

"Oh yeah… hmm, it kinda feels like that's what happened." I couldn't actually remember exactly how it happened though, since I was sleepy now.

"Not quite, but that's fine. That's the way I can tell Lane it happened, anyway." He smirked like he thought he was cute.

I wasn't going to bring it back up again, but since we were somewhat on the subject, I figured I'd ask him about Xavier. "Why is it you don't like Hernandez, like for real, not just you're rivals or whatever Lane said?"

Jake looked less than enthusiastic about the subject but went on, willing to humor me. "Well, we were rivals, so Lane was right… to a point. We'd worked together for the last couple of years before I left New York. It was a competition at first—who could capture the most Gypsyins. Then in turned into who would ascend rank fastest. Well, one day when I found out the way they were treating the ones we were bringing in, I told him I was going to switch units. I didn't want to do T&C anymore, so I was considering applying to be a personal guard for an Elite rank… But… before I got a chance to do that, because I gave him the idea, he applied to the only open position there was at the time and got accepted." Jake paused for a moment to sweep the hair out of my face before he continued. "So, because that position wasn't available, and I didn't want to do T&C here in New York anymore, I left to go to Nashville."

"Was that position guarding Ellie?"

"I don't know, maybe… When we apply, we don't get to choose who we guard. If it was, then it'd have been just by chance that it was the First Rank's daughter… if that's who he was originally assigned to, anyway."

"So are you still mad he took that position from you? Cause I mean… my sister might not be as much work as I am." I grinned.

"Oh, stop it… She's probably not as fun as you are either." He said, now smiling back. "I mean, is she as sexy as you? Yeah! But as fun… probably not." He smirked.

"You think you're funny?"

"Umm-hmm," he nodded, still with a big grin.

"I guess you'll have to ask Lane just how sexy she is after they fall in love..."

"Too late," he said quickly.

"What? He can't be in—"

"No," he interrupted to clarify. "He's already told me how sexy he thought she was. You don't have to love a woman to appreciate her beauty."

"Oh, I know that. I was just saying... So he likes her?" I felt the little girl inside me getting giddy at the idea of them being together.

Jake laughed, "Well, I think it's a bit early for that, especially since the only opportunity he got to see her awake was while she was swinging at him and calling him names. But, you know... I think since she looks like you, it wouldn't take much for her to woo him. When she's sober, that is."

"What do you mean, because she looks like me?" I understood everything else he was saying but thought that was an odd statement for him to throw in there.

He half-smiled, then looked away like I'd caught something he hadn't intended for me to. "Lane loves you, baby." He said, looking back at me.

I was confused since I thought I already knew that. "Like a brother... right?"

"No..." He shook his head slightly. "Like he told me, I better never break up with you, because you won't be available anymore by the time I realize I made a mistake."

I didn't say anything. I just stared at him, wondering why he was telling me all of this.

"You seem surprised..." He said, seeing my face.

"Uh, yeah... I mean... I am. Why is it you don't seem to be, um, like—"

"Concerned?" He finished my sentence.

"Yeah!" I said, emphasizing that was exactly the word I was thinking.

Jake smiled again as he rolled to his back, "'Cause he knows you're mine."

"Okay?" It didn't seem that simple to me.

"And he knows I'd kill him if he ever tried anything," He grinned as he turned his head to look back at me. "But really, he loves me and respects me, so he knows you're off limits, simple as that."

"Oh," I nodded slowly like I got it, "okay…"

"Should I have not told you that? I mean, you're kinda acting weird now."

"Hmm," I giggled as I moved over and rested my head on his arm while throwing my arm over his chest. "No… you don't have to worry about me, baby. I just think it's interesting, that's all." I intended to drop the subject, but then felt more intrigued the longer I thought about it. "What else has he said about me, though? I mean, 'cause now I wanna know more."

Jake laughed again as he ran his fingers though my hair, "Nothing else… that was it."

"You're lying," I said as I slapped his chest lightly.

"Yep," he chuckled.

"Do you think he's comfortable… I mean having to sleep in the guardroom, not in his big fancy bed he has at home?"

"What, now you're concerned about him all of a sudden?" Jake said, teasing me.

"No… we just have so much room in this bed, you know… I mean, I could sleep in the middle and he could have the other side." I said, teasing him back. "I'm totally cool with being shared."

He laughed out loud as he squeezed my head and shoulder with his arm. "No, he's good where he's at, but I'm sure he'd appreciate you thinking of him."

"I'm sure," I whispered as I closed my eyes. I was ready to go back to sleep.

"I spoke with your father again earlier… when you sent us away to eat." He said, prompting me to open my eyes again and reengage.

"Really? He wasn't too busy to have a conversation with you?" I asked, remembering that he had acted like he didn't have much time to chat when we'd first arrived.

"He wants you to go get your tag soon." Jake said it like he either didn't approve or was expecting me not to. I couldn't tell which.

"Okay?" I said, hoping he'd go on, maybe giving me insight on why he had said it the way he did.

"I didn't know how you felt about that… finally becoming a Coldier."

"Yeah…" I said, thinking about it myself, "to be honest, I don't know."

"You don't seem scared…" He rolled back to his side so he could look at me while we talked.

"Why would I be scared?"

He looked at me oddly. "It's an operation."

"What? It is?" I had no clue, but realized the more I thought about it, that made sense. Now, suddenly, I was scared as he suspected I would be.

"Yeah, baby, they have to put you out so they can insert the tag and tracker into your arm. It'd be too painful to do it while you're awake. I mean, I guess they could use local anesthesia, but with your track record as far as being around doctors… uh, I just don't think you'd be able to handle it mentally, if you know what I mean. I doubt you could sit there and hold still while they—"

"I get it, that's enough!" He was right, just listening to him talk about it was bothering me, let alone being awake through it.

"I'm sorry, baby."

"I know…" I sighed, trying to shake off the anxiety that had begun to build. "I didn't know it was a surgery but I guess it makes sense… It doesn't matter though, I don't think I need it. I mean, I have a tracker. Why do I need another one?"

"The Sicari may be able to track you, but we can't. We don't have the equipment that detects whatever frequency their trackers use. When you get a Coldier tag, the tracker is inside it… it's a good thing. That way, if you get kidnapped again, which won't happen by the way, but then we can find you sooner."

"Okay… that sounds great, but I changed my mind now. I really mean it. I don't want one anymore." The idea of being around any doctor again was well past my comfort zone. So having to be put out by one was definitely not going to happen.

"You have to have one, baby." Jake said softly, knowing it wasn't an option.

I knew he meant the best by it, but all I could think of was when Marcus said the same thing, right before he cuffed me and took me to Parker to have it done. "No! I can't do it. I… I… you don't get it, I just can't." I said, sitting up and moving to sit on the side of the bed.

"Eva, what's the matter?" He moved behind me like he was getting up to sit beside me.

"No," I said, standing up so he wouldn't touch me. The anxiety from thinking about being around a doctor again on top of the memories of what Marcus did was overwhelming me. "I don't wanna be tracked anymore. I don't even want the one that I have."

"Okay… baby, it's okay. Just calm down, here come sit back down. Let's talk about it."

"I can't." I said as I started to pace from the bed to the fireplace. *Breathe*, I thought, trying to keep myself calm though I could feel my chest beginning to feel tight.

"You'll be all right. Is that what's wrong? Are you scared of the operation? I'll be there. I won't let anything happen to you. Come here, baby, let's tal—."

"No, Jake…" Even if I wanted to, I couldn't talk about it, not when I felt my pulse in my throat. *Breathe…*

"Do you want them to remove the Sicari's tracker? I'm sure they can do that while you're in there." He said, assuming that would be a good incentive for me to agree to it.

"No, Jake!" I said louder since he wasn't getting the idea.

He didn't have a chance to respond when I heard banging on the door. "Jayde! Are you all right?" It was Xavier. He must have woken up when he heard me yelling.

I walked over to unlock the door and tell him I was fine when suddenly the knob turned and it opened without me. "Jayde?" He said, taking a step inside and looking around.

"Hernandez, she's fine, now leave!" Jake didn't sound happy that he'd come in without me saying he could.

I thought I locked it, but when I looked down at the knob, I saw that a key was sticking out of the lock. "Jayde?" He said again, totally ignoring Jake. His eyes narrowed on me like he could tell there was something wrong.

"Yes... I..." *Breathe!* I was having a hard time thinking of what to say, since I was surprised to see him as well as I was still trying to calm myself.

"Are you all right?" He asked again, but slower.

"Yes!" I said finally, looking back up at him, trying to fake a smile.

"Okay..." He said calmly, "Then do you mind if I speak with you in the hall for a moment?"

I looked over at Jake. He didn't look thrilled, but nodded, showing he was fine with it. "Okay," I said, then followed him just outside the door, into the hall.

Xavier gently rested his hand on my shoulder as he leaned in to talk to me under his breath, "I heard you yelling *no* at him... You can be honest with me and he won't know you said anything... Is there a problem?"

I suddenly realized how it must have looked. "Oh my gosh, no, not at all." I said as I pulled his hand off my shoulder. "I'm fine, Xavier... Really!"

He squinted a little, probably afraid I wasn't being honest, then relaxed and nodded, "All right... If you change your mind, you can tell me."

I didn't know what else to say to make him believe me, so I just nodded, thanked him for checking on me, and returned to my room.

Jake was waiting on the other side of the door for me when I stepped in. "You're tired, baby. Why don't you come lie back down and let me help you relax?" He said softly after he shut the door, then wrapped his arm around my waist and walked me back to the bed. "We don't have to talk about it again until you're ready to."

I took a deep breath, willing myself to relax and forget about it. "Okay…"

Before I pulled the covers back to get in, he leaned down and kissed me. "I know just what you need." He murmured against my mouth.

"Sleep?" I said dryly.

He laughed. "No, a massage," he said as he gently pushed me back to lie flat on the bed.

"Oh really?" I asked, suspicious to his real motives.

He grinned. "Really. Just a nice relaxing massage, nothing else."

I rolled my eyes, not believing him. "Fine, then start with this," I said, then lifted my foot up to his chest.

"Whatever you need, baby… What. Ever. You. Need." He winked, then started to rub it.

7

FORGING NEW BONDS

"What does Ellie normally do around here all day?" I asked as I sat and stared out a bay window in one of the great rooms. I thought I'd speak to Xavier and break the awkward silence that had built up in the room since Jake had left to go to the restroom.

"Well…" he pointed to the upstairs. "Just down the hall from your room is a library. She doesn't normally go in there. I don't think she enjoys reading… but if you're bored, it's an option."

"I'm not bored… I'm just asking." I enjoyed looking out the window. It was entertaining to watch as the guards scurried around the courtyard outside.

"She asked to see you this morning." Xavier said, probably knowing that would get my attention away from the window for a moment, so I turned to look at him.

"She did?" I felt excited at the idea of seeing her un-inebriated, but slightly scared, too.

"Yes… She's probably in the East wing corridor if you'd like for me to take you to her." He said, taking a step back and motioning toward his right. "That's her favorite place to be. It's a hall full of

windows. She's like you; she enjoys the sunlight she gets from them."
He said, assuming that's why I was sitting next to one.

"When Jake comes back then, yes, please." I smiled, then looked
over at Lane to see how he would react to that.

"Why do you need to wait on Agent Miles?" Xavier asked, pulling
my attention back to him.

I looked at him oddly, not sure why he'd even ask that. "Um…
because… I feel like it." I didn't need to give him any more of an
explanation than that, and I didn't intend to either.

He nodded once, then shrugged slightly. "Fair enough," he said,
then returned to his guard stance with his hands behind his back,
looking away from me like he knew I was done talking to him.

"Kaleah," Lane said as he walked over and sat down in the chair
next to mine. "If you want, I can go look through the library later and
find something you might like to read."

It was a sweet suggestion, but I was suspicious he was using it
more as an excuse to go see the library himself, rather than just for me.

"I'd love that, Lane," I said, smiling even though I honestly didn't
care about the books.

He looked happy that I accepted his offer, but didn't get to respond
before we both saw Jake come back into the room.

"Hey, baby…" I stood up and walking over to Jake. "Ellie asked to
see me, so Xavier is going to take us to the East wing." I said it like he
knew he had the option to tell me if he didn't think it was a good idea,
though he didn't say anything like that at all.

"All right… Are you ready to see her again?"

"Yeah," I said quickly as I looked at Xavier, so he knew I was
ready to go.

"Follow me this way then," he said, moving away from the wall.
As he walked, he looked at the other agents that were standing around
the room and made a gesture, instructing them to follow us as well.

We walked from one room to another, each appearing to
effortlessly blend in with the next. The ceilings and walls were all full
of delicately engraved woodwork, set apart by large panels of what

looked like textured plaster. I didn't know what the building was before my father got a hold of it and had it turned into his own private mansion, but it was massive and beautiful, to say the least. It was so large and elaborate; his house in Nashville paled in comparison.

As we followed Xavier's winding navigation through the house, we entered a dark hall. I could barely make out a ceiling light fixture as we walked past, but I had no idea where the switch would be and none of the agents with me appeared to be in a hurry to find it so we continued walking. Upon rounding a corner at the end of the hall, a flood of light hit my senses suddenly. It was almost so bright that it was hard to distinguish initially what was what and where I was going. Soon though, once my eyes had fully adjusted, I saw her. There Ellie was, like an angel, peacefully sitting on a small window seat farther down the corridor. She was facing away from us, gazing out one of the windows.

Xavier, who had been leading us, suddenly came to a halt. Without saying anything, he turned toward me and motioned for me to go on ahead. Then he made eye contact with Jake and Lane as he slowly backed himself up to the wall and took his guard stance. I looked over at Jake before proceeding, but almost like he had read Xavier's look, he too motioned for me to go ahead while he took a similar stance as Xavier, backing himself up to the wall to wait. Lane and the other agents quickly followed suit, lining up along the wall on my left and right. Thinking it odd, and feeling a little nervous, I turned back to look at Lane, who also didn't say anything, just smiled a large smile and nodded while making a shoo motion for me to go on by myself.

Seeing I was on my own, I turned back toward Ellie and slowly moved closer to her until I was standing almost behind her. I was about to say her name when I noticed her reflection in the glass. She noticed mine at the same time and turned around to see me. "Jayde?" She looked like she'd been crying.

"Ellie…" I said softly, not knowing what to expect.

She didn't say anything else, she just stood up suddenly and threw her arms around me.

"I missed you," I said, trying not to cry, but I could feel tears already rolling down my cheeks as I returned her embrace.

"I didn't know if I would ever see you again," she whispered as she held on to me like she was afraid I wasn't really there and it was all an illusion.

I didn't know what to say, so I just moved my head in agreement where she could feel it and rubbed her back to comfort her.

"But you're back now... for good, right? You're not going to go away again?" She asked, like she was desperate to know. She sounded so sweet, nothing like the woman I'd seen the day before, but just like the girl I'd left.

"Ellie..." I said, pulling back to see her face. "I'm sorry..." I couldn't contain it any longer. As the words slipped from my mouth, the tears poured like a damn breaking, letting me release a whole mess of emotions I didn't even know I had contained in there. "I'm sorry, Ellie. I'm so sorry..." I couldn't say anything else. The only words I could conjure up were those three over and over as I repeated them between breaths and tears.

"Jayde..." She said pushing the hair back out of my face, "It wasn't your fault... I'm sorry I was upset with you..." Then she leaned in to hug me again and let me continue to cry against her shoulder. "I was just scared. I lost you, then Mom... I never thought I'd see either of you again." She continued as she struggled with losing breath herself from crying. "One day you were there, then the next thing I know, you were gone... I thought they'd killed you."

"No..." I shook my head against her, "They tried, Ellie, so many have tried... but they couldn't... I'm think I'm invincible." I sniffed, trying not to laugh.

I could feel her take a deep breath in, like she wanted to laugh as well, but she didn't either. "You won't leave again, right, Jayde? If so, I don't think I could handle it... I can barely keep myself together these days as it is." She said softly, as her tears began to wane.

"I won't ever leave you like that again..." I said as I thought about what she needed to do as well. "Will you agree to stop drinking like you do?" I knew it could be hard for her, but I was committed, so I wanted her to be as well.

She didn't say anything for a moment, she just clung to me like she didn't want to let go. "Do you promise?" She asked like she knew I wouldn't say yes if I didn't intend to keep it.

"Yes, Ellie… I promise. You have my word."

She let go of me and pulled back, sliding her hands down my arms. "Then I promise—," she started to say something else before she stopped and looked down at my forearm. She didn't say anything for a second. She just paused, staring at it. Then she looked up suddenly, like she was confused. "I thought they made you a Sicari… Dad said they forced you to be a spy… Where's your tag?" I assumed she meant my Sicari tag.

"Ellie…" I wanted to tell her I thought it was my idea to leave, but I didn't have the heart to. "It's in my head… They put it in my head."

"Oh," she said, looking from my hairline to my arm like she was sad, "this makes you look like a Gypsyin."

"I know… that's what I thought I was for years after I'd been erased."

"Erased?" Her eyes widened as she took in a sharp breath. She really didn't know the things I'd been through. "They erased you too?" She asked like she couldn't bear the thought of it.

I figured she was referring to the Sicari. "Yeah, something like that," I said, not wanting her to know it was actually the Coldiers who'd done it first, and then continued repeatedly until I was freed.

"Well, how do you remember me then… and Dad and… who you are?"

"Jake," I said, looking over toward where the men were standing. "A Coldier agent found me… He saved me."

She looked at them when I did, but didn't turn her head back toward me when I turned to look at her. "Really?" She said like she was looking for him. "Which one is he?"

"The tall one."

"Then who's the other guy? I don't recognize him either?" She asked, finally turning to look at me again.

"His brother, Lane." I said, then turned to look at the window seat before sitting down.

She looked back down the hall toward them as she nodded like she was taking it all in, then turned to see I'd sat and moved over to sit down next to me.

"You're going to get a Coldier tag now that you remember who you are again, right?" She asked as she picked up my wrist and swept her hand slowly down the smooth skin of my forearm.

I didn't respond for a second, I just sat there staring at my arm, watching her move her hand slowly up and down it until finally I had enough gumption to tell her the truth. "I can't…"

"Why?" She looked up quickly, like she hadn't expected that answer.

"I… I just can't." I didn't want to tell her why. I didn't think she'd understand.

"But, Jayde… you have to." She said like she was mimicking Jake from the night before. "You are father's daughter…" She must have had her own reasons that meant I had to, but I didn't think it did.

"It's not that easy," I said, looking at my arm. "I'm—"

"I'll stop drinking," she said suddenly, like she figured that would do it, like that's all I wanted and in exchange, I'd agree.

I looked over at Jake. He was acting like he wasn't listening, but I knew he was. There were many reasons I needed that tag, and marrying him was the main one. I turned back around and looked at my arm again, thinking about what all it would entail and if I could make myself do it, even though everything in me deep down was terrified to.

"You love him…" she said, reaching for my hand to hold it.

"Yes." I looked up at her, trying to smile.

"He can't be with a Gypsyin… it's illegal." She whispered, like she thought she had figured something out.

"I know," I said, thinking about it, thinking about him and how much he'd already sacrificed just to be with me. "Okay… I'll get the tag." I said, looking back at him, knowing he could hear me. "I wanna be with him, so I'll do what I have to do."

She squeezed my hand, then leaned in to hug me again like she was proud of me. In that moment, for the first time in a long time, I felt proud of myself as well.

"Jayde, dear, you're not eating… you need to eat!" Dad ordered as he looked at my practically untouched plate.

"Oh, yeah… sorry," I realized he was right when I looked down and saw I'd barely taken more than a couple spoonfuls of the soup that had been served to us first and none of the main course.

"Jacob," Dad continued. "I'm glad we're able to sit down like this as a family, finally. Sometimes it's nice to put business aside and just enjoy each other's company."

Jake, who was sitting across from me with Lane next to him, nodded and smiled, showing he appreciated that they were both allowed to sit with Dad, Ellie, and me. "It is, Sir."

"So, you said you two were family. How so?" Dad asked, gesturing between them. I'm sure he already knew everything about both men and already had them thoroughly background checked before allowing them to be in the same house with his daughters, but it was nice of him to try to be cordial.

"Yes, Sir, Henry is actually my first cousin. Our mothers are sisters, but we were raised more like brothers." Jake said before taking another bite of his meatloaf.

"Oh well, that's nice." Dad said like he really did already know.

"Henry…" Ellie said suddenly, thinking out loud, like she was tasting how the name rolled off her tongue. "I've never met anyone with that name before."

Lane looked across the table at her like a deer in headlights. He didn't say anything, he just stared for a moment, almost in shock that she would speak his name. Then, almost as if Jake silently kicked him under the table, his trance finally broke and he spoke. "Oh, yes… it's…

uh, it's an English name, I believe." He said like it was the first thing that came to mind, then swiftly moved his eyes from her to me. I wondered if he was checking to see if I was going to laugh at him. I wanted to, but I knew he was probably just nervous and needed grace, so I didn't even smirk, even though deep down, I did think it was funny.

Suddenly, I was startled when an arm from someone behind me reached over to grab my bowl of soup, assuming I was done. "Oh, I'm sorry, miss," an older man's voice followed. "Were you not finished?"

I was about to look up at him to tell him 'no go ahead', when something about his arm caught my attention—he didn't have a tag. *He's a Gypsyin.*

Dad suddenly cleared his throat. "I think she's done, Thomas. Thank you."

Thomas nodded, took my bowl, and walked away.

"Dad?" I blinked a few times to bring myself back and clear my thoughts.

"Yes, sweetheart?" He said before taking another bite of food.

"Why would you have Gypsyins? People shouldn't be owned."

He furrowed his brow, slowly lifting his eyes back to mine. "Jayde… I don't have Gypsyins and for that very reason, I agree with you."

I was suddenly extremely confused. "If you don't have any, then what's Thomas? His arm didn't have a tag. Not only that, but if you agree with me then why is that even a law here? Just make New York do what Nashville does with them."

"Jayde, it's not—" Jake started to say something before Dad gently raised his hand to dismiss him like he realized I didn't know something that apparently everyone else did.

"Jayde, honey… Thomas does have a tag. It's in his other arm. He was one of the first Coldiers to receive his tag. It was before they standardized the tagging system and determined a set location for the tag. And as for the laws… I am just the chief military officer in the eastern division. I don't make the laws, I only do my best to enforce them."

"Uh… okay… But then why do New York and Nashville have different Gypsyin laws?"

"Members of the Governing Council make the laws. Each council member represents one of the Coldier cities and has the freedom to enact laws specific to their jurisdiction within certain guidelines."

"Oh…" I looked up to see Lane now grinning at me. I narrowed my eyes at him, and like he got the idea, he suddenly quit.

"It's okay, Jayde." Ellie said probably realizing I felt stupid for not knowing that. "A lot has changed since you've been gone."

Before I had a chance to respond, Jake spoke up. "It's okay, we'll catch her up. She's a quick study." He said it to them but was lovingly looking at me.

"Jayde," Dad said, changing the conversation. "Have you thought about where you would like to have your wedding?" He asked with a proud father's smile, probably happy to be discussing pleasure rather than business for once.

"Wedding?" Ellie asked, gasping in surprised, "I didn't know it was already that serious." She said, elbowing me.

I could feel myself blush. "Uh, yeah… I, um… No, Dad, actually… I haven't had a chance to think about where I'd like to have it. I don't really know the city well enough and, well, to be honest, I didn't know when it would be safe to have a ceremony. Not to mention, Jake's family doesn't really—" I stopped myself. I didn't know how much Jake would want me to tell him, so I didn't go on. "Um, I mean… never mind."

"Jake's family, what?" Dad asked, not willing to let it go.

I had intended to say they didn't approve, but I changed my mind and didn't want to throw them under the bus even though I whole heartedly felt like his mother and sister deserved it. "They don't know me as Jayde, that's all. They don't know that you're my father." I said, trying to cover for myself. When I looked up, Jake looked like he appreciated my forethought to tippy-toe around the subject.

"Oh, well, we can fix that!" Dad said, apparently already knowing a way to correct the issue.

"Have you not met them yet?" Ellie asked, sounding confused.

"No, she has." Jake said, stepping in to help me navigate the murky waters, "That was just when she didn't remember who she was yet, that's all."

"Oh, well, how did you get your memory back then?" She asked, looking at me again.

I wanted to answer her honestly, but knew the story was far too complicated to give her exact details. "Well, the first time Jake was able to get a special medicine from a Coldier doctor to counteract the serum." I said, hoping that answer would be enough to fix her confusion.

"He did?" Dad quickly piped up like this was news to him and he'd not heard that part of our story before.

"Uh," I looked at Jake, afraid that I had said something I shouldn't have.

"I did." He said, willing to accept whatever consequences, if there were any, that resulted from doing such a thing.

Dad leaned back and rested his hands in his lap like he was thinking, then looked back at Jake. "So let me get this correct, when she lost her memory initially from the Coldiers serum, you gave her a medicine that brought it back?"

Jake hesitantly replied. "Yes, that is correct, Sir."

"Jayde," Dad looked back at me, "how many times were you erased before that time… after you had the intel?"

I couldn't figure out why he was asking, but I tried to think of the most accurate answer to give him, anyway. "Um," I swallowed. It wasn't pleasant having to think about all the sessions I'd spent with Miller and each of the times he'd erased me himself or had a doctor do it for him. "I… umm… I…"

"Too many, Sir," Jake said, answering for me.

Dad looked at him and nodded. "I understand." He said, then looked back at me. "Jayde, sweetie, how certain are you that you knew the entire code to the vault in Knoxville?"

I furrowed my brow a little when I realized why he was asking. "Oh my gosh, you think I forgot some of it?"

"Is that so hard to believe?" He said point blank, like that was precisely what he thought.

"But I didn't forget, Dad. I know that I know the code, I'm certain."

"It's twelve digits, Jayde, not eleven." He said like he'd suspected this all along.

"What? No, that's not true… It's eleven, I know it."

"Miles…" He turned to address Jake, now ignoring my denial. "Do you remember the doctor that you got the medicine from?"

Jake stiffened, knowing why Dad was asking, but couldn't lie. "Um, Yes… Yes, Sir, I do."

"Good, then first thing next week, you can travel to where the Coldier doctor is and acquire more of that medicine. If Jayde is in danger because everyone wants the missing piece of code that she's forgotten, then the best way to resolve this is for her to remember so that I can have the rest of the code first. Once I have it and send men to retrieve what's in the vault, then there will be no need for anyone to come after Jayde any longer." Dad acted like it was just that easy even though I think Jake and I probably both knew it was absolutely not that simple.

"What? Dad, no, you can't send him away… I need him here!" Not to mention the countless other reasons I didn't like Dad's plan. That was the one I felt I needed to verbalize.

"Sir…" I could tell Jake wasn't happy with this plan either. "I'm not certain that's the best idea right now."

"It's settled, Agent Miles." Dad said, not willing to budge. "If you're leery of traveling so far, I can send men to escort you. You may take a team of however many agents you'd like."

"But her protection while she's here, Sir, I'm—"

"I understand your position, son. I really do. I lost my wife, the love of my life, in a situation similar to this. If it eases your mind, you can leave Lane with his own team under him to guard her in tandem with Hernandez and his men. Besides, now with the girls together, and looking as similar as they do, I wouldn't mind more men to help keep them both safe, anyway. The last thing I want would be for something to happen to my Ellie if the Sicari come thinking she's Jayde."

Probably for the same reason as me, Jake didn't continue arguing. It was futile. Although he still looked dejected, he just leaned back in his seat and nodded his head to agree, even though it probably about killed him to do so.

8

DANGERS IN THE DARK

"Miles… What are you gonna do?" Lane asked Jake as soon as we had returned to my room and shut the door behind us.

"I'm gonna do what I was ordered to do." Jake said stiffly, like he didn't really want to think about it.

"But—"

"But nothing, Lane!" Jake quickly cut him off. "I'm going to do what I need to and you are, too. You're gonna stay here and watch Eva. You're not gonna let anything happen to her and I'll be back as soon as I can, hear me?"

Lane didn't say anything else. He just slowly nodded, then looked over at me like it was my turn to try.

"He ain't gonna listen to me." I said, addressing Lane's look. "Believe me, I don't want him to leave any more than you do."

"Lane," Jake continued, "start thinking about which men you want under you. You have three days. You should have no less than ten men. Twelve would be better. Mr. Prescott has given us an opportunity to bring in our own guys, so I'd say let's use it wisely. Maybe when I return, he'll let us keep the guard in tandem with Hernandez, as he mentioned. Or better yet, Hernandez and his team can watch Ellie and you and me can watch Eva with our own men."

"What if I go with you?" I said suddenly as soon as the thought popped into my head. "It'd make me a moving target... harder to catch, ya know? Especially if Miller is already in New York. I'd say, me leaving to go with you would be safer than me staying here."

"No," Jake said without even acting like he really thought about it. "You're staying, end of discussion."

"But Jake..." I didn't care that he said *end of discussion*. I intended to keep discussing it as long as I felt like it. "You haven't even thought about it. I think it's a good idea."

"I have, Eva." He said as he turned toward me fully, raising his voice a little. "Between dinner and now I've thought about a lot of things, and that was one of them. If you think I'm taking you, without a Coldier tag or tracker, out of this city into Sicari territory and then into another city where they'd just have to go on our word that you are who we say you are, you're sadly mistaken. This is the safest place for you, even if I'm not here, so *here* is where you're gonna stay." He said, lowering his tone like it was an order. "Understand?"

"Yes," I mumbled, then gave Lane a *see I told you* look before I turned and sat down on the bed.

"What if she had her tag?" Lane asked cautiously.

"What is your problem, Lane? Why is it that you can't just follow orders?" Jake asked, motioning with his hands like he was confused.

Lane didn't respond.

"He's scared to be in charge of me again." I figured Lane wouldn't admit to it so I would throw it out there and see if he denied it.

Both men looked at me suddenly before slowly looking back at each other. "She's right..." Lane said calmly as he took a seat in one of the armchairs by the fireplace.

Jake nodded as he looked toward the ground like he was thinking about it. "All right... that's fair enough," he said, then paused. "But I'm sorry, you're just gonna have to man up and do it. I don't like this any more than you do, but it was an order. So we have no choice."

"Would you take me if I had my tag?" I wasn't ready to get it, but I wanted to know if it was even an option.

Jake brought his eyes up to mine, then quickly glanced away before taking a seat in the other armchair. "I thought you weren't ready to get a tag yet?"

"I'm not… I'm just asking." I said, intentionally not committing to anything.

"Maybe she can get a special one with her name on it somewhere so people will know who she is." Lane said, probably thinking he was being cute.

Jake didn't say anything, he just looked away like what Lane said had sparked a thought. "No, never mind. Even if you had a tag, baby, it wouldn't keep you safe if you went with me. It might even make you a target for other men like Miller that have something against your father."

"Ugh… Lane!?" I said exaggeratively, as I threw my hands up and threw myself backwards onto the bed like I was blaming him for Jake changing his mind.

I didn't hear anything for a minute when suddenly I saw Lane standing next to the bed, looking down at me. "Are you done being dramatic?"

I smiled at him. "You've known him longer than me. How do you get him to change his mind on stuff?" I asked, sitting back up.

Lane quickly looked down at my chest before turning to look back at Jake. "He's a man… maybe he'll respond to… uh… your womanly charm… I'm sure you've mastered that already, Kaleah." He walked over to open the door. "I'll leave you to work your magic," he said with a wink, then turned to walk out, shutting the door behind him.

I looked over at Jake, sitting there, not paying any attention to us, just still thinking about everything. "Hey!" I said to get his attention, so he'd look up at me. "Lane said you'll change your mind if I *persuade* you." I smiled with a wink so he'd get the innuendo.

"Lane's an idiot sometimes," he said without smiling, letting his eyes slowly drift back down to the floor.

I got the idea he was stuck in a serious mood and not feeling playful at all. "Maybe he is an idiot..." I said, getting up from the bed and walking over to him. "But I'm sure he's a happy idiot."

Jake didn't respond. He just continued to stare at the floor, lost in thought.

"What are you thinking about?" I asked, sitting down on the floor in front of him between his legs so he would have to look at me.

"A lot, baby... I'm sorry, I'm not in the mood right now." He said as he reached up to run his hand over my hair.

"Okay... like what, though?"

He looked at me as he let out a deep sigh, willing to relax for a moment to talk. "First, I'm trying to think of what men I trust for Lane to have under him. Then, well... I'm trying to think of who I want to travel with me down to Charlotte. Plus, I have to think about how I'm going to find that doctor and make her give me the medicine again. Not to mention, I don't even know if it's all for nothing, since you're certain you didn't forget any of the intel..." He paused like he was thinking about all of it, then went on. "I really don't want to give you that medicine again, either. I remember what it did to you last time and how sick it made you there for a while... I don't want to see you go through that again, baby. And I don't even know if your dad's idea about getting the intel first to stop them from coming after you is even realistic."

By the time he had finished, it was easy to see why he was still so serious. I didn't say anything. I just leaned my head against his thigh and reached up to rub his side, so he knew I was listening.

"Trust me, baby... I want you with me, I really do. But it'd be selfish of me to take you just so I have you with me, when I know it's safer for you to be here, watched over by way more agents than I'd have with me." He said, reaching up to stroke my cheek with the back of his fingers.

"Okay." I smiled, so he knew I wouldn't try to fight him about it anymore.

"You're gonna be fine. Lane will protect you. Even if he's scared that he'll screw it up somehow, he won't. And..." He leaned forward and readjusted himself in the seat, "I won't be gone long. It's a few days there, and hopefully not long until I can find her, then a few days back. You'll be fine." He said it again, probably reassuring himself just as much as he was trying to reassure me.

"Okay…"

"Do you mind going and telling Lane he can come back in now? We need to go over details and discuss which agents he's going to use."

"Sure," I said, as I got up and walked over to the door, then called out into the hall for Lane.

"He went to the East corridor, Ma'am." Xavier said after I stepped out and said Lane's name again with no response.

"What? Why… I mean… How do you even know that?" I asked, looking around, thinking surely he was mistaken.

"Probably to visit with your sister, Ma'am… I sent a man to follow him. He returned and told me that's where he went." Xavier said, acting like he didn't want to admit he'd done it, but he wasn't sorry that he had either.

"Oh, um… okay…" I thought that was odd. "Well…" I turned to look back into the room at Jake. "Hey, Lane left, I'm gonna go get him, okay?"

Jake seemed to be lost in thought again, then looked up finally to answer. "Sure… Just don't go far…"

"Okay," I said, as I slowly shut the door behind me. "It's not far, it's just the East wing… I remember how to get there." I mumbled to myself.

"Jayde?" Xavier asked, as I walked past him and started down the stairs.

"Yes?" I knew what he wanted. He wanted to follow me, but I acted like that wasn't necessary. If Lane was talking to Ellie, I didn't really want Xavier there to hear them and potentially screw anything up between the two.

"Are you going to the East wing?"

"Yes, I'm going to see my sister. The house is safe, right? I don't need you to follow me."

"Well, um…" I could see he wanted an excuse to follow me but couldn't deny the house being safe, so then, in reality, he didn't have one.

"Okay, good… you stay here and I'll be right back." I smiled. "I don't need any of your men following me either, Xavier. I have Lane, he's enough."

He made a face suggesting he was used to that order—probably something Ellie told him a lot—and he didn't like it, but was willing to comply, anyway. "Yes, Ma'am," he said, then returned to standing against the wall at to the top of the stairs.

"Thanks!" I smiled, then turned to continue down the stairs.

I had an excellent visual memory, so even though I'd only been to the East wing's corridor one time, I remembered exactly how to get there again without help. I walked through the same great rooms that Xavier had taken us through, then weaved my way through a few other smaller rooms until I saw the darkened hallway that was just before the corridor with all the windows. Because it was after dark, there wasn't much if any light so I couldn't see where I was walking whatsoever, but I figured there was some light on the other side, so I would be fine. I walked into it slowly, trying to feel for where I was going. At the same time, I stepped lightly to avoid making any noise that might disturb Lane and Ellie if they were in the corridor talking.

As I neared the other end of the hall, I began to faintly hear Lane's voice. *Atta boy, Lane.* I stayed hidden in the darkness of the hall, but moved close enough to hear what they were talking about.

"Nah, I'm an only child… Jake's the closest thing I've got to a sibling. You're lucky to have Kal… I mean Jayde, as your sister. She's an amazing person."

"What were you about to call her?" Ellie asked him, like she'd caught his slip of tongue.

"Oh, um… Well, when Jake first met her she thought her name was Kaleah, then he found out it was Eva before we knew she was Jayde." Lane didn't really explain it all that well but I figured I could go over it again later with her if I really needed to.

"Oh, okay… so have you known her for a long time?" Ellie asked.

"For a while now, yeah…" Lane said, then paused. "Are you always out here by yourself? It doesn't seem safe for you to be alone."

"Well…" Ellie started to reply, but then stopped like she was considering what to say. "Xavier used to guard me, but he… um… he stopped when we got into a fight a few weeks ago."

"About what, if you don't mind me asking?" Lane asked, no longer sounding shy or tripping over his words.

"Um… well… we'd been together, you know… dating, for a while and um…" She didn't sound like she felt as comfortable talking to him as much just yet, though. "He just wasn't happy with me, that's all."

"Because you were drinking?" Lane pressed her to continue.

"Well… not exactly. He's just um…"

"You don't have to tell me, it's okay." Lane said, getting the idea she didn't really want to talk about it. But now I was curious what their fight was about, since it didn't sound like it'd happened the way Xavier told me it did.

"Oh ok, I'm sorry."

"You don't have to apologize…" Lane said sweetly, then paused. "Wow, I just can't get over how much you look like Jayde."

"Yeah… we didn't use to as much when we were in our teens, so um… I don't know, maybe we just both had to grow into it. We looked a lot alike when we were little, though. I remember people thought we were twins. To this day, Dad still can't tell us apart in some of the pictures he had of us when we were little girls… You kind of look like Jake, I mean not exactly, but I can tell that you're both family."

Lane laughed, "Yeah… we've never been mistaken for twins but when we were both in high school, I did have a girlfriend break up with me when she thought she saw me kissing another girl when in fact it was actually him."

Ellie giggled like she thought that was funny. I did too, then caught myself before I got loud enough for them to hear me.

"So, are you and Xavier still together?" Lane asked.

"Um… well, it's complicated, but the last time we talked, he said he was done with me so… um no, I guess not."

I wished I could peek around the corner to see them, but I knew I'd be caught if I tried. I didn't know how long I should stay and eavesdrop on them either because I knew before long Jake would notice my absence and come looking for me. I felt like I'd heard enough at that point to turn around and go back. I didn't want to disturb them and break up their conversation, so I hoped Jake understood when I returned without Lane.

I slowly tippy-toed backward, about to turn around, when I suddenly ran into something behind me. It was a person because I heard a grunt as I bumped into him. I didn't have a chance to think before I started to scream on impulse.

"Elliceva… Shhh," he hissed as his hand covered my mouth. I tried to swing for where I thought he'd be, but I couldn't see him. Then suddenly, his other arm wrapped around me from behind and dragged me backwards.

"Kaleah?" Lane yelled for me, sounding like he'd just rounded the corner. "Was that yo… Holy shit!" He must have been able to see something by the way he sounded, but I was still clearly impaired because I'd yet to see anything but faint shadows as I continued to fight against whoever was holding onto me.

"I'll go get the men!" Ellie yelled, then I heard a whooshing sound like she'd run past us.

Lane yelled again, sounding much closer. "Let her go, or I'll shoot!"

I tried to elbow the man, but it didn't seem to matter. He had to be much larger than me because I couldn't break free. Then I had a thought—*bite him!*

After Lane yelled, the man froze, so I bit down, making him scream as he pulled his hand off my mouth.

"Lane!" I said, so he'd know it was me, just in case his vision wasn't as clear either.

"Debo proteger el intel," the man quickly spoke to me in Latin, then I heard the sound of metal against leather as he brought his hand up to my forehead, pulling my head back toward him to expose my throat.

"No!" Lane yelled again. Then, suddenly, I saw a bright flash of light followed by a deafening crack that pierced the air, forcing my ears into a void of silence and leaving me stunned and reeling without sight or sound to give me direction.

"Kaleah!"

I was shaking when I faintly heard my name. The initial silence in my ears slowly morphed into a muffled ringing.

"Kaleah!" I heard it again, then felt arms wrap around me and move me to sit on the floor. "Kaleah, answer me…"

"Jake?"

"No, Kaleah… It's Lane… Are you all right? Tell me you're all right!" He was so muffled I could barely hear him.

"Jake…" I breathed. I wanted Jake.

"Oh my gosh, Kaleah… Tell me if you're hurt! Did he hurt you?" He asked as he pulled away, while keeping a hand on my shoulder.

"I… uh…"

"Here…" He scooped me up and walked around to the corridor where there were different shades of orange and blue hues of light shining through the windows from the glow of the city's skyline. He set me down on the floor and leaned me up against the wall. "Look at me, Kaleah. Can you hear me?" He said as he cupped my face in his hands and guided me to look at him, probably so I could read his lips.

I shook my head a little. I was confused and only half knew what was going on and why I was there.

"Are you hurt?" He said loudly, then looked down at my body, checking for himself.

"Lane…"

"Yeah?" He took his hands and ran them down my arms, then reached up and felt around my neck before moving them up to sweep down my hair at my temples.

I didn't say anything else when suddenly the light in the hall came on, brightening up the corridor as well.

"Jayde?" Jake was yelling out my name.

"Miles, she's in here." Lane said quickly as he stood up, then returned to me when he saw them coming. "I shot him… I think she's okay!" He said as Jake rounded the corner.

"Okay…" Jake quickly knelt down in front of me. "Jayde…" He leaned in to catch my wandering gaze so he could look into my eyes. "I'm here. Okay, baby… I'm here now…"

9

SHARED PAIN

"Jayde?" Xavier called as he rounded the corner a few moments after Jake, then walked over and looked down at me.

"What happened, Lane?" Jake asked as he started to do what Lane had, taking his hands and running them over me every which way, checking for where I was hurt.

"I was in here talking to Ellie when I heard Kaleah scream like she was in the hall. When I went to check on her, it looked like he was trying to take her, but when I pulled my gun and told him to let her go, he yelled something in another language and pulled a knife. It looked like he was about to slit her throat when I shot him. I don't know if she's hurt… she won't answer me. I think she's confused."

"She's in shock," Jake said, still staring at me. "Did he hurt you, baby?"

I looked around, trying to think about what had happened. Everything had happened so quickly it was hard to remember. "Um… I'm… I don't know."

"I think she's fine. I don't see anything that looks like she's bleeding… I think all this is his blood." Jake said as he motioned to my shoulder.

"Who is he?" Lane asked, looking over at Xavier.

"His arm has a Coldier tag. It's hard to tell by looking at his face now, but it looks like he could have been one of the cooking staff. Or he might be one of Miller's men, I'm not sure." Xavier looked from Lane back to me, "Jayde… Did you recognize him?"

"She can't see in the dark… not that well, anyway." Jake spoke up as he leaned forward to pull me toward him so he could hold me. "That's probably the only reason he was able to grab her."

"What was she doing in the hall… *by herself?*" Lane asked angrily as he looked at Xavier.

"Coming to find you!" Xavier snapped back, like he thought Lane was accusing him of something. "She ordered both me and my men to stay near her room. She said that you were *enough*, and that she didn't need us."

"Ohhh, well…" Lane nodded with a pleased smile as he looked back down at me like that was acceptable.

"It's not Miller's man." Jake said, cradling my head to rest it against his shoulder. "They wouldn't have spoken another language. That sounds like a Sicari."

"Whoever he was, why would he want to kill her? I thought they were all looking for the intel." Lane asked.

"Another reason it's probably a Sicari," Jake said. "You're right… Miller wouldn't have ordered for his men to do anything but take her. He wants her alive… she's no good to him dead."

"It was Latin." I mumbled, thinking about what all the men were saying.

"What?" Jake pulled back, happy I was ready to talk.

"He spoke Latin…" I said again under my breath.

"Okay… Baby, do you know what he said?" Jake asked slowly, like he wasn't sure if it was hard for me to understand him.

"Debo proteger el intel… I must protect the intel."

"Holy shit…" Lane whisper-shouted, "He *was* gonna kill her!"

I heard Ellie suddenly gasp and make a noise like she was about to cry. She was so silent before that I don't think anyone else knew she was standing behind them, listening.

"Oh… Uh…" Lane turned when he heard her, "I'm sorry…" He

said, walking toward her with one arm out as an invitation for a comforting hug.

"Miles, how would a Sicari get a Coldier's tag?" Xavier asked, still trying to figure it all out.

"Jayde? Ellice?" Dad called out from the hall before he rounded the corner, prompting everyone to stiffen and stand more at attention. "Are they both all right… who's hurt?"

Jake squeezed me, then stood, pulling me up with him, holding me tight to his chest.

"It was Jayde, Sir…" Xavier said, "But we believe she's all right, just shaken up, that's all."

Dad looked from Xavier over to Ellie, then over to me as he stepped forward with his arms out as Jake released me to him. "Jayde, sweetheart?" He didn't say anything else. He just wrapped his arms around me for a moment before turning back toward the men. "How'd this happen? Who was guarding her?" He didn't sound happy.

No one said anything initially until finally Lane stepped forward, "I was, Sir." He said lowering his head, willing to accept the blame.

"It was my fault, Dad," I said softly. I didn't want Lane in trouble. I knew he was only taking the blame so Jake wouldn't be the one to suffer the consequences.

"Good work, son!" Dad said, ignoring me and stepping forward to pat Lane on the shoulder. "Hernandez!" Dad said as he swiftly turned to look at him, "Investigate who the man was and how he got inside my house… Brief me when you know something." Then Dad turned to look at me again and lower his voice to sound softer. "Jayde… sweetie, do you need a doctor?"

I didn't say anything. I just stood there, thinking. I could feel my right eye beginning to twitch. Then I heard him speak again. "Jayde?"

"No… uh no, Sir," I said softly as I let my eyes slowly drift back toward the floor to think again.

"All right…" Dad said, giving me another hug, then let go and turned toward Jake. "Take her back to her room, Miles. Take Ellice as well… They should stay together for the night until I can increase the guard detail. Neither girl is to be left alone under any circumstance, do you understand?"

"Yes, Sir!" Jake said, accepting the order.

"Good man!" Dad said as he firmly patted him on the upper arm, then turned around to walk away.

Xavier quickly gave Lane a dirty look before turning around to order his men to clean up the body and move the man to an area where they could investigate him further.

"What?" Lane said passively, returning the look before turning to look back at me and Jake.

"Ellie," Jake said, looking over at her. "Do you need anything from your room before you come to Jayde's for the night?"

"Um… well…" She hesitated while she looked at me, "I don't suppose it'd be acceptable to drink right now…" she said, almost like she was asking me if she could.

Jake didn't respond. He just looked at me as well, but when I didn't answer, he turned back toward her. "I don't think that'd be the best idea right now."

"If you want to take Jayde back to her room, I can take Ellie to hers to get what she needs really quick." Lane offered.

Jake hesitated as he looked at them both, probably deciding whether that was a good idea or not.

"She's been by herself this whole time and no one has bothered her. It's Jayde they want…" Lane said, suggesting she wasn't in danger, so only one person guarding her should be sufficient.

"No…" Jake shook his head after thinking about it for a moment, "I'm sorry, Lane. It's not my call. We'll all go together."

"I don't need anything," Ellie said suddenly.

Jake gave her an odd look. "You sure?" He asked.

"Yeah…" she said softly, looking over at Lane. "Will um… you both be in the room with us tonight?" She asked shyly like she might not have felt comfortable with that, but it was hard to tell.

"Yep," Lane said, giving Jake the side eye, probably hoping that was the plan because that's what he intended.

"Okay, good." I could hear in her voice she was scared. Other than when Mom was taken, I bet she never really had much like this happen so close to home.

"Jayde," Jake said softly as he ran his fingers through my hair while he sat on the bed next to me. "You're still so quiet, baby."

I didn't respond. I just nodded while I watched as Xavier's men carried more furniture into the room so everyone would have a place to sleep.

"Is she going to be all right?" Ellie asked as she leaned against the bedpost at my feet.

"Yeah," Jake said optimistically, but I could hear the uncertainty in his voice. "She's been through worse."

"Like what?" Ellie asked.

Jake hesitated, like he didn't know if it was a good idea to bring it all up again at the moment.

"When I first met her, she'd just lost their baby." Lane said as he leaned against the opposite bed post.

"Lane!" Jake huffed, tensing up, upset that Lane would mention that.

"It's okay…" I whispered as I reached out to hold Jake's hand.

Jake nodded, then stroked my hair again.

"She was pregnant?" Ellie asked, her voice saturated with sympathy.

"Yes," Jake said softly, looking up at her, then he paused. "Wait a second…" he froze and stared at her for a moment. "Have you always had that mark under your chin?"

"What? This?" Ellie reached up and rubbed a scar at the bottom of her chin that she'd gotten from falling in the gravel when she was two. "Oh… uh, yeah… It's just a scar… I normally try to hide it with makeup but it must have rubbed off while I was crying earlier."

"Oh my gosh… Jayde, baby…" Jake looked down at me again,

excited about something. "The little girl… the one in the picture that Miller had. You know, the one he said was your daughter? She had that scar." He smiled, happy to have figured it out. "So she's not real… I knew it! I knew he was lying! Now we know, baby!"

I was relieved and wanted to feel as excited as he was, but it was still hard for me to express it. I didn't know why, but I still felt numb inside and didn't feel like I could really do anything except lie there, listening to them all. "Good…" I whispered, so he knew I'd heard him.

"That is good," he said, leaning down and kissing my temple. "Very good," he whispered into my ear before nuzzling his face against it for a moment.

"I don't understand?" Ellie said like she was confused why her chin had anything to do with me and a man named Miller.

Jake sat up again and looked at her, then looked back down at me before replying. "A lot of bad things have happened to your sister, Ellie. It's incredible that she's still able to function… One of the men that's after her for the intel is a Coldier Agent named Miller. He's a third rank that used to work under your father in Nashville."

Jake acted like he was about to go on when Ellie interrupted him with a gasp. "Miller? You mean the Miller everyone is talking about is *that* Agent Miller?"

"You know him?" Lane asked suddenly, looking surprised.

"Yeah… I mean—" She stopped and looked around, then nodded silently.

"How?" Jake asked, squinting his eyes a little, now concerned.

"Um…" She quickly looked down, "I don't know… I just…" She stopped again.

"How do you know him, Ellie?" Lane continued to push.

"I…" She froze as she looked down at me, "I don't wanna talk about it." She said, then got up quickly to walk out.

"Ellie, you can't leave." Jake said kindly, reminding her.

Lane stood up at the same time and walked in front of the door before she got there. "Ellie, I'm sorry. You don't have to talk about him if you don't want to." He said as he stood in the way to stop her from passing.

"I need to use the bathroom," she said like that was her excuse to leave.

Lane quickly looked over at Jake not knowing how to proceed.

"I'll go in with her," I said as I sat up. "You can stand outside the door." I looked over at Jake as I said it.

"All right," he nodded, then helped me stand to my feet.

"Have you ever told anyone?" I asked as she hesitantly turned around to sit on the toilet, like she felt uncomfortable with me being in there with her.

"What are you talking about, Jayde?" She quickly looked away.

"What did he do to you, Ellie?" I asked, feeling the same twitch in my eye that I'd felt earlier.

She didn't respond. She just sat there, staring at her legs.

"Ellie, you can tell me… I'm safe, okay?" I turned and pulled myself up to sit on the counter next to the sink beside the door.

"Nothing," she said finally, lying.

"He raped me." I said, staring at my legs now too. "Then he erased me so he could do it all over again." There was so much more that I wasn't telling her, but I thought that was enough.

"Really?" she said faintly, not looking surprised. "Is that how you got pregnant?"

"No…" I said, thinking back. "Not by him anyway… The first time it was from another man that I thought I was in love with, but I lost that baby right after Miller captured me. He tried to get me pregnant again, but he couldn't. I never remember thinking he did anyway until he told Jake that he had and was holding my daughter as leverage until I came back to him."

"Did you believe him?" She asked as she stood, pulled her pants up and flushed the toilet, then walked over to lean against the wall in front of me.

"I didn't wanna believe it but I knew I'd been erased so many times, anything was possible. I even had nightmares about it after Jake told me. I thought I had a daughter out there somewhere, missing her mommy... It tore me up inside."

"That's awful..." she said, her eyes now glistening with oncoming tears.

"He must have used your picture to show to Jake." I said, thinking out loud.

"Oh, was it the scar that made Jake not think it was you or..."

"He didn't know I had a sister." I paused. "I didn't want you in danger so I never told anyone about you."

She nodded, understanding. "He raped me too," she said softly under her breath, probably not wanting to voice the words, but needing to share the pain.

"When?" I asked calmly, so she felt safe to tell me more.

"When I was sixteen... Dad just made High Rank, and we were staying in Nashville for a while."

"Just once?" I asked calmly again.

"Yeah... It was when I visited Dad's office. Miller was there as one of the guards. He asked if I wanted to see the loft upstairs. He said it'd been remodeled and had a great view."

I didn't ask anything else. I just nodded, so she knew I was listening.

"I never went back there again after that... I was too scared to."

"Does Dad know?"

"No!" She looked up at me suddenly, "Please don't tell him... I don't want him to know!"

"It's okay!" I said quickly, trying to calm her down. "I won't tell him if you don't want me to. I understand." I hopped down from the counter and stepped forward to give her a hug. "You can tell me anything, Ellie. I want you to know that."

She squeezed my shoulder. "Okay," she said sweetly.

"Are you scared Miller will try to come for you, too?" I asked.

She hesitated before she shook her head, then released the hug. "No... Henry will protect me like he did you, right?"

"Of course he will," I smiled. "And you have Xavier... He's going to be watching us both, too."

Her face turned timid suddenly as she looked away again.

"When you guys broke up, what was your fight really about?" I asked, remembering what she'd almost told Lane before she stopped.

She looked at me, face turned down as she leaned up against the wall again. "Are you still considered a virgin if you've been... you know... raped?" She asked, then reached up to brush away tears that had fallen onto her cheek.

I didn't know how to answer her. "Um..." Her question took me off guard. I wanted to be honest, but I didn't actually know the answer myself. "I don't know... I'm sorry."

"It's okay," she smiled like she knew it was a hard one and hadn't expected me to know either. "Xavier is a great guy... he just..." she paused. "He wanted things from me that I wasn't quite ready for, you know? I mean... I don't think he understood when I said I couldn't. I think he thought that meant that I didn't want to or like I was rejecting him... Which I mean..." She paused again.

"Did he make you do things?" I asked, feeling slightly confused.

"No! Oh no... no, that's not what I was saying." She said, shaking her head. "When I told him to stop, he did. We didn't do anything then, but I think he just couldn't understand what was wrong with me."

"Oh, okay," I said, feeling thankful she clarified for me before I went out to kick his ass.

"That's while Dad was away and we were here alone... But then after that, I got Dad's letter about you and, well... I started drinking more, you know. So that didn't help anything." she said like she felt ashamed.

I was about to respond when I heard a small knock on the door. "Jayde, baby? I don't mean to rush you. I just wanna check on you both to make sure you're all right." It was Jake.

"It's okay," Ellie said, motioning for the door. "We can go back out there now."

"Okay," I smiled, then unlocked the door to step out with her behind me.

When we reentered my room, it almost looked like it wasn't the same place as before, with all the new pieces of furniture sitting around and the old ones being rearranged.

Lane didn't say anything when he saw us, he just smiled.

"Do you like to read, Ellie?" I asked, not remembering if she had or not from when we were in school.

"I don't," she said softly, ashamed to admit it. "I can't ever find anything good."

"I can help you." Lane sat up in his seat and looked at me like he'd caught on and was thankful.

I looked over at Jake, who was now sitting on the edge of our bed again. "Maybe in the morning, Lane… It's getting late and we should all get some sleep."

Lane's expression quickly deflated, "Oh, okay."

"Where are you sleeping, Henry?" Ellie asked as she looked at the way the beds were arranged while I walked over to my side of my bed and crawled into it.

"Ellie," Jake said before Lane could reply. "Do you want to sleep with Jayde tonight, in this bed?" He asked standing up, willing to relinquish his claim.

She smiled and nodded timidly, "Yes, that would actually be nice, thank you!"

"Of course," Jake said as he walked around to my side, ready to say goodnight. I caught Lane giving him a dirty look, but it quickly dissolved when he saw me watching.

"I love you, baby," Jake said as he sat on the edge next to me and leaned over for a hug. "Is this all right, or do you need me to sleep closer?" He whispered in my ear before letting go.

"I would love for you to sleep next to me. You could move the other bed up next to mine on this side so we can still be close. Would that work?"

"Absolutely," he said with a smile then kissed my forehead.

IO

EVA'S BACK

It'd been three days since Jake had left. I wanted to tell myself that he was all right and safe and likely to return soon, but I knew he'd probably only just arrived at Charlotte. Lane seemed optimistic too but I think we both knew we probably wouldn't see him for at least another week.

Initially, I thought after the incident with the Sicari, Dad would have called off Jake's trip, but it didn't seem to do anything but encourage him to believe he was on the right path. The next day, he insisted that every man and agent in the house go through a secondary screening process, one that was more thorough than the last.

The idea that a man with a Coldier's tag would somehow turn and align himself with the Sicari, was beyond him. He acted like he could understand a spy and their mission, but to have men planted, acting perfectly normal for years ready to betray their own, seemed to perplex him. Or maybe what really bothered my dad was that this was the second time it'd happened. Maybe he started to feel the old adage: fool me once, shame on you, fool me twice, shame on me. I don't know for sure what it was, but he hadn't acted the same since that night.

"Hernandez," Dad was sitting at his desk, shuffling through papers. "Have your men do their rounds again and make sure they fully check the premises!" He acted almost paranoid, having the entire house and grounds checked more frequently. Then he would order it again almost right after it was completed. Every time Xavier complied, but I could see in his face he also knew something about Dad wasn't the same as it had been.

"Jayde," Dad would address me next, almost exactly in the same pattern, every time. "Come, look at these men…" He said, motioning for me to walk over to his desk to look at more pictures of the men he had working for him. "Do any of them look familiar?"

After trying to explain to him the first three times that there were very few Sicari that I would recognize, I gave it up and just did what he asked. I stood there analyzing one photo after another, one face at a time, until I ran through them all before handing the stack back to him. "No, I don't recognize any of them."

"Okay," he said, letting the stack gently hit the desk to re-square them all together again. "Charles, bring in the next two men."—Was his next order, the same one I'd heard seven times already as I continued to sit in his office as he'd asked.

I waited and watched out the window until before long I saw another two men dressed in black slowly file into the room and stop at a wall next to me.

"Men, my daughter is going to speak to each of you. If you understand her, please let me know." Dad would say each time right before he motioned for me to go on.

"Si vos intelligere me scio, et me, occidet te." I said the same thing every time very slowly, as I watched each of their faces and their body language as they heard each word leave my mouth. I was telling them, 'If you understand me, I will know and I will kill you.' It was the best I could think of to elicit the perfect response. If they didn't understand, then they wouldn't do anything but stare at me, maybe look down at my chest before bashfully looking away, sometimes smile like they thought I was cute. However, if they did understand what I said, I was expecting them to look scared or surprised. At that point, however, I had yet to see any man that looked like they knew what I was saying to them.

"No," I shook my head, looking at Dad so he knew neither of these two showed any indication of understanding.

"All right, men, you are free to go. Charles, bring in the next two." Dad ordered again, but this time broke the pattern. He stood up, walked around from his desk, then came over to sit down next to me.

"What are you doing?" I couldn't help but ask, wondering why the change up with such an elaborate rhythmic method he had going on.

"I want to see what you see. This time, when they leave, you can tell me what you were watching for, but I want to see if I can catch something myself first."

"Oh, okay," I shrugged. I didn't see how having a second pair of eyes could hurt.

Before long, two more men entered the room slowly, one at a time. They each walked like they were nervous and scared to be in trouble, which was understandable. Dad said the same thing to them, prefacing what I was going to do. So I repeated the same words, again watching their faces and again seeing nothing to indicate understanding, prompting Dad to send yet another two away.

"Ok, Jayde… What are you trying to see?" He asked, looking at me.

"If you understand me, I will know and I will kill you." I said suddenly, keeping direct eye contact with my face stone cold.

His eyes widened ever so slightly for a split second, followed by the smallest furrow of his eyebrows. "Is that what you're telling them?" He asked as he let his face relax again.

"Yes, it's all in your eyes. If they understand me, they'll always show it, even if they try not to, then I'll know by them over-correcting."

"What do you mean?" He seemed intrigued.

"If they don't show it in their eyes because they were trained like I was, then they know what I am looking for, so they'll intentionally not make any expression. Which in and of itself wouldn't happen if they didn't understand me. Almost everyone who doesn't understand either looks at me relieved when I am done or like they are confused because they don't know what's about to happen next."

He didn't say anything. He just brought his arm up to gently rest his other elbow on, so he could rub his chin with his thumb like he was deep in thought.

"How many men are there? Will I have to be here much longer?" I tried to ask it respectfully, but I was getting bored and hoping it would be over soon.

He broke his concentration to stand up and return to his seat at his desk. "Only a few more, then we can break for lunch." He said, making a motion for Agent Charles to go fetch two more. "Hernandez, have your men do their rounds again."

Xavier nodded, then stepped out of the room just past the doorway into the hall before quickly returning after passing off the orders to one of his men.

After another few moments of staring out the window, Dad loudly cleared his throat to get my attention. I looked over to see another two men had come in and again stand adjacent to the wall next to me. Dad said the same thing he usually said when I looked up at their faces, fully expecting to see the same as I had the last few sets of men— absolutely no recognition at all. This time, though, there was something about the man standing on the right. I didn't know what it was, but I thought it was familiar.

"Jayde," Dad said, prompting me to go on and say what I was supposed to.

"Oh, yeah..." I said straightening my face, "Si vos intelligere me scio, et me, occidet te." I stared at each man again as I said it slowly, and again neither man showed any sign they knew what I was saying. "Keep this one," I said, pointing to the man on the right.

Dad furrowed his brow, looking surprised, then quickly stood up again to walk over and around to stand next to me.

"Um... Sir... I..." The man started to babble but was quickly hushed by Dad as he raised his hand, motioning for his silence.

"What's your name, Agent?" I asked, like I had the full authority of my father at my disposal.

"Um... Agent Burgess, Ma'am..." He said hesitantly, not sure what all was going on and why I had called him out.

"Burgess?" I asked, when suddenly I realized why it sounded familiar and what likely it was that I noticed about him. That was Katherine's last name. I stood up so I could get a better look at his face.

"Yes, Ma'am," he said as he stood at attention.

"Are you from New York, Agent Burgess?"

"Um… Yes, Ma'am." He was becoming more and more uncomfortable the longer I continued to ask questions.

"Do you know any Sicari?"

"Uh, no, of course not, Ma'am!"

"Do you have family here in New York?"

"Uh, yes, Ma'am, I do. I have my father and my sister, Ma'am."

"Oh, really?" I knew I was getting close, so I figured I might as well press him to see if I was right, even if it wasn't exactly what Dad had me in there for. "What are their names, Agent?"

"Um… My father is David Burgess, and my sister is Katherine Burgess… Ma'am."

"Oh, well, that sounds realistic enough… but we'll see." I said, then turned to look at Dad. "It's a lengthy process, this whole thing. I really need to meet his family to make sure he isn't lying about them. It's kind of hard to tell, ya know? I don't want to condemn an innocent man just because his eyes twitched."

Dad looked a little confused, but then quickly straightened his face like he understood.

"If you could just have him call in the sister, that'd be good enough. I'll know more if I get a chance to question her." I said, as I turned back around to smile at the man.

"Um…" Suddenly his face grew extremely concerned as he glanced over at my dad, awaiting his orders.

Dad nodded at me, then looked over at Agent Charles. "Take this man to make a call to his sister. She's to be brought here to be questioned. I don't want him telling her anything else over the phone. Just have her come straight here."

Agent Charles nodded that he received the order and quickly walked over to Agent Burgess to detain him before escorting him from the room.

"Do you think he is one of them?" Dad asked as he walked back over behind his desk again to sit down.

"Well…" I shrugged, "if he isn't, his sister might be. I don't know. There was something about him though… better safe than sorry."

Dad furrowed his brow, then blinked a few times like it was hard for him to grasp. "All right. I'll call you back in here when his sister arrives. Right now, you can go have lunch."

"Okay," I said, happy to leave as I turned toward the door, but stopped and turned back to say one more thing. "Oh and uh, when you bring her in, I'm gonna need to talk to her without her brother there though… Actually, if it could just be myself and Agent Lane, that would be best. If you're concerned that she's a Sicari, just have her detained before we speak. That way I won't be in any danger."

"That's fine," Dad said only half paying attention, likely ready to move on to other things.

"Great!" I turned, gesturing for Xavier to follow me, then walked out.

"Jayde," Xavier said, as he walked beside me down the hall leading to the great room. "I've worked with Agent Burgess for a few years now and I don't personally believe he has anything to do with the Sicari."

"But what if he does, Hernandez?" I asked as I continued to walk toward the dining room.

"I mean, it's always a possibility, but… I just… I think I would know and I don't see him being that kind of individual, Ma'am."

I stopped and turned toward him. "What kind of individual is it we're looking for, Hernandez? What exactly do you think they look like, or act like… please tell me!"

His face froze for a moment like I took him off guard. "Um… Well…" He paused.

"Exactly. If you were so good at finding them, then the cook wouldn't have had a chance to try to slit my throat the other night, would he?" I huffed, then turned to walk again.

"Ma'am…" Xavier said, trying to catch up with me. "What happened the other night, I'm sure was an isolated incident and I can assure you it won't happen again. But that doesn't mean we need to go on a witch hurt with all the other agents, trying to find something that isn't there."

I stopped to look at him again, "You know, that's exactly what the warlock would say." I said, widening my eyes for emphasis.

"Jayde! That's not... I mean... I didn't—"

"They're not my orders, Hernandez!" I turned to walk again. "I'm doing the same thing as Miles, and you and everyone else. I'm just following the First Rank's orders. He says find the mole... and I find the mole... He says jump, we all jump. I'd think you'd see that by now."

"Would you just stop?" he said suddenly as he firmly grabbed a hold of my arm and stopped me to look at him. "I didn't mean it like that."

I calmly looked down at his hand, then back up at him as he slowly released it, realizing he shouldn't have done that. "Look," I said, keeping a calm demeanor, "I don't know how you and my sister interacted when you guarded her, but I'm not Ellie... I'm Jayde. Put your hand on me again and I'll twist your arm, wrap it around your neck and use it to cut off your air supply until you're passed out on the ground."

His eyes widened as he stiffened and took a small step back. "I'm sorry, Jayde. You're correct, that was inappropriate. I won't do it again."

I didn't get a chance to respond when I heard Ellie's voice coming from another room talking to Lane.

"Not again, hear me?" I whispered, giving Xavier a stern look.

"Yes, Ma'am," he said quickly, happy I was willing to let it go.

"Good," I smiled pleasantly, then turned to continue walking as he followed beside me. We walked past the room where Lane and Ellie were sitting, but neither of them seemed to notice.

"Can I ask you a question, Jayde?" Apparently, Xavier wasn't done talking.

"What?"

"Why are you with Miles?"

I thought he was going to ask me something about the Sicari, about me being one or something else more relevant to what we had just been discussing, but not that.

"What?" I was confused. I didn't stop walking, but I slowed down. "Why would you ask me that?"

"I didn't realize you were such a strong, motivated woman. The whole time you've been here, you've been a different person. When you're around Miles, you seem weak and… well, if I'm being honest, defenseless. I'd have never thought you were an agent until today. But in your father's office, the way I watched as you talked to those men, then to me here in the hall… I'm just a little taken aback by you."

"What does any of that have to do with Miles?" I asked, as we finally made it to the dining room. I pulled out a chair and took a seat, motioning for him to sit across from me.

He quickly shook his head, suggesting he couldn't, as he continued talking. "You can have anyone. Why him? I mean, with your position and who your father is, I just don't understand what Agent Miles has to offer you."

I tilted my head and squinted my eyes, trying to figure him out. He wasn't really asking me to list the things I saw in Jake, or what things I loved about Jake. What he was doing was trying to get me to think about who I was so I would reconsider what my options were. Too bad for him, I didn't need to reconsider. "You're a fourth rank, right, Hernandez?"

"Yes, Ma'am," he said, looking unsure of why I'd ask.

"Do you think I'm with Miles because he ranks so high?"

"Well… I don't know. Possibly." He said, looking hopeful.

I bit my lip and nodded as I looked away, trying to think of the best way to respond. "Do you think that's why Ellie was with you?" I asked, genuinely curious.

"No… I think Ellice needed a friend. She was lonely, and I was around. She's not the kind of woman you are, Jayde. She's…" He paused, likely picking his words wisely. "She's a bit childish."

"Hmm… What… and you like *real* women?" I asked as a server walked out with a plate of food and started toward me.

Xavier lowered his head as he watched the server with his eyes, then after he set my food down and left the room, Xavier finally responded. "I like a woman who knows what she wants."

"Hmm…" I said as I picked up my fork to get a bite of food. "Too bad I'm indecisive."

"Not at all," he said, taking a few steps back to lean against the wall. "You know exactly what you want… Just like you knew you wanted to speak with Katherine because she's Miles' ex-fiancée." He said as he squinted his eyes a little, watching for how I would react.

I squinted mine back, wondering which angle he was trying to play with that comment. "You know, I'm glad you said that. It's good that you know who she is because I was gonna say I know just the perfect woman for you, Hernandez…"

He chuckled as he looked at the floor. "Never…" He said under his breath where I could barely hear it.

"Too bad…" I smirked. "I could have hooked you up." Then I took another bite of food and swallowed. "But say anything to my father and you're a dead man." I said, as I looked up at him and smiled.

He smiled back. "Let me be in the room when you talk with her and I won't say a word."

I stared at him for a minute. "Deal." I said, then took another bite of food.

II
JUST DESSERTS

"How long has she been here?" I asked.

Lane looked puzzled. "Kaleah, I don't know how long. *Why* is she here? That's what I wanna know?"

"You'll see. Right now, I'm going to finish eating my meal. Then when I'm done, you and Hernandez can take me to her."

"She's really upset…" Lane acted like he felt bad for her.

I looked at him without lifting my head as I continued to chew my food.

"Do you know what this is all about?" Lane asked, turning to look at Xavier.

Xavier smirked, looked at me as he shook his head slightly, then looked down at the floor like he wasn't getting involved.

"Kaleah… I don't know what you're doing, but this isn't you. If Miles knew about this, he'd—"

"Miles isn't here, Lane." I stopped him as I set my silverware on my plate and wiped my mouth with my napkin. "Are you done?" I asked as I stood up.

"What do you mean?" He looked confused.

"Lecturing me?"

"I… um… yes," He said quietly, knowing he wasn't going to win.

"Good." I walked around the table to stand between them. "Is Ellie being guarded?"

"Yes, she's currently in with your father and Andry." Lane said, still with a bit of attitude.

"Good, then take me to Katherine."

Lane took a deep breath as he stared at me, then nodded like he felt defeated before he turned to lead the way.

"I don't care what he says, I like this side of you, Jayde." Xavier whispered as he walked beside me down the hall.

"You shouldn't," I said, knowing the side he was referring to was actually almost entirely Eva. Someone with little remorse and enough strategic intellect to lead a coup.

"Why, because you're with Miles?" He asked, remembering our previous conversation.

"No… because…" I wanted to tell him because he shouldn't trust me, because Eva wasn't Jayde nor Kaleah and didn't hold the same loyalties as either. "Because *I'm* the Sicari."

He didn't respond right away. He just looked at me oddly. "That's not your fault… Besides, your father's going to remedy that. He already scheduled for you to have your Coldier tag put in next week."

"Why didn't you tell me that before now?" I asked, not giving him the kindest look.

"I knew you wouldn't respond well." He said, being frank.

I didn't say anything. I just glared at him as I continued to follow Lane.

"See… I was right." Xavier said.

"We're here," Lane stopped suddenly outside a large set of doors, then turned around to look at me. "Kal… Jayde, would you mind if I spoke with you alone first? Hernandez can go on in."

"Sure," I said, then motioned with my eyes for Xavier to go ahead.

"You wanna talk to me now about what exactly she's doing here?" Lane said, after waiting for the doors to shut behind Xavier.

"Lane…" I closed my eyes and took a deep breath, then slowly exhaled it as I opened them. "What do you see in me?"

He furrowed his brow. "What?"

"Just answer it, please."

He looked around like he was slightly caught off guard but willing to think about it. "Um... you're kind and gentle and funny... Uh, you're beautiful, and smart and um... I don't know, Kaleah, why are you asking me that?"

"Because you're wrong," I said, trying to smile but unable to accomplish it. "I'm weak and broken and vindictive... and I'm scared, Lane. I'm freakin' scared... And honestly, I don't think you really know me at all. 'Cause if you did... then you'd know exactly why she was here."

He didn't respond for a moment, he just stared at me. "Okay..." he said slowly, still confused.

"If you don't want to go in with me, you don't have to... I would understand." I said, trying to relax.

"No..." he put a hand on my shoulder. "I'm going in with you." He said, then pulled me in to hug him. "I'm sorry, Kaleah. I shouldn't have questioned you. Even if I don't always understand you, I do trust that you'll do the right thing. Miles wouldn't be with you if he didn't trust you... so I should, too."

I squeezed my eyelids as tight as they could go to stop my eyes from tearing up. Even if I felt weak at the moment, I couldn't show it. I had to stay strong. "Thank you," I said as I let go of him and stepped back.

"You ready?" He asked as he put his hand on the knob.

I nodded, then quickly rubbed each of my eyes to make sure there was no moisture in them as he opened the door and stepped in, then held it open for me.

"H-Henry?" Kat stammered. She sounded like she'd just seen him for the first time since arriving and was now confused. "Henry, why am I h—" She stopped mid-sentence when she saw me walk in behind him. "What the hell is she doing here?"

No one said anything as I walked over to the table and sat down across from her.

"Henry... I don't understand. Please, I haven't done anything." She said, looking at him again.

"Katherine? Why do you think you're here?" I asked in a calm, low voice.

"I'm not talking to you," she said as she got louder. "Henry, where is Jacob? I want to see Jacob!"

"I'm the one in charge, Katherine… Jacob isn't here to save you. Now, I need you to answer my question."

"What the hell?!" She looked at me like she thought I was joking, or maybe she was dreaming. "I'm not talking to you, you're nothing but a freakin' Gypsyin…" She paused, seeing if the words stung. "Yeah, you heard me… I know what you are. You're not fooling anyone!"

I nodded, "You're right!" I said, pulling up my sleeve to show her my arm.

"What the…" She acted like she was suspicious, but hadn't really known it to be a fact until that moment. "Why… I don't…" She looked over at Lane, "Henry… why am I here? Please?"

I looked at Lane, motioning so he knew he could speak if he wanted.

He didn't change his stance. "Answer her," he said, keeping a straight face.

"What? This is insane. You have no authority to keep me here. Who do you think you even are?"

"Who do you think I am, Katherine?"

"I don't know, a freakin' nut job…" she said like she was starting to actually wonder.

"You remember when you called and reported me for being a Gypsyin?"

"Yeah and I plan on doing it again… I'll do it until you're taken and put where you belong… as an erased little slave, serving someone like me in my house. You don't deserve to be with Jacob! He doesn't love you!" She continued to babble like she thought she was getting somewhere with it.

"How did you know I was a Gypsyin?"

"Ha! Wouldn't you like to know, you li'l shit!" She yelled, leaning forward as far as she could until she hit the end of the cuffs around the back of the chair, prompting her to lean back again.

I nodded slowly, like I was listening to her before I continued. "Agent Lane told me about you visiting him…" I left it at that, knowing she'd easily fill in the blanks since she wasn't smart enough to control her anger.

"Yeah, so what? He's a putz," she said, looking at him, not even apologetic. "I just went over there to see Jacob. Henry is the one dumb enough to think we could have something together."

I could handle it when she said what she did about me, but hearing what she said about him made me angry. I shook my head like I was thinking. "Okay, Hernandez, I've decided…" I said as I stood up, pretending I was going to walk out.

"Wait, what?" She yelled out, suddenly desperate. "You've decided what?"

I didn't say anything. I just motioned like I was done and Lane could follow me out.

"Wait… Wait… All right… All right, stop and I'll talk…"

I turned like I was willing to listen again.

"I'll talk… I'll talk, all right?" She continued.

"How did you know I was a Gypsyin?" I asked, raising my voice, showing her I was more serious than before and she wouldn't have another chance.

"I didn't, okay? I swear… It was a guess, just a lucky guess. I told Jacob's mom, and she said she would take care of it. I don't know what she meant. She said something about papers. I'm sorry…"

"If you're so sorry, then why did you report me?" I asked, still not returning to the previous calm demeanor that I originally had just yet.

"That was her plan. She said she gave you a chance to leave on your own but you didn't go, so you forced her hand… But she said she'd handled it where you'd just get put back through the system again, that's all. She told me to report you. She said it was anonymous and Jacob wouldn't ever find out…"

"The papers were counterfeit." I paused to watch her face to see if she knew that. "Lane, care to tell her what happens when you're caught with counterfeit papers?"

"Death!" He said like he was quickly catching on now to what I was doing.

"What? I didn't know that… Please, I swear, I didn't know that."

I knew by looking at her that she wasn't lying. Even though I wished it was her and not Jacob's mother, I knew I couldn't pin this one on her.

I didn't say anything else. I just nodded while staring down at her.

"Lane?" I said, keeping my eyes on her.

"Yes, Ma'am?"

"What? You really are in charge?" Her eyes widened like she thought she was screwed. "Who the hell are you?"

"Do you have any questions for her?" I asked, still talking to Lane, ignoring what she asked me.

"Yes," he said as he stepped up to stand beside me at the table. "Katherine, you were never interested in me, were you?"

She looked scared, like she didn't know if she should be honest or if she should lie.

"Be honest," I said, warning her.

"Um…" she looked from me back to him, "no… I wasn't. I only did things with you because I thought it would make Jacob jealous when he returned."

Lane looked relieved, then turned and nodded at me, indicating he was done before returning to stand behind me.

"Okay," I said as I continued to stand. "I'm going to give you two options, Katherine. Both options consist of you never talking to Jacob Miles or any of his family ever again. And… neither you nor any of your family will ever be allowed to come to any elite Coldier functions ever again. Do you hear me?"

"What? You can't do that… no!"

"I can do whatever the hell I want. Now, before I give you the two options, tell me… how high does your brother rank?"

"What? Christopher?" She said still sounding scared.

"Answer me!" I wasn't in the mood to play games. If she only had one brother, it was a simple question.

"I'm sorry, um… he's um, up to ninth rank I believe."

I looked over at Xavier, who nodded to confirm what she said, then I looked back at her. "Okay, option number one, I can tell you who I really am, but your brother loses his full ranking and is dismissed from being an agent."

"What?" She acted like that was asking a lot, almost too much.

"Option number two, I don't tell you who I am. You never find out, and you just live the rest of your life thinking Jacob replaced you with a stupid Gypsyin nut job. Your brother gets to keep his rank, but has to move to work with a different agency."

"What? You can't do that," she said again like she thought I was bluffing.

"Pick one, Katherine, because I'm pretty sure you won't like option number three."

"Okay… Okay… wait a minute, I don't know… okay? Just wait." She began to act frantic. "Where's Jacob, please can I just see him one more time? I need to talk to him."

I rolled my eyes as I exaggeratively sat down again across from her. "Oh my gosh, woman! You're seriously testing my patience… Jacob isn't anywhere around here, and even if he were, he wouldn't want to see you again or talk to you. Now decide!"

Her face looked saddened when she realized I wasn't making stuff up, and it was true; she would never see him again.

"I wanna know who you really are…" she said finally, having decided. "I don't give a shit about my brother's rank."

"Okay!" I said, happy that she didn't keep dragging it out. Too bad she's an idiot and really thought she got to decide, though. I smiled as I stood up again. "I'm Eva, a Sicari." I said, giving her a wink, then turned to look at Lane. "Wait in the hall for me."

"What? You're lying! What the hell… that's not true… it can't be." She started to ramble and continued as I turned to address Xavier next.

"Hernandez, her brother is now a security risk. Don't demote him, but have him moved to another city's agency."

"Yes, Ma'am," Xavier said. "And what would you like done with her?" He asked, as if I actually got to decide. I wasn't sure if I was pressing my luck with my power play, but I could feel it becoming short lived. I didn't want to go overboard before my short bungee broke and made me go splat on Father's doorstep.

"Release her. She knows the rules, what she is and isn't allowed to do now… She'll behave. Won't you Katherine?" I said, looking back at her, hoping it would scare her more, but I really was just bluffing this time.

"Yes…" she said now shaking slightly.

"If I find out you've had any more contact with Jacob or Lane's family and I have to haul your ass back in here, you won't like what I'll be willing to do to you."

"Okay, okay, I won't… I promise. I won't, all right!"

I smiled as I relaxed my shoulders. "Good!" I said, then turned around and stepped out.

"How do you know how to do that?" Lane asked quietly when the doors had finished closing behind me.

"Do what?" I motioned for him to walk with me as I turned to head back to the dining room for some dessert.

"Interrogate someone…" He said it like he was realizing I was right and maybe he didn't know me as well as he thought he did.

"I know how to do a lot of things, Lane. Are you surprised?"

"Yes and no, Miles has told me a lot but I just…" He paused for a second. "I don't know."

"Are you scared of me now? Is that your problem?" He was acting weird, and I wasn't sure why.

He laughed. "Of course not!" He said like that was out of the question.

"Then what's wrong?"

He got quiet as we continued to walk. "Um… well, I… um… nothing, it's nothing." He said with a forced smile.

"Bullshit," I said, smiling back.

He quickly lost his smile, but still didn't say anything.

"Lane, what's wrong?" I asked as I stopped walking and turned toward him, seeing it was serious.

"I love you, Kaleah," He said it so softly, I almost didn't hear him. His eyes looked broken, like he felt guilty—like he didn't think he should feel it and probably shouldn't have said it either.

I didn't know what to say. I just stood there staring at him until finally I nodded my head and slowly turned to walk again. "I know, Lane."

"What?" He sounded confused.

"I love you too. You know… like I love being around you, and I love having fun with you and talking to you and messing with you… and…"

"That's not what I meant," he gently touched my arm to stop me from walking away. I turned back to look at him.

"I know…" I said softly.

"You do?" He asked, holding my gaze.

"Yeah… but the person you think you love isn't who I am, Lane… You love someone who's sweet and kind and…" I stopped to look away for a moment. "The things about me you think you love, the person who acted like Kaleah… that's not the real me. That's actually Ellie… She's all those things and right now she needs you. She needs someone to love her like Jake loves me."

I could feel myself tear up the more I talked about her. "She's not broken like I am… and neither are you. That's why Jake understands me. He's been through so much shit with me. He's the only one who knows how to handle me. But not her, Lane…" I looked back at him. "She's still so innocent. She needs someone like you… you know… to protect her so the same things don't happen to her that have happened to me."

Lane just stared at me for a moment before nodding like he was starting to understand, then closed his eyes for a second before quickly pulling me in to hug him. "If anything ever happens to him, I want you to know I'm going to take care of you…" The sincerity in his voice was thicker than I'd ever heard it.

I let myself relax as I hugged him back. "What if something

happens to me, though? Will you promise to take care of *him*... make sure *he's* okay?"

He pulled back to look at me. "Of course," he said softly, then lowered his brow, trying to see why I'd say that. "You're not hearing voices again, are you?"

I tried to smile as I shook my head slightly. "No, nothing like that."

"Then what's wrong?"

"Why does something have to be wrong?" I did a better job of smiling this time, but figured he might still see through it.

"He's gonna come back, Kaleah... and until he gets back, you're gonna be safe... I'm here, no one's going to get you... I won't let that happen again. You don't need to worry about him, either. He's more than capable of taking care of himself."

I wasn't worried about Jake, or my safety. I was worried about the person I was when Jake wasn't with me. Eva scared me. I couldn't control her or what she wanted to do before, not as Kaleah and I was afraid now, not as Jayde either. I smiled again. "I know." I said, hoping he could let it go now as I turned to walk again. "Did it bother you what Katherine said about you?" I wanted to change the subject just to make sure he wouldn't keep prodding.

"No," he said, not having to think about it. "I knew she had ulterior motives... that's why initially I didn't feel so bad about using her like I did either. She was trying to use me first, so I figured why not... What's good for the Kat is good for the dog." He smiled, thinking he was clever. "What about you? With everything she said, are you all right?"

I knew he was probably referring to what she'd said about Jake's mom, but I hadn't had a chance to let myself really absorb it yet. "I'm fine." I said, trying to dismiss his concerns.

"Okay..." He paused as he continued to walk, "I wish Miles could have seen you in there... He'd be proud to see how well you held it together, you know?"

"Miles wouldn't have let me do that... He would've stopped me like you tried to do." I stopped to look at him again right before we got to the dining room. "Don't tell him about it, all right? I don't want him to know."

"Why, it's already happ—"

"I don't want him to know, Lane… Please?" I interrupted him.

He slowly let his look of confusion dissipate as he nodded. "Okay…"

"Thank you," I said with a small smile, then turned to walk into the dining room and around the table to sit down. "Here, why don't you have some dessert with me?"

12

A COLDIER KILLER

"It's Wednesday, Ma'am…" Xavier said, reminding me it was the date my father had set for me to have my tag placed.

"I don't care what day it is, Jake isn't back yet," I said as I stared out one of the windows in the East corridor.

"So… uh, you need Agent Miles here first? Because he might not be back for days or maybe longer, we don't know. But I'm certain your father doesn't want to wait any longer. It's important that you get your tag."

"It's almost been two weeks, Hernandez. He could be back any minute. I told him I wouldn't do the surgery until he returned." It was actually Jake that told me I didn't have to do it until he was with me, by my side again, but I didn't want to have to explain to Xavier why I was scared, so I lied.

"Well, you can tell that to your father, but the last I heard, he's already brought in the doctor. The staff were already getting one of the spare rooms set up as a surgical suite for you, too. Didn't you discuss this with Agent Lane already? This morning, he told me his men were ready to provide any extra support you needed today."

"Him and his men are busy watching Ellie. I don't need them."

"I understand, Ma'am, but he said—"

"Hernandez," I stopped him, "I don't care what he said. None of his men are to leave Ellie, hear me?"

"They're his men, Ma'am… They follow his orders, not mine."

I didn't respond. I just turned to look back out the window.

"Jayde?" Xavier walked over and sat down beside me.

"What?" I asked, still not turning to look at him.

"Why don't you want your tag?" He asked like he'd caught on. "You seem tense. Just try to relax."

"I'm not a Coldier." I said, keeping my eyes out the window.

"If you're not a Coldier, what are you?" I heard skepticism in his voice.

"A ghost."

"I don't understand." He said, hoping I'd clarify.

"Jayde died, Hernandez… The Sicari changed me…" I finally turned to look at him. "I can look like Jayde and talk like Jayde, but the things I went through during training…" I paused, then turned to look back out the window. "They purged me of her… every ounce, everything I was… it's gone. They turned me into Eva, a heartless, soulless body… trained for only one thing…"

"What's that?" He asked softly.

"A Coldier killer." I said, as I turned to look at him.

His eyes widened, probably not sure if he should take me seriously, but then they quickly changed, like something about my face started to scare him. "Jayde, wait!" He blurted out, but before I knew what I was doing, I had already reached over, pulled his gun and was now standing, aiming it at him. "Holy shit, Jayde. What the hell are you doing?" He said as he quickly backed away from me.

I wanted to tell him I had no idea, but I couldn't make myself say it.

"You don't have to get your tag, all right… No one's going to force you to get it!" He said as he held his hands up. "Please… we can talk about this. Just lower the weapon. I'm on your side, Jayde!"

"I can't!" I wanted to tell him more, but I couldn't. Whatever was happening wasn't Jayde doing it, it felt like I was stuck inside another person's body. Like Eva's instincts of self preservation had finally hit their max and completely taken over.

"What do you mean, you can't? Of course you can, just put it down!" He said, backing up a few more steps.

I didn't have a chance to respond when something sharp stuck me in the back, prompting me to quickly turn around.

"No!" Xavier screamed as I spun to see one of his men standing there holding something in his hand that looked like a needle.

Xavier quickly moved to me and took his gun back as I stood there staring at the man. "What the hell have you done, Stevens!?" He said as he walked around me.

"Sir, she was going to shoot you. It's the only thing I could think of."

"What?" I asked, feeling frantic. "What was that?" I hoped it was nothing more than a simple sedative for when things got out of hand, as they had in this case.

"Holy shit…" Xavier quickly ran his hand from his forehead back through his hair, not sure what to do. "She wasn't going to shoot me, you freakin' idiot. She was just freaked out about her surgery and acting out, that's all. It's no worse than the shit Ellice used to do to me while she was drunk."

"Sir, I'm sorry!" The man said as he looked around. There were now four other men there that had probably come when they heard us yelling.

"What was that!?" I asked again as I reached down to grab what he was still holding in his hand.

"Quit!" He quickly pulled his hand away from me and held it up high where I couldn't reach. "It's nothing!"

"Stevens, get your ass out of here! Go home! I don't want to see you again until I get this shit straightened out! Sims, go tell the doctor Jayde will be ready for surgery here in a minute. I'll bring her to him. The rest of you go find something to do and if I hear you tell anyone about this, I'll have your rank!" Xavier barked the orders, now in a hurry.

"What?" I looked from the men to Xavier, "What was…" I started to ask again what it was when I began to feel dizzy. *Shit!*

"Get out of here, now!" Xavier yelled at the men again, when finally they all turned to leave like they knew he was serious.

"Xavier…"

"Sit down, Jayde…" He said as he re-holstered his gun then put his hand on my shoulder to guide me back down to my seat.

I wanted to fight him. I wanted to kick and scream and yell, but I couldn't. Now all I could do was stare at the floor as I watched the light around my eyes slowly fade until I didn't see or hear anything else.

"Jayde?" I heard a woman's voice. It was soft and dainty, like she was young. "Hey, sleepyhead… wake up…" I opened my eyes when I heard her again. "Hey… there you are… how do you feel?"

I didn't answer her. I was too busy staring, studying her face. I'd never seen her before. She was pretty, though.

"Jayde?" She looked confused. "What's wrong?"

I thought that was odd. "What?" I said finally.

"Why are you looking at me like that?"

"Who are you?" I asked.

Her face went from one level of confusion to another before it changed to disbelief, then back to a smile. "Oh my gosh, Jayde… nice try, silly. Henry told me you like to do that with him, too. I'm not going to fall for it, though." She said, keeping her smile only until I didn't smile back. "You're joking, right? 'Cause you're starting to scare me."

"No," I said, trying to sit up a little to look around. "Where am I?"

"What?" she took a step back. "Y-you… you really are good at this." she said, trying to smile, then stopped like she still wasn't sure. "Henry said you took it too far sometimes."

"Who's Henry?" I asked, looking around again before something down at my side caught my attention. I had a clear cord attached to my arm leading up to a bag filled with clear liquid. I turned to look at my other arm, which hurt but had a bandage around it. "Did I get hurt?" I asked, looking back up at her.

"Uh…" She was frozen. "Henry!" She yelled out as she quickly turned to walk toward the door.

"Yes," the door opened suddenly, like whoever she was yelling for was right on the other side, waiting. "Is she ready to see me already? I thought you'd want to spend more time with her alone first?" He said, looking from me over to the girl as he walked in. He must have noticed something was wrong though, because she didn't have to say anything else before his face quickly changed. "What's wrong, Ellie?" He said as he quickly looked from her back to me. "Kaleah, you all right?" He asked as he walked closer.

I didn't respond. I just stared at him, trying to analyze his face. I had never met him either. Why did they both act like they knew me when I had no clue who either of them were?

"What, did she say something that bothered you, Ellie?" He asked, looking back at her. "'Cause anesthesia can do that… the doctor said she might say weird things initially as she woke up." He smiled as he looked back at me, certain that's all it was.

"She doesn't know who I am, Henry… or you!" The girl said suddenly.

"What?" He quickly lost his smile. "Are you sure?" He asked as he turned toward me and moved closer. "Kaleah, are you feeling all right?"

"I… um… Why are you calling me that when she called me Jayde?" If I had remembered who they were, I would have been suspicious that something was wrong anyway, since neither of them seemed to have their story straight on who I was supposed to be.

"Are you shitting me?" He said like he was talking to himself, though he was still looking at me.

"Hernandez!" He yelled as he suddenly spun around and walked out of the room.

"You're not joking with us, are you?" The girl asked, letting her shoulders fall forward.

I shook my head gently as I continued to watch her. "Who am I?"

"You're my sister…" she said, her eyes quickly glossing over.

Before I could ask her anything else, someone pushed the door open so suddenly it swung back and hit the wall, making a loud thud sound. A man dressed in all black walked in with Henry.

"Jayde," the man said as he got close to the bed, "what do you remember?"

I was going to respond when I stopped to think. I let my eyes roam around the room as I tried to think of something, anything, that might spark a memory, but no matter how hard I tried, thinking didn't do any good. "Um… nothing…"

"Holy shit!" The man said like he too was in shock and upset to hear it. "Lane, stay with her… I'll go inform her father. The surgery must have done this somehow." He said as he started to turn around.

"Wait!" Henry held up his hand as the man walked into it, stopping him from continuing to leave. "I've never heard of surgery making you lose your memory. She's acting like she's been erased."

The man turned like he was going to look at me when he stopped, "Maybe you're right, but we vetted the doctor and the staff… You yourself talked to them all first!"

Henry's shoulders slumped as he looked at the floor. "It had to be one of them. If not, who else has been around her?" He asked, standing back up straight again, determined to solve this mystery.

The other man shook his head. "I don't know, but I have to go tell Mr. Prescott." He said, then quickly walked out again.

Henry turned back around and looked at me, then swallowed.

"What will your brother say?" The girl asked, reaching over and resting her hand against Henry's back.

Henry's eyes enlarged, like he hadn't thought of that yet. "Oh, my gosh…" He inhaled sharply. "Holy shit… Kaleah…" He started to breathe harder.

"I'm sorry…" I don't know why I said it, but I felt bad. I had no idea who I was or who any of these people were, but apparently me not remembering seemed to be a problem for more than just me.

"Isn't he supposed to be back soon?" She asked.

He seemed deflated again as he looked toward the floor and nodded. "Yeah… He just called about an hour ago. He said he was back in the city."

"Does he know she was having the surgery today?" She asked as she took a few steps backward toward a seat next to the door and sat down in it.

"No…" He said, tensing up, then began to rub his face with both hands. "I didn't tell him. It was already over with when we talked, so I figured he'd just be pleasantly surprised when he got here and saw she had her tag."

"My tag? What?" I asked, looking down at my arm, wondering what the hell they'd done to me and if that's what was making it hurt.

"It's okay, just calm down." Henry said as he paced from where he was standing to the other end of the room. "Oh my gosh, I can't even go back and check the staff to see who it was because we sent them all away already. The only one who's left is an after care nurse who wasn't even here during the surgery… so she wouldn't know anything." He said then squatted down like he felt lightheaded.

"Jayde?" An older man walked into the room, quickly looked around until he saw me, then walked over to the bed. "You're all right… right? You're not hurt, or… uh…" He paused, lost for words. "You're fine?"

I didn't know what to say, but I got the idea from hearing them talk that this was likely my father, seeing that he'd returned with the man in black, who said he'd go get him. He looked old and frightened and I didn't want him to feel worse than he was already acting, so I nodded to let him know I was all right.

"Oh, good… okay… well…" he said, looking down and away to think. "It could have been worse, we have the medicine coming that will reverse this… Hernandez," he looked up finally to speak to the man next to the door, "how did this happen?"

The man briefly glanced at me before looking away quickly.

"We're not certain, Sir. I don't believe it was from the staff, though. I think it's probably just a simple side effect of the surgery, Sir."

The older man nodded his head as he rested his chin against his hand to think. "Well… it's indeed unfortunate, but from what she'd expressed to me over the past couple months, I believe it's not entirely the worst thing that could have happened. Plus, until she gets the medicine, this should help hide her signal from the Sicari being able to track it."

As soon as he said what he had, I could see almost everyone in the room sigh or relax, like they were relieved to some extent, except Henry. Henry had stood back up but looked just as stiff and on edge as he had from the moment he saw I wasn't pretending.

"Agent Lane," the older man said as he turned to look at Henry, "Continue to have your men sweep the perimeter, even though we're less likely to deal with Sicari now I still want to keep the guard detail sharp, the girls are still in danger, despite what has happened here."

"Yes, Sir," Henry said.

"Oh, and as soon as you see Agent Miles return, bring him to me first before he comes to see Jayde." The older man said again, adding on to his order.

"I will, Sir," the man in black, who they called Hernandez, spoke up to agree even though the older man was speaking to Henry.

"Good," the older man said, then turned around to look at me again. He didn't say anything else, he just stared at me for a second, gave me a warm smile then patted the back of my hand a couple of times before he quickly turned to walk back out of the room.

Hernandez looked at Henry, who looked back at him like they were making a special pact with their eyes, then turned to speak to the girl. "Ellice, sweetie… Let's let Lane have a moment alone with Jayde."

The girl looked at him, confused, but then quickly nodded to agree before walking over to follow him out the door.

"You all act like I've died." I said as I watched Henry slowly walk closer to me to stand next to the bed.

He reached down to hold my hand. "It feels like you have, Kaleah." He said somberly, his eyes now glossy.

"Why do you call me Kaleah, when they've all called me Jayde? Which one am I?"

His eyes trailed from mine slowly down and away as he thought about how to respond. "I know how he felt now, I didn't get it but now I do." Henry said like he hadn't heard my question.

"Who?"

"The man who loves you more than the world itself…" He said before clenching his lower jaw.

"What?" I didn't understand.

"This is how it feels to lose you… I didn't get it when he tried to explain it. I just thought he was being sensitive… I mean, I thought, it's just her memories… You can make new ones." Henry sounded like he was talking to himself now. "He's gone through so much, and lost you so many times… now again, on my watch… I can't do this, Kaleah. I don't know what to do…"

"What man?" I asked again.

"The one that's about to walk in here and break into a thousand pieces when he sees you're gone again." He said as he stared off into space.

I didn't say anything, I just squeezed his hand, which broke him from his stare to look at me again. "It's going to be all right, Henry," I said, then smiled.

Something about that must have been hard for him to hear. He looked at me for a second before he finally broke. His face, taut with tension, finally relaxed allowing tears to shed freely from his pain packed eyes. He didn't respond. He just quickly turned away, bringing his other arm up to hold his sleeve against his eyes.

He still hadn't responded when we heard a knock at the door, quickly followed by it opening and a man I hadn't seen yet walking in.

13
WHO KNOWS WHAT?

"Jayde, baby?" The man said before Henry walked over to him to stop him from coming closer. "Lane, why are you crying?" The man's tone quickly changed as he turned from Henry to look at me. "Eva?"

"Hang on, Miles," Henry said, placing his palm on the man's chest.

"What do you mean, hang on?" The man seemed confused and now irritated.

"Have you talked to Mr. Prescott yet?" Henry asked as he brought his sleeve up to quickly wipe his face again.

"No, why is she in here?" The man looked from Henry back to me again as he swept Henry's arm from his chest and moved forward toward me. "Eva… what's going on?" He said looking down at my arm then up at the bag hanging above the bed. "Oh, you got your tag?" He looked surprised. "Is that what this is all about, Lane?" He asked quickly as he turned to speak with him before turning back toward me.

"I need to talk to you before you talk to her!" Henry said as he sat down in the chair next to the door.

The man had grabbed my hand, but hadn't had time to do more than look at me when he realized what Henry had said. "Is everything all right, baby?" He asked as he smiled at me, ignoring Henry. In that moment, I realized who he must have been—the one Henry was referring to earlier.

I was afraid to say anything to him. His eyes were so kind and his smile so sweet. I didn't want to see it go away when he realized I had no clue who he was.

"Jacob, I'm serious!" Henry spoke louder.

"I'm fine," I said finally, looking up at the man and smiling back.

He smiled bigger apparently relieved, nodded then turned to look at Henry. "All right, man… What's your problem?"

"What did she just say to you?" Henry asked, standing up again, looking puzzled like the man wasn't acting how Henry expected he should.

"She's fine… Now hurry up. What did you need to talk to me about so badly? It's been a long trip, and I'd really like to spend some time with her now that I'm back."

Henry looked at me suspiciously, then hesitated before looking back at the man. "How'd you know we were in here?" He asked.

"Hernandez told me."

"He didn't tell you Prescott asked to see you as soon as you got here?"

"No… Why? What does Mr. Prescott need?" He asked, then before waiting for a reply he continued. "Lane, first… why were you crying when I walked in?" The man quickly looked back at me, then back at Henry. "Did Eva say something that hurt your feelings or… I mean… It's just weird to see you cry."

"She was erased again, Jacob," Henry said suddenly.

"What… Who you talking about?"

Henry looked over at me slowly while he took in a breath, preparing to sigh.

"Who… Eva?" The man asked, ready to laugh as he turned to look at me again. "No, she's not…" He said, taking his eyes back to Henry, "Look, she's fine!"

"You got the medicine Prescott sent you for, right?" Henry asked, keeping a serious look on his face.

"Lane, this isn't funny… I don't know what you're trying to do, but that's not something to joke about." The man quickly lost his smile as he turned to look at me. "Eva, you said you're fine… Tell him you're fine." He sounded desperate, like if I didn't say it he'd freak out.

I looked at him again, trying to study his face. I wanted to give in and tell him Henry was right and I didn't remember anything about him, but I couldn't. I hated to think I would break his heart. "I'm fine," I said again, staring at him. Then I turned to look at Henry, "I'm fine, Henry."

I didn't get a chance to see the look on Henry's face when the man spoke up suddenly like there was something wrong. "Wait? What did you call him?" He said, turning to look straight at me.

I froze. I thought his name was Henry. Wasn't that what everyone had been calling him? "Um… Lane?" I said, hoping that was right.

The man looked at me confused, then nodded slightly like that was right before turning to look at Henry again. "If she's acting weird, it's probably just from the surgery, Lane… Man, I know a lot has happened, but you're probably just paranoid. I know you didn't really want me to leave and all; you didn't want the responsibility, but seriously, it's fine. You can take it easy now… She's all right and I'm back."

"No, she's not all right," Henry seemed to suddenly break from a moment of silent disbelief. He looked at me like he thought either he was going insane or I was, but either way, something was wrong. "You can talk to Ellie, she was here… She saw it… or Hernandez…" Henry turned to open the door as he continued to talk. "Ellie… Ellie, you still out here?" He paused before he continued to walk out of the room to look for her.

The man turned back toward me, looking suspicious now. "Eva, baby… What's going on? Did you say something trying to freak him out, 'cause I know you guys like to play like that but this isn't—"

"No," I said, stopping him as I continued to stare at his face.

"Okay… then what is this?" He asked, then gently pushed my legs over so he could sit on the bed next to me.

"I don't know," I said as I continued to stare at him. He was large and well built, but seemed gentle and kind. I had no reference to what his face reminded me of, but something about it was comforting. Maybe it was his smile or the way his eyes looked at me, but I liked it and I didn't want it to stop. At that moment, I realized I was afraid for him to find out the truth. I was scared he wouldn't keep looking at me the same as he had when he first came into the room.

He nodded, believing me, then reached over to hold my hand again. "I'm surprised you got your tag without me. I mean, I'm not mad, I don't mind. You just seemed like you were pretty adamant you weren't going to get it, so I thought there was no way you would if I wasn't here pressuring you to."

"Yeah…" I said with a sigh as I looked down at my arm, still not sure what a tag was.

"You don't seem very talkative. Are you still tired? Anesthesia can do that to ya…" He asked as he let go of my hand to rest his on my thigh.

I smiled and was about to respond when I heard Henry and the girl coming back. "Tell him! He doesn't believe me." Henry said as they walked back through the door.

"Um…" The girl stopped midway into the room and froze as she and Jacob looked at each other.

"Tell him," Henry said.

"She um…" The girl seemed nervous, like Jacob intimidated her. "She didn't recognize me." She said finally.

"Okay… but she does now, right?" Jacob asked, like he still thought it was a side effect from waking up after surgery.

"I don't… know…" she said slowly as she turned to look at me.

"Yeah… she's my sister." I said with a smile.

"Hernandez, get in here!" Henry yelled out the door, then turned back around and stared at me like he couldn't believe I would do this.

"What… what's wrong?" the man in black asked as he walked in slowly.

"Who is this man, Kaleah?" Henry asked, still looking at me, ready for me to cut it out.

"Um…" I hesitated as I tried to think back to the point he was initially in the room.

"Lane, come on man, she's had a rough morning..." the man in black said, then looked over at Jacob quickly before his eyes went back to Lane. "I told you it's probably just something temporary from the surgery."

"Bullshit!" Lane said as he looked toward the ceiling and threw up his hands like he couldn't believe no one was listening to him.

"Lane..." Jacob stood up to walk over to him. "You need to calm down. I'm sure it's been a hard couple weeks for you, maybe if—"

"No, man!" He stopped him, drew in a large breath then set his hands on his hips. "It's all right... I'm calm, okay..." He said before looking up at me again. "Kaleah... just answer one thing for me, and I'll let this all go." He said calmly. "You still want me to keep it a secret what you did to Kat last week?"

"Really, man?" The man in black huffed, insinuating that was a low blow.

"Um..." I didn't know how to respond when suddenly Jacob turned to look at me, confused and waiting for my answer as well. "I... I... Um..."

"See! She doesn't even know who the hell Kat is!" Henry said, having just proved his point.

I started to cry when I realized I'd been caught. "I'm sorry..." I said as I looked down and away from everyone to stare at my blankets.

"Lane, get the hell out! You've done enough!" The man in black said suddenly, then looked over at Jacob, trying to gauge his reaction. "Ellice, come on, you too... Let's go... Let's let him talk to her alone for a bit. He'll know if she remembers him or not."

Jacob turned around to look at me like he wasn't sure what to believe.

"Miles?" Henry said, not willing to leave just yet.

"Just go, Lane..." Jacob said softly.

Henry nodded silently, then looked at me with regret in his eyes before turning to walk out, followed by Hernandez and my sister.

"Eva... look at me," Jacob said as he sat back down on the bed next to me.

I slowly let my eyes wander upward until they connected with his.

He looked upset, but not like I had expected. Almost like he'd been through this with me before.

"You don't remember me, do you?" He said finally.

"No," I mumbled as I tried to look away again.

"Stop… please look at me."

I lifted my head again as he brought his hand up to my face. "Eva, baby… Why would you lie?" He asked as he gently swept the hair away from my eyes.

"I was scared."

"Scared of what?"

"I don't know…"

He nodded slowly as he looked away to think. "I wonder how this happened…" He said then paused. "What's the first thing you remember? Was it when you woke up from surgery?"

"Uh… no…"

"It wasn't?" He looked back at me, surprised.

I shook my head, "I heard men talking… but I couldn't open my eyes so I don't know what they looked like."

"Okay… What did they say? Do you remember that?"

"Something about a medicine… and they had to get it first or… um… I don't know it's kinda fuzzy after that."

"It's okay… you're doing good… just try to remember." He said as he let his hand rest on my thigh again.

"I don't know."

"Okay. Do you remember if anyone had a name or did you hear them say anyone's name?"

"No."

"Okay," he said, still thinking.

"Why aren't you more mad?" I asked hesitantly as I watched him. "Henry said you'd be really mad."

"I am mad," he said as he patted my thigh gently.

"Agent Miles?" the older man called as he walked through the doorway. "You didn't report to me when you arrived."

"Yes, Sir," Jacob stood up. "Permission to speak freely, Sir?"

The man nodded to agree.

"Because you sent me away, your men failed to protect her, yet again!" Jacob sounded a lot more mad when he spoke this time.

"Agent!" the older man scolded.

"Do you even care?" Jacob went on.

"Not another word, Agent!" The older man rebuked him again. "Of course I care… But I also care about the other millions of lives that are affected by my decisions. I love my daughters dearly. You have no idea the lengths I've gone through to find Jayde and have her brought back to me. Her and Ellie's safety is paramount. I'm just thankful the only thing that has happened is a memory wipe. Now that you have the medicine, her having been erased again isn't nearly as critical. We'll simply give it—"

"I don't have it!" Jacob interrupted him. "I don't have it, Sir!" That time he sounded more distraught when he said it.

"What?" The man stopped and stared at him for a moment, then stared at me like the gravity of the situation had just hit him a little harder than it previously had. "But that's what I sent you to retrieve. That was your mission…" His speech trailed off as his eyes glossed over.

"I can't retrieve something from someone who isn't still alive, Sir."

The man had no words as he stared blankly at Jacob.

"I'm sorry, Sir!"

The man slowly nodded like he understood, then turned to me. "Jayde, sweetheart…" His eyes were looking at mine but almost as if he was still stuck in a trance, looking through me. "I… I…" He blinked and briefly looked away. "I love you…" He murmured softly, then quickly leaned in to kiss me on the forehead before turning sharply and leaving the room.

"Lane!" Jacob walked over to the doorway and called for Henry to come back in, then when he had, he shut and locked the door behind them.

"That didn't sound like it went well." Henry noted. "What are you gonna do now if there's no way to bring her back again?" He asked, then looked over at me, realizing it was worse than he thought.

"Who was she with last? Were you watching her or was it Hernandez?" Jacob asked, not addressing anything Henry had just said.

Henry hesitated, probably not sure why Jacob was asking, then he answered. "Hernandez, why? You think he did this... that doesn't really make sense. Why would he want her erased?"

"He wouldn't... I wouldn't think." Jacob looked toward the ground as he started to pace back and forth in deep thought. "And who carries that shit with them, anyway?"

"What, the serum?" Henry asked.

"Yeah... It'd have to have been the doct—"

"His second would have." Henry interrupted him.

"What?"

"His second in command... Stevens... Last week, when I sat down with Hernandez, we discussed who would watch which woman on which days. We discussed our routines and the guarding positions, who would have rounds and when. Then the last thing we went over was the best method for a non-lethal take down. So, you know... what happened with the Sicari didn't happen again. Hernandez said because he couldn't question him, he didn't know where he came from or how he got in. Stevens spoke up and said he figured we should just all carry the serum around since it'd be an easy take down. I told him that was asinine since after they passed out, you can't question them, anyway. But Hernandez didn't say anything, like... I wonder if he knew his men were carrying it and he didn't stop them."

"Okay... that's got to be just an excuse though, because a tranquilizer would work. So if he just made that up, what's the real reason he would be carrying it?"

Henry looked at him like he knew, but was hesitating to answer. "Well... only the leads do... or in this case his second... It's just for intimidation, they know their men will follow orders better if they're scared one day they might wake up and not remember anything about who they are or how they got there."

"Why do you act like you know all about this?" Jacob asked, looking at Henry suspiciously.

"Because the CO in my pillar does it… When the doctor wasn't looking, he took a vial with him. He's threatened us with it before."

Jacob cocked his jaw, afraid Henry might have been right. "All right… Who's currently guarding Ellie?"

"My men," Henry said, looking curious as to why Jacob asked.

"All right… and tomorrow it's his? Then you're back to Eva?"

Henry nodded.

"Okay, don't ask any questions. I'll explain everything later, but right now I need you to take this and keep it safe, just in case someone tries to go through my stuff." Jacob said, pulling out a small piece of paper from his inner jacket pocket, handing it to Henry.

"What's—" Henry started to ask when he looked up at Jacob's face and stopped. "Right, no questions… never mind."

"All right, now go watch Ellie… and don't tell anyone about that. We might not have to worry about someone on the outside finding Eva anymore, but now I'm wondering if someone on the inside's done something to her, and she's been erased to cover it up."

"Holy shit…" Henry made a face like he hadn't thought about that. "You think Hernandez did something?" He said low so no one outside the room could hear.

"I wouldn't put it past him." Jacob said like it hurt him to think about it.

"Well… he *was* flirting with her the other day when we were going to talk to… uh… Ellie."

"Did she flirt back?" Jacob asked. It felt weird to hear them speaking about me like I wasn't in the room listening, but I was actually more intrigued at this point than anything, so I didn't mind.

Henry's eyes quickly glanced over at me for a moment, likely thinking the same thing I just had. Then he looked back at Jacob. "No… she actually shot him down pretty good."

"Okay," Jacob said softly, looking away from him. "Maybe that's what happened then. Before I left, Eva told me the real reason he broke it off with Ellie was because she refused to get physical with him… Maybe he uh…" Jacob stopped. "You get where I'm going."

Henry nodded. "I'm sorry, man."

"It'll be all right. Just keep that paper safe and she'll be fine. We'll bring her back."

Henry didn't say anything. He just looked at him, confused. Then, after a moment, having realized something, his face changed to look surprised."Oooh…" He said finally, relaxing to look relieved.

"You should go now. Ellie might need you." Jacob said, giving him a look like there was hidden meaning behind it.

Henry nodded, briefly glanced at me with a caring smile, then turned to walk out.

Jacob turned around, walked back over to the bed, and sat down beside me again. "I don't guess you'd feel comfortable with me looking you over to see if you've been messed with, would you?" He asked, like he already knew the answer.

"No," his suspicions were correct.

"Okay, I understand." He shrugged. "Can I at least kiss you, though?"

"No."

He smiled, knowing I'd answer that way again.

"What was on the paper?" I asked, since I was now curious from getting to eavesdrop on their conversation.

"Just a recipe," He said, reaching down to hold my hand again. "Grandma Ming makes a killer herbal soup." He smiled.

14

FRACTURED DEVOTION

"Hey, you mind if I sit down?"

I knew Jacob had been watching me from afar for a while before he came over. I wasn't sure what I still had to talk to him about, though. "Sure, go ahead." I said as I let my toes frolic in the fountain water.

"It's nice out today…" I could tell he didn't know what there was to still talk about, either. "Autumn's really pretty up here this time of year. You always enjoyed seeing the leaves change and fall." He reached down and swished the water with his fingers. "It's nice to see you outside again. I know you don't remember it but you used to love sitting by the water at the falls when we were in the grotto lands too. You said the sound was soothing."

"Jacob," I wanted to stop him before he got carried away. "I'm sorry I'm not her. It's been almost two months now, and I… I'm just…" I looked away from him, trying to think of the best way to tell him what I was thinking. "I know you already told me what you both had together, but… I… um… you're a great guy… you just—"

"Stop," he said suddenly, afraid for me to continue. Then he looked like he was about to say something else, but paused while he stared at me for a second, making a face like he didn't know what to do. "Can I ask you something?" He asked finally.

"What?" I said, then someone behind him caught my eye, making me smile.

He turned to see who it was before looking back at me. "Why not me?"

"What do you mean?" I asked, bringing my attention back to him.

"I'm supposed to be guarding you but you won't let me in your room anymore... You ask me not to follow you... You barely want to speak to me... You act like—"

"I don't know you." I interrupted him.

"But that's the thing... you don't even act like you want to again, either. We were supposed to be getting married, bab... ugh Jayde... I just don't understand. I still love you... What is it about me that... Ugh... Why do you not even wanna try to be with me again?"

"It has nothing to do with you Jacob... it's me... it's—"

"Call me Jake, please... That's what you called me... I don't want it to be Jacob."

"Okay... Jake... I don't think it's that there's anything wrong with you, it's just... I don't even know who *I* really am yet. So how am I supposed to still love someone when I don't—"

"I'm not asking you to love me again yet. I just want you to pay attention to me, give *me* a chance instead of... whoever the hell that is." He said, turning around again to see if the man was still there.

I didn't respond. I just looked at him, trying to understand why he'd raise his voice.

"I'm sorry... I... I shouldn't have said it like that... I just... you're not the same, Eva... Ugh... Jayde... You're not the same and I just don't know what to do..." He said, looking tense as he leaned forward and rested his forehead in his palms.

"There are other women out there... I'm sure you—"

"Are you serious?" He looked up at me again suddenly, with a furrowed brow. "I don't want anyone else! I want you, all of you, baby... I want you back!" I could see the pain in his eyes—a mixture of intensity and desperation. He clenched his jaw and sharply looked away like he was stopping himself from shedding tears.

"Jacob, maybe you shouldn't be guarding me anymore." I said softly, wondering if him being around me so much was causing more issues than not.

"It's Jake!" He stood up suddenly. His expression said he was choking back the urge to say more. "I can't do this…" He said softly, as he closed his eyes and let out a ragged breath. "I'm not gonna keep doing this, Jayde… You don't even realize it but you're tearing me up inside…" He let his eyes settle on me for a moment then he turned slowly to walk off.

I sat there for a while, just thinking about what he said and what he meant. I felt so bad for him. I knew what he wanted, but it wasn't something I could give him.

"Jayde? You alone?" Pierce called from behind me.

I turned to smile. "Yeah," I said as I stood up to give him a hug. "I talked to Jacob. He's not happy with me again."

"Yeah, I saw he was here for a minute." He said as he moved over to sit down, motioning for me to again as well. "Is he still trying to convince you to love him again?"

"It's not like that… I'm sure this is all hard for him, you know?" I said, trying to give him grace. "Jacob isn't a bad guy. He just… he wants things from me that I can't give him."

"Yeah, but sometimes you just gotta move on. I mean, I've had to before… it's part of life. When you break up with someone, you just have to realize it's over and let them go."

"We didn't break up." I knew he knew that, but I thought I'd clarify.

"Well… yeah, but… you know what I mean. You're not with him anymore… or am I wrong?"

"I'm not with anybody." I said it to remind him that we weren't a thing either.

"We can change that," he said with a small grin.

I shook my head, "Pierce, I already told you, we're just friends. That's all—"

"I know," he quickly stopped me, "But a guy can hope, you know?" He smirked again.

I was about to respond when I saw Henry over Pierce's shoulder, standing next to the building, waiting so we could talk.

"I'm sorry, I have to go." I said as I stood up.

"You what?" He stood up with me, then turned to see what I was looking at. "What... Lane? He can wait."

"It looks like it's important," I said, reaching up to hug him again. "We'll talk later, Pierce." Then I moved away to walk to Lane.

"Is Ellie all right?" I asked.

"She's fine," he said calmly. "I'm not here to talk about her, though."

"Oh," I sighed as I looked away. I knew what else he was there for then.

"Do you mind if we sit?" He asked as he motioned toward a bench on the far side of the courtyard away from Pierce.

"Look, Henry, we already went over this. I don't know what you're gonna say that he hasn't already..." I said, referring to Jacob.

"Please?" He asked like he wanted a shot, anyway.

I sighed. "Okay..." I said as I walked with him over to the bench and sat.

"I know you don't remember anything about before. Well... what we haven't told you anyway, that's expected... But do you remember what it feels like to love someone, Jayde?"

I didn't want to respond hastily, so I thought about it for a moment before answering him. "I don't remember loving him, no... but I think I know what love feels like, yes."

"I'm not talking about puppy love, like when you're in high school." He looked over at Pierce, then back at me. "I'm talking about real love, like when you've been through hell and back with someone and you'd do anything for them."

I didn't say anything, I just shook my head no.

"Right... that's what I thought." He said as he took in a large breath, about to get to the point. "Jake would never say this to you, and he probably wouldn't even want me to but I'm going to anyway." He leaned forward, trying to collect his thoughts. "He has the stuff to bring your memories back, Jayde… But he loves you more than he loves himself. That's why he hasn't told you… That's why he hasn't done anything about it, except sit here and watch every day as you push him farther and farther away." He narrowed his eyes as he glanced back at me, stopping with a stern look.

"What? What are you talking about? He told my dad he didn't have the medicine."

"He didn't… or well doesn't… but he knows how to get it… make it, that is."

"Why are you telling me this?"

"Because you don't understand what you're doing to him, and I need you to understand."

"Fine, then explain it."

"After he got back and found out you'd been erased again, when I knew he could make the medicine, I figured he'd just do it, you know? He'd have you back and then you both could proceed like you were before he left. But then that first night, when you didn't have any nightmares and then the following week, you weren't consumed anymore with Miller and wanting to find him… Not to mention all of a sudden you're safe from the Sicari again, more safe than you've ever been… He wouldn't do it."

"I don't understand."

"Jake would rather risk the chance of you never loving him again than force you to remember all the shit you've been through… to re-live every night with every dream, all the trauma that'd happened to you… I'd watch you lay there screaming until he held you… He'd cradle and rock you until it'd pass. The problems you had from your past were hard on him too, but he dealt with it. He never complained either, not even once, because he loved you that much! He'd do anything for you! Apparently, even sit aside while you flirt with other men." As he finished, he gave me a look, clearly upset with me.

"That's not fair," I said, returning his look.

"No, it is, Jayde… It's very fair. You act like he was nothing to you, when he's tried… every freakin' day, he's tried. He won't give you the medicine. Even if he has to suffer watching you be with someone else, he won't do it… Because he loves you too damn much!" He said, then swallowed. "What's not fair is you not even giving yourself a chance to fall in love with him again. That's all he's wanted… He's willing to lose all the memories you shared together, everything you had up to this point… But losing you all together… ugh… Jayde! You don't even get it… You're freakin' *killing* him…" He paused to make himself settle back down.

"What Henry… what do you want from me? Do you want me to pretend? Is that it? Do you want—"

"Stop, just stop…" He said as he stood up and turned to look down at me. "I don't want anything from you… not this you… I want Eva, that's what I want. The woman that was a pain in the ass, shoot it straight like it is, kick your ass if you look at her wrong, Eva… And I want Kaleah, despite how broken and messed up she was, I freakin' loved her… But not you Jayde, not *this* you… I don't know *this* you, but what I do know is… I don't like it."

"Get away from me, Henry." He'd made me feel bad enough. I didn't want to hear any more. "I don't need you to like me. Go back to Ellie. You seem to like her enough for both of us."

He didn't say anything else. He just looked at me solemnly for a moment, then looked toward the ground, nodded slowly, then turned and walked away.

I wanted to sit there and cry, but I didn't want anyone to see me. I didn't intend to hurt Jacob with how I was acting, but I didn't know how to act any other way, either. I sat there trying to think about what Henry said. Even though some of his words seemed harsh, I could see past them to what he meant. But the person who I was now didn't feel like I had the capacity to love anyone or even be loved back, for that matter. I wasn't ready for a relationship. So the idea of letting Jacob in like that was hard for me to grasp. The only way I felt like I could ever be with him was if Henry was right. I couldn't be me. I'd have to go back to being Kaleah Eva.

"Jayde?" It didn't seem to take long for Pierce to find me again. Even though he wasn't on my guard detail, he had a knack for knowing where I was and finding a way to come and talk to me almost every day.

"Pierce, I don't wanna talk right—"

"Jayde, why are you crying? What'd Lane say to you?" He acted concerned, though I knew he probably wouldn't understand even if I tried to explain it.

"Please… Just leave me alone."

"But Jayde, he shouldn't—"

"I want left alone, Pierce!" I didn't want to yell at him, but he never really was good at listening to me.

"All right… sorry," he didn't continue to argue. He just turned and walked away exactly like Henry had.

"You won't tell anyone, will you?" I didn't know where else to turn, so I figured I'd find Ellie and talk to her about what I should do. Even though it didn't feel like we'd technically known each other for very long, there was some kind of sisterly bond I still felt when I talked to her.

"No… Of course I won't tell anyone. You can talk to me about anything, Jayde."

We were alone in her room. I hadn't been in there all that much, but from looking around, it didn't look like Henry had a way to hear us, so I felt comfortable enough to discuss it with her there.

"It's about Henry…" I started until I saw her face, when I stopped.

"You have an issue with Henry?" She asked defensively, like she was already on his side.

I knew they'd been spending almost every day together, but I hoped she'd still be able to put their relationship aside long enough to listen to me. "And Jacob…" I clarified, then I saw her face change again.

"Oh, yeah," she said, like she already knew what I was going to talk to her about.

"I can't love Jacob," I said finally, just to get it out before I stopped myself.

"Why?" she asked, looking surprised.

"I... um... I..." I didn't know if she'd understand my actual reasoning. "I just can't."

"Don't you think he's cute... I mean... I think he's cute. He looks like Henry... who's tall and handsome and funny..." She started to list all the things she could see in him when I stopped to remind her we weren't talking about Henry. "Oh yeah," she blushed. "Sorry..."

"Can I tell you something and you not tell Dad?"

She nodded like she was eager to hear what it was.

"Jacob has the medicine... I mean... Well, he has a way to make it. So he... um—"

"He can bring your memory back!" She said it like she was excited about the idea, but quickly lost her enthusiasm when she saw my face. "Don't you want that?"

"I don't know... I'm scared. I'm not sure I want the memory of my past back, really. Not after they initially told me about it and what all happened to me."

She nodded like she understood. Then I heard a quick knock at the door, followed by Henry talking, unaware that she wasn't alone. He hadn't rounded the corner past her hall yet to see me. "Ellie, babe, you ready to go get some supper? Your dad's there, waiting. Miles can't find Jayde, though. She's probably in a corner somewhere making out with Pierce. I'm not sure what the cook's made, but—" he stopped when he finally raised his head to see me sitting with her on the bed.

"Jayde?" He froze, his face looking more than surprised.

I didn't say anything. I just quietly moved over to the edge to stand up and slip my shoes back on to walk out when I heard Ellie. "Jayde, don't go..."

"Jayde, I'm sorry... I was... I shouldn't have said that. It wasn't nice." He said, raising a hand to stop me as I walked past him.

"Jayde?" He tried again, but I didn't respond. I just continued down her hall and opened the door to walk out.

"Henry!" Ellie huffed, knowing what he said wasn't helpful for how I was feeling or why I was there.

I shut the door quietly behind me and proceeded to walk down the corridor toward my room. I didn't feel like going to supper anymore. After that, I really wasn't sure I could eat and didn't want to see or talk to anyone for a while, either.

I slowly passed the large panes of glass in the East corridor that overlooked the courtyard, then turned to go down the creepy dark hall that stood between me and the West side of the house. I only made it halfway when I ran into someone suddenly that I couldn't see was there, standing in my path. I didn't get a chance to make any sound or even try to talk to him when whoever it was wrapped his hand around the back of my head and quickly leaned down, bringing his lips firmly to mine in an unexpected kiss.

I was about to push him away when I realized I didn't remember being kissed before or what it felt like. I didn't know who it was, Jacob or maybe even Pierce, but I relaxed and allowed it to continue. His hand felt large against the back of my head and his lips felt soft against mine. The short hairs of his beard tickled the bottom of my mouth just below my lip. After a moment when I didn't try to pull away or stop him, he reached around and rested his other hand against the back of my waist, gently pulling me up against him.

His lips were warm and tasted slightly sweet. The longer it went on, the more I didn't want it to end, the more I kissed him back. He slowly swept his mouth up, then pulled it away just to push back again to suck on my lower lip ever so slightly. I felt lost in the moment like the rest of the world had disappeared until I heard speaking from down the corridor like Henry and Ellie were on their way and close to turning the corner and catching us.

I didn't know if it was Pierce, but if so, the last thing I wanted was for Henry to walk around and catch us kissing and think he was right for what he'd already accused me of doing. I quickly pulled away and looked up at the face standing in front of me, trying to see who it was, with no luck.

He didn't speak, and I didn't ask. I just turned to quickly make sure I hadn't been seen yet before I pulled away and walked around him to continue to my room. Before I left the hall, I turned one more time to get another glance at the man's silhouette, but then quickly turned and trotted away before anyone saw me.

15

BREAKING POINT

"Come in." I didn't know who was knocking, but I wiped my face quickly so whoever it was couldn't see that I'd been crying. Just to be safe though, I figured I wouldn't turn to look at them. I would just keep laying in the bed facing the windows.

"Jayde?" It was Jacob's voice.

"What?" I asked, hearing the gravel in my own voice.

"Am I allowed to come in?"

I hesitated to answer him. I didn't want him to see me like that, but I didn't want to keep pushing him away, either. "Okay…" I mumbled, hoping he wouldn't come around the bed.

"Are you feeling all right?" He asked. When I didn't see his feet, I assumed I was in the clear, but before I could answer, I felt him sit at the end of the bed.

"Yeah, I'm fine." I said quickly, so maybe he wouldn't hear the lie in my tone.

"Are you hungry? You weren't down at breakfast again this morning, so I thought I'd bring you some. You haven't been eating a whole lot, and I'm just concerned. Here, it's your favorite—biscuits and gravy."

"I don't like biscuits and gravy," I said, then realized that sounded ungrateful, so I turned to look at him finally to apologize. "Sorry, I mean… thank you, but um… I'm not really hungry."

He didn't respond for a moment, he just looked at me, lost in his thoughts, then nodded before looking away. "Okay?" He acted like he didn't know what else to say.

"We're not together anymore, are we?" I asked as I pulled myself up to lean against the headboard.

"Is that what you want?" He continued to stare at the floor like he couldn't look at me.

I didn't answer him. I just let my eyes dance around while I thought about what to say.

"Jayde?" He said, looking up at me finally like I'd taken too long to answer him.

I nodded, but for whatever reason, I started to cry as I did.

"Oh, hey… come here…" He said quickly, scooting toward me to let my head rest against him as he rubbed my back. "Why're you crying, baby?" He asked softly.

"Because I don't want you to hate me," I said, trying to stop the tears, but I couldn't.

"Shh…" He rested his hand against the back of my head to pull me closer to him. "You could never do anything to make me hate you, Jayde."

"Not be with you again… Henry said I was killing you." I couldn't help but cry harder, thinking about what I was doing to him and feeling helpless to change it.

"Don't worry about Henry… He's just… Henry…" He said as he continued to hold me.

"I wanna love you. I just can't. I'm sorry, Jacob… I really am…"

"Do you know why you can't?" He asked softly.

"No," I said, bursting out again with more tears.

"Shh… okay… it's okay, baby… you're fine… shh…" He began to stroke my hair as he pulled me closer so my face could rest against his chest.

"Miles, you up here?" Henry called out from down the hall. "Oh, wow umm… Sorry, man… I can talk to you later." He said softer from the doorway.

I felt Jacob turn to look that way. "Shut the door, please." He said, then after a moment, I heard the door click like Henry had closed it.

"I'm sorry…" I said as I pulled back to wipe my eyes and look down at the mess I'd made on his shirt.

"For what?" He asked as he reached up to push my hair back and tuck it behind my ear.

"Everything…" I said, feeling myself start to lose it again.

"Jayde… you're all right." He put his hand under my chin to gently lift my face so I'd look at him.

"No, I'm not, Jacob…" I said, crying again. "I'm not all right… I'm not happy and I don't even know why. Not having my memories makes me feel like I came in at the end of a movie everyone's in the middle of watching. Everyone knows what's going on, except for me. Everyone knows how they feel, except for me. They know who they're with and who they love… but not me." I said, breaking down again, even though I tried harder this time to contain it. "I can't love you because I don't even know how to love."

"Jayde," He said, pulling me toward him again, "It's okay… just relax, you're getting yourself all worked up, honey… You're gonna make yourself sick."

"I can't…" Even when I tried to stop, I just cried harder, "I can't love you, Jacob… I can't love anyone right now. I just can't…"

"Okay," He began to gently rub the back of my head again while I leaned my forehead into his chest. "Okay, baby… you don't have to, okay? You don't have to love me again… You don't have to do anything, all right? Nobody's forcing you… it's okay." He said, probably hoping that would help me calm down.

I was too upset to speak, so I just nodded and turned my body where I could lie back down and rest my head in his lap. I didn't know if it was from all the crying or what, but I felt extremely tired suddenly and needed to rest.

"There ya go, just relax, baby… It's okay." He said as he helped guide me to rest against him. "You don't have to love me… it's okay."

I wanted to respond, but I didn't. I just closed my eyes and tried to relax like he'd said.

"You're so beautiful," he murmured softly, but I couldn't respond. I could feel myself slowly slipping into a deep sleep.

"Here boy… come here boy!" I said, patting my hands as I called out for Reggie.

He barked a few times, looking at the fence like he'd seen something and wasn't ready to come back to me just yet.

"What's wrong, boy?" I asked as I walked over to him to see what he was barking at.

He pounced his paws against the ground and wagged his tail quicker, like whatever he saw made him want to play.

"What is it? You got a toy over here?" I asked as I looked down at where he was looking.

He barked again, then pawed at the ground a little, wanting to go under the fence.

I didn't see anything. "What are you looking for, boy?" I asked him again as I tried to look harder at what it was.

"Jayde? Dinner!"

"I don't see anything, Reggie. Come on… we gotta go eat." I said, trying to reach for his collar when he pounced on the ground again, now wanting to play.

"Jayde!" I was awakened by a loud knock on the door and someone loudly calling my name. When I opened my eyes, I saw Jacob sitting on the floor leaning against the wall, then he looked over at the door as he got up quickly to address whoever was calling for me.

Jacob opened the door and leaned against the frame, blocking whoever was there from coming in. "She's resting. What are you doing here?"

"Dude… what are *you* doing here?" It was Xavier's voice. He hadn't been to my room again since Dad had him reassigned to his own personal detail a couple of weeks back, so I wasn't sure why he'd be here now.

"My job... guarding her!" Jacob scoffed. I'm sure he was confused as well why Xavier was visiting me.

"Hasn't it been like over a month since she's let you in her room? What'd you say to weasel your way in now?" Xavier snapped back, acting surprised to see him as well.

"Why are you here?" Jacob raised his voice, ignoring Xavier's comment.

"To check on her. Why else would I be here?" Xavier said, as he looked past Jacob over at me.

Jacob looked back and forth between us, probably suspicious of Xaviers motives. "She's fine, see? She was just taking a nap." Jacob said as he reached for the door, ready to shut it in Xavier's face.

"Wait," Xavier said, as he shot out his hand to stop it, then he looked back over at me. "Jayde, sweetie... you sure you're good? He's not bothering you?"

"Are you serious, man?" Jacob didn't let me reply before he blew up on him. "Who the hell do you think you are? Of course she's fine. What the hell would I be doing with her in here?"

"Oh... I don't know..." Xavier continued, intentionally pushing Jacob's buttons. "You know she doesn't want you anymore, so why you're still even at this house is a mystery to me."

I wanted to yell at them to stop arguing, but I couldn't. I was too scared to get between them.

As soon as Xavier said it, a tension built up in Jacob's shoulders, making it obvious he was getting angry. Then, before I realized what had even happened, he cocked his arm back and slung his fist forward, hitting Xavier somewhere in his face.

"Jacob, no!" I yelled suddenly, finding my voice, as I quickly got out of the bed and ran over to them.

Xavier stumbled back a little, then stood back up straight as he wiped his face with the back of his hand and looked at it. The expression on his face as his eyes lifted to look back at Jacob was menacing but his silent glare was beyond eery, almost like a calm before the storm.

"Xavier, please…" I said, stepping in front of Jacob, "just stop this!" I could tell by the look on his face though, he wasn't about to have it end there.

"Move, Jayde…" Xavier growled.

"No! Please…" I said as I took a step back into Jacob with my hands out to the side and back, making sure he was squarely behind me. Then I felt his hands on my shoulders, slowly moving me over.

As soon as I wasn't in the way, Xavier launched himself forward, hitting Jacob in the stomach with his shoulder, forcing him to the ground.

"Stop it!" I yelled at them but they continued to tussle and throw punches at each other. "Jacob! Please…" It didn't seem to matter which name I called out, neither of them were listening.

I turned to run out the door; I needed to get help. "Henry!?" I called out, wondering if he was still close. "Lawson, Rogers…" I tried yelling a couple other names of the men that were usually around as I turned to run down the stairs.

"Cupcake? What's the matter?" Andry, one of Henry's men, was walking into the great room as I hit the bottom step.

"It's…" I tried to point since I was out of breath. "It's Ja…" I didn't know why, but all of a sudden, I didn't feel well. "Jacob…" I said finally, before turning to look back at Andry.

"You all right, Cup…"

"Move her over here… lay her down… What happened? Eva… uh… Jayde, baby? Can you hear me?"

"She just passed out, Boss. I mean, it looked like she was trying to get someone to come stop you two."

"This is your fault, Miles… You constantly forcing her to be with you again is stressing her out!"

"Shut the hell up, Hernandez! Jayde, baby… wake up, sweetie… We're done fighting, everything's all right."

I felt a warm hand rubbing briskly up and down my thigh. I opened my eyes to see Jacob, Andry, and Xavier all hovering above me. "You're hurt…" I said, lifting my hand to touch the corner of Jacob's eye.

"It's fine," he said as he reached up to squeeze my hand, then hold it. "You should see the other guy," he said with a smirk and a quick glance at Xavier's glowering and battered face. Then, returning his attention to me. "Are you all right? What happened?"

I looked around at each of their faces while I thought about what he'd asked. "Um… I, uh… don't know. Everything just went black."

Jacob furrowed his brow, apparently thinking that was odd. "Andry, where's Lane?" He asked, glancing up at him.

"Xavier…" I said, noticing his face looked worse than Jacob's. "You're bleeding. You should—"

"I'll be fine, Jayde." He quickly dismissed my concern.

"Lane's with Ellie, in the atrium, I believe." Andry said, responding to Jacob. "You want me to go get him, Boss?"

"No… but next time you see him, tell him I need to talk to him about something."

Andry nodded.

"Jayde, do you need me to call the doctor?" Xavier asked, as he used his sleeve to wipe away the blood that kept appearing under his nose.

"You need the doctor, not me." I said as I sat up. I still felt a little woozy, but not bad enough to mention it to them.

"No, really, you should probably get yourself checked out… this could be anything."

"He's right, Jayde." Jacob said as he placed his hand on my back to steady me. "You just passing out like this isn't normal."

"Well, didn't she have issues with something like that when she was pregnant last?" Andry asked, standing back up.

"No…" Jacob said, then looked down at me, seeing how I took the reminder that at one point, I had carried his baby. "It was something else you're thinking about, Andry."

"Well, I guess she could be pregnant again," Xavier said, like I wasn't sitting there listening to them trying to diagnose me.

"What? No, I can't!" I said, then thought about it. "Can I?" I asked, slightly feeling freaked out by the idea.

"No… no… Don't worry about that, baby, you're fine. You had a long-lasting birth control just a few… um… months ago…" He initially said it trying to make me feel better, but then it sounded like he wasn't sure he wanted to mention it in front of Xavier, as his words slowly trailed off.

"Why do you keep calling her baby? Dude, can't you see that makes her uncomfortable?" Xavier said as he stood up, now looking down at Jacob.

Jacob tensed up and turned to stare at him, ready to punch him in the mouth again if he kept going.

"Boss!" Andry said suddenly, then cleared his throat.

Jacob blinked a couple times, then gave Xavier a side-eye before turning back around to look at me. "Don't worry, you're not pregnant. Not by—" He stopped and shook his head a little, stopping himself from whatever he was going to say. "Do you want to see the doctor? I'll have him come to your room if you do."

"No," I shook my head. "I'm fine."

"Okay, do you want me to carry you back up there?"

"Geez, Miles…" Xavier threw his hands up. "She can walk. She didn't break her leg!"

Jacob stood up and turned to face him, clearly done hearing his mouth.

"Stop!" I yelled out and quickly stood up to try to get between them again. I didn't want them to fight anymore. I took a step, putting both my arms out toward each of their torsos like I was going to push them away from each other, but before I could, my vision went dark again.

"Jayde?"

"Oh my gosh, why isn't she waking up? Henry, you said she'd be fine."

"She will, Ellie… well, I mean…"

"After she wakes up, you and me are gonna have a talk, Lane!"

"Uh… yeah… sure thing, Miles…"

"Jayde, baby? Can you hear me?"

"All right, Boss… Hernandez said the doctor's on his way."

"Thanks, Andry… Ellie, Jayde's gonna be fine. This has happened to her before. It's probably nothing. Would you mind if I talked to Lane for a minute, though… alone?"

"Uh… Okay…"

"Thanks, Ellie! Andry, would you escort her back to her room, then? Lane will be there in a few."

"Sure, Boss!"

"Jayde… baby… Can you hear me?"

"She looks fine… like she's just in a really deep sleep, you know? I'm sure it's nothing serious, Miles."

"I know it's nothing serious, Lane… You wanna tell me what you've been up to the last few days?"

"Um… nothing, you know, just a little bit of—"

"Cooking? Where's that recipe I gave you?"

"Uh… What are you talking about, Miles?"

"She was talking in her sleep again earlier when she was taking a nap… I thought it was odd but didn't think anything of it until I thought about how tired she seemed suddenly, then next thing I know she's passing out left and right!"

"Uh, yeah… that sure does sound awfully odd…"

"Cut the crap, Lane! Why would you do this when I told you not to? This wasn't what I wanted."

"I'm sorry, man… I… um… I just… I don't know."

"Lane, dammit! How much have you given her?"

"Well, *I* haven't given her anything… technically… It's actually Ellie that's been giving it to her… so…"

"Are you freakin' serious? You got her in on this now?"

"Sorry?"

"You're gonna stop it. I don't want her getting any more, hear me?"

"No… I won't…"

"What?"

"You heard me, Miles. I'm sorry, I know you don't like it but it's not your choice to make. You guys aren't even together anymore… hell, for all you know she could be doing shit with Hernandez or that li'l prick, Pierce… So it's Ellie's decision now… She's her sister, and this is what she wants for her. We've talked, this is—"

"It *is* my choice, Lane!"

"Jacob? Are you all right?" I opened my eyes to see him and Henry yelling at each other at the far end of my room.

"Oh, hey…" He turned toward me suddenly and changed his tone. "You awake now? How're you feeling?" He asked as he came to sit next to me on the bed.

"Yeah, I'm fine. Just really tired." I said, trying to sit up to see the room. "Why are you and Henry yelling at each other?"

Jacob looked around unsure how to answer that, then looked up at Henry.

"Where's Xavier?" I asked, since I didn't see him in the room anymore.

"See!" Henry raised his hand to point at me and make a weird face, looking at Miles. "Told ya!"

Jacob stood up suddenly, "You need to leave… I'll talk to you about this later, now get out!" He said as he walked over to open the door and wait on him.

"Fine!" Henry looked over at me briefly, then turned to walk out.

Jacob shut the door behind him, then turned to look at me. "The doctor will be here soon, then if you're feeling well I can take you down to get some lunch… We need to be careful with what you're eating, something in it could be what's causing you to feel sick."

I thought that was odd, but I didn't say anything. I just nodded to agree.

16

FLIES TO HONEY

"Where's Miles?" Henry asked like he didn't already know, which I found unrealistic.

"I sent him home." I said as I flipped a page in the book I was reading.

"Why would you do that?" The way he asked it was precisely as I expected. He likely already knew where Jacob went and now just wanted my reasoning behind it.

"I don't need guarded anymore. I'm no longer in danger."

"Kaleah, look at me."

I brought my eyes from the book up to him. "My name isn't Kaleah, Henry. I've told you that before."

"You *do* need guarded!" He didn't act happy with me, but what was new? "You're a Prescott. Even if you don't remember stuff and can't be tracked by the Sicari anymore, there are still multitudes of people that would love to take you or hurt you."

"That's the same thing Jacob said, but I'm pretty sure I'm fine. Nothing has happened to me since I woke up with my tag."

"I swear, you're so freakin' stubborn." He said like he was about to lose his temper, but quickly calmed himself down.

"Please… feel free to speak your mind." I said sarcastically as I looked back down at my book.

"I know why you sent him away… It's so you can be with Pierce without Miles getting in the way."

I looked at him suddenly in disbelief. I was appalled that he'd even say what he did. I slowly set the book down and stood up, thinking about how I should respond before I walked away.

"Or maybe it's Hernandez you've gone to bed with, huh, Jayde?"

"What?" I gasped, then reached up to slap him, but he stopped my arm mid swing and quickly used it to pull me toward him. He wrapped his other arm around my waist and held me tight against him while he planted a kiss squarely on my lips. It wasn't anything like the kiss from the man in the hall. It wasn't slow and sensual. It was deep and desperate. I used my other hand to push myself back, then pulled my arm away from his grasp. "What the hell was that?" I asked, almost frozen with shock as I took a couple of steps back.

His eyes widened, suddenly realizing something. "Jayde?" He furrowed his brow. "How many people have you been with?"

"What??" I scoffed, clearly taken aback at that question on top of the kiss. I didn't understand what that had to do with anything or why he even thought he should kiss me in the first place.

"How many people have you slept with… like after you were erased last… how many?"

"I don't have to answer you. That's none of your business!" I said as I pushed past him to walk out, but he quickly caught my arm and swung me around to look at him again.

"Miles thinks you're cheating on him!"

"You can't cheat on someone you're not with, Henry!" I said, trying to pull my arm away again with no luck.

"He only left because he thought you were fooling around with someone else, otherwise he wouldn't have listened when you ordered him to." He said softly as he let go of my arm. "But you haven't been with anyone else, have you?"

I didn't know what to say. I just looked away. "Why did you just kiss me?"

"To prove to myself I was right… even though I didn't want to believe it."

"How does kissing me prove anything?" I asked as I looked at him again.

"It didn't… because I was wrong. You haven't been with a man since you were erased. You don't kiss like it, anyway."

"I don't appreciate you accusing me like you did." I said as I turned around to sit back down and curl up in the chair.

"Why didn't you tell Miles you hadn't been with anyone else?"

"I did. I told him I couldn't love anyone, *including* him."

"Not loving someone doesn't stop you from letting them in your bed…" He said, rubbing the back of his head and looking around like this somehow changed things. "So you haven't been with Pierce… *or* Hernandez?" He asked, apparently needing confirmation that he was wrong.

"No!" I said, irritated that it was even implied. "Why would Jacob even think I had?"

Henry wouldn't look at me. He just sat down and leaned against the wall while he stared at the floor. "I don't know… maybe 'cause I told him so," he said softly before running his hands over his face as he exhaled loudly.

"Why would you do that?"

"Why don't you want to be with him?" He looked up at me finally. "I couldn't think of any other reason you wouldn't want to be with him. That's why! Not to mention, you let both of those assholes constantly flirt with you… How was I supposed to know?"

I didn't respond. I just shook my head like I didn't know what to say.

"They won't love you… neither of them will ever love you like he does!"

"I don't want them to." I said softly as I leaned my face against the back of the leather chair while I fidgeted with the buttons on my blouse.

"You don't?" He sounded surprised.

"No, I don't like them anymore than I do him… You don't get it, it's not as easy as what you think it is. I wake up, don't know who I am, but everyone else does. But no one tells me the same story. Jacob says I'm supposed to be with him and he loves me. Xavier says Jacob isn't who I think he is and that he just wants to be with me because of who my father is. Pierce… well, he said he just wants to be friends, but then is constantly talking about how we can be together. Now you… I thought you were with my sister, but then you infer that I'm a whore right before you kiss me… What the hell am I supposed to think, Henry?" I could feel myself getting wound up the more I let it all out.

He looked stunned, unsure of what to say. "Jayde… oh my gosh, I'm sorry… I never realized you felt like that." He said finally, like he genuinely meant it.

"No… instead of asking me how I feel or what I'm thinking, you'd rather yell at me and tell me how much you don't like me… All right before you go back to my sister and tell her you think I'm in a corner cheating on your brother." I couldn't help but cry as I said it.

"Jayde… no… ugh, dammit…" He said softly under his breath as he got up on his knees to move over to the chair. "I'm sorry… please… will you look at me?"

I lifted my eyes to meet his.

"You're right, I didn't know any of that… I'm sorry… I shouldn't have said what I did. There's no excuse, I just… I love my brother and I can't stand to see him like he is. He's never loved anyone like he loves you. He's never wanted to be with anyone else like he does you, either. And as far as what Hernandez said, that's a freakin' lie. Jacob loved you before he ever knew who you really were."

I didn't say anything. I just wiped the tears from my eyes as I continued to listen.

"As far as me and your sister… she's the best thing that's ever happened to me." He paused as he leaned back to rest on his heels. "Before I met her, I envied what I saw you and Miles had. Every time I saw you both together, laughing, smiling, just loving each other… I thought how lucky he was to have you. But now that I have that with her, I don't feel like I can enjoy it 'cause when I look at either of you, you both seem miserable… I'm sorry I kissed you." He looked away.

"It didn't mean anything and it won't happen again." He said, then sat flat on the floor, waiting for a reply.

"Does Jacob really think I'm cheating on him?"

He looked back at me like he was curious why I asked, then nodded slightly. "Yeah."

I could feel everything in me I had been suppressing deep inside begin to bubble up like it was about to flow out. I didn't say anything else. I just quickly wiped my eyes and stood up.

"Where are you going?" Apparently, he didn't think we were done.

"I can't talk anymore." I said, trying to hold back the river of tears I felt coming as I stepped around him.

"Jayde, I'm sorry! I'll fix this!" He said behind me as I walked toward the door. "Dammit," I heard him sigh, then mumble something else I didn't quite catch as I walked out.

"Hey, Jayde!" Ellie peaked her head around the corner of the great-room's fireplace. "You in here all alone?"

"Yeah," I said, trying to smile as I watched flames dance back and forth over the logs.

"It's getting chilly outside again, so I brought you some soup." She said cheerfully as she slowly revealed her hands with the bowl of soup tightly clutched between them.

"Okay?" I watched her bring it around and set it down on the end table next to me. "Is this the same soup you made me a few weeks ago when you and Henry were practicing cooking together?"

"Yeah," she said like she was excited for me to try it again. "Why? Do you not like it?"

"No, I do… I just—"

"I'm sorry I haven't made it for a couple of weeks." She said before I could finish. "It's just, there's been a lot going on with Henry and Jake and all, and I got busy. But since I know how much you like it, I wanna make it for you more often if you don't mind. I really enjoy it when Henry teaches me how to make different dishes. I've never really been taught how to cook before. It's super fun."

"Oh… uh, okay…" I didn't love the soup, but I didn't hate it either, so I figured if it made her happy to make it, I would do my best to eat it.

"Yay!" She sounded enthused. "I'll make you more tomorrow, then." She said with a big smile, then looked at me like she wasn't sure why I wasn't smiling back. "What's wrong?"

"Oh, uh… nothing," I didn't feel like talking about it so I lied.

"Do you miss Jake?" She asked, like she could read my mind.

"Hmm…" I tried to smile as I shook my head and reached down to pick up the soup.

"You can tell me, Jayde… I won't tell no one."

I didn't want to cry again, so I tried not to think about it. "I'm fine." I said quickly, hoping she wouldn't continue.

"When did he leave? Just a few days ago?" She asked, like she fully intended to keep going.

"Four days, tomorrow," I mumbled as I took the spoon and ladled the broth into my mouth.

"Oh…" she said like she hadn't realized it'd been that long. "Do you know when he'll be back?"

"He's not coming back…" I said softly. "I'm sure he hates me now, since he thinks I've been cheating on him."

She didn't say anything at first. She just looked at me oddly, then walked back toward the direction she had come from. "I'm sure if you wanted to see him again, he'd come back."

I didn't respond. I just nodded as I sipped more soup.

"I can bring you breakfast tomorrow too if you'd like. Henry said he'd teach me how to make an herb infused quiche."

"Okay… Hey, I need to tell you something before you go." I said, stopping her from walking out.

"Sure," She took a step back toward me, looking a little puzzled.

"It's been bothering me, so… I don't know. I just don't want to keep anything from you." I paused to work up the courage to go on. "Henry kissed me earlier."

She nodded. "I know."

"Uhh… what?"

"It's okay, Jayde. He already told me."

"He did?"

"Yeah," she smiled. "He explained everything and why he did it. He really is the sweetest guy. I wished you two had a better relationship than you do. I mean, I know you used to before you were erased, but… well… I know you probably don't realize it but he's been going through a lot since then. He still blames himself for what happened since Jake left you in his care. He feels like it's his fault that you and Jake aren't together anymore. Not to mention, Henry misses the old you, too. You guys used to be really close. I actually caught him crying one night. Don't tell him I told you…" She paused with a long sigh. "He tells me everything, Jayde… and well… I love him."

"Oh…" I didn't know what to say, so I just stared at her for a moment.

"Anyway…" she shrugged, "I'll see you bright and early in the morning." She smiled, then turned to walk out.

"Kaleah?" I thought I heard Jacob, but when I opened my eyes there was nobody there, only a pitch black room. It was clear that I was alone, and now I felt lonely as well. I realized I had done it to myself, but I didn't know what to do to reverse it. I closed my eyes and rested my head back against the pillow.

"It won't happen again." Jake said with a little more strength behind the tone. He must have known I was crying. He released my hand and brought his up to my face, resting his palm against my cheek as he wiped the tears under my eyes away with his thumb. Then he tightened his grip slightly against my face and pushed himself closer to me with his other arm. His face was now closer to mine, with the whites of his eyes bigger than before. "I won't let it happen again." He said once more with a sweet yet stern voice.

"Jacob?" I opened my eyes again as I sat up in the bed. "Are you there?" I thought I heard his voice again, but wasn't sure if it was real or if I had just dreamed it. I still didn't see anything or hear anyone either. I felt around in the bed next to me but didn't feel him. That's when I realized it had to be a dream. I was close to crying again when I laid my head back against the pillow and closed my eyes before they could fully tear up.

"Please don't hurt me." I cried out. "P... Please," the shivering started to deepen. "Don't h... hurt me. P... Please," I cried out again, feeling close now to the edge of passing out.

Two hands gently gripped my arms, then they shook me slightly to rock me back a little. "P... Please don't h... hurt me." I begged.

Slowly, as if my hearing had started to fade back into my thoughts I could hear a small voice every time the hands shook me. "Kal..." the volume of the voice slowly increased. "Kale..." Then as if all at once "Kaleah," said a soft, gentle voice.

I opened my eyes, still hesitating to lift my head. "Kaleah, it's me. Kaleah..." The hands moved down and around to my back as a large warm body pulled himself closer to mine.

"Kaleah... you're okay. It's me, Jake. You're okay now. I've got you. You're okay now."

"Jake?!" I woke up screaming his name. "Jacob?" I yelled out again as I opened my eyes, hoping to see him sitting there next to me, but still there was nothing but complete darkness. "Jacob, please answer me!" I cried out one more time but knew he wasn't there and it again was nothing more than just another dream.

I sat there for a moment staring into the darkness, then turned to reach for my bedside lamp to pull the chain. When the light came on, I saw exactly what I had expected to see. There was no one in the room with me. I didn't even want to try to go to sleep again; I knew I would just wind up caught in the same dream-wake-scream cycle, inevitably realizing that I was still completely alone.

I turned to sit on the edge of the bed while I thought about what to do. I wanted Jake, but knew I couldn't have him. He wasn't anywhere around and even if he was; I was certain he wouldn't want to see me again since I'd sent him away. The longer I sat there thinking about it, the more I regretted it and wondered why I had even done what I did. Ellie was right. I did miss him. I missed him terribly and wanted nothing more than to see him again.

I began to cry as I reached down to grab my slippers and put them on my feet. When I had them on, I stood up and reached for my robe that was draped across a chair next to the window. I didn't know where I intended to go, but I didn't want to stay in my room anymore. I put the robe on and walked out into the hall.

There wasn't a lot of light, but there was enough. I figured I would go back to the library. I hoped maybe reading would distract me.

"He won't be back," I stopped when I heard Xavier's voice speaking from below in the great room.

"How do you know?" I didn't recognize the other man's voice, but I assumed it was one of Xavier's men. I didn't move, I just kept listening to the conversation.

"Because she ordered him to leave finally. Her being erased worked out better than I thought it would. Now that he's out of the way, it won't take long before I convince her to hook up with me."

"What makes you think she'll wanna be with you if it didn't work out between you and Ellie? They're practically the same person now that she doesn't remember anything. It's like she mirrors her sister's personality."

"Because I'm available and she's desperate. It's that simple.

Pretend to be the princess's knight in shining armor and she can't get enough of you."

I couldn't keep listening. For whatever reason, when I heard him call me princess, I instantly felt severely sick to my stomach. I turned to go back to my room when random memories suddenly flashed through my mind. I saw a man; he was an agent, all dressed in black like the others. There was something about him that didn't remind me of the others, though. There was something wrong with him. Something about him was sickening to me. Maybe it was the way he looked at me, maybe it was his mustache. I wasn't sure, but I felt like I needed to lie down.

I began to feel dizzy the more worked up I got when I thought about what I saw. I hurried back toward the doorway of my room when suddenly I didn't see anything anymore.

"Jayde? Ah shit, she's bleeding…"

"What do you think happened?"

"I don't know… it looks like she passed out again… probably hit her head on the door frame when she fell. Jayde? Wake up, sweetie…"

"What did the doctor say when this happened last time?"

"I don't know. I wasn't in the room with her. Miles was but he wouldn't tell me anything when I asked him how it went. Go get Lane, maybe he knows."

"All right… you got her?"

"Of course I got her!"

"Jayde… it's Xavier… I'm here… wake up, honey…"

"Holy shit, Hernandez, what the hell did you do to her?"

"Shut the hell up, Lane. I didn't do shit to her. I wasn't even up here when she fell. What did the doctor tell Miles was wrong with her?"

"Lawson, go get the doc. She's gonna need stitches."

"I already sent a man for the doc, Lane… Now answer me, what did he tell Miles?"

"Why would I tell *you* that? You're not her guard… It's none of your business."

"Because we're together now, so it *is* my business."

"Bull freakin' shit, you are! Miles will be back in the morning. Tell *him* you're together and see what he says."

"What? She told him to leave. She doesn't want to be with him anymore!"

"Well, try telling her that when she wakes up and see if she agrees!"

17

NOT SO PLATONIC

"Lane… oh my gosh, is she all right? I came as soon as you called… When did she ask for me?"

"Uh… yeah… about that, um… technically she didn't, but I figured you should be here for her."

"How long has she been like this?"

"The doc gave her a sedative earlier after she woke up a few times screaming for you… She's been out since then."

"What happened?"

"I'm not totally sure. Sims came to get me, told me him and Hernandez were downstairs when they thought they heard her. Hernandez said when they went to check on her she was laying in the doorway. It looked like she fell and hit her head."

"The doc stitched her up nicely…"

"Yeah… doesn't look like it'll leave a scar, that's good."

"Okay, Lane… so now you wanna tell me why she fell? I thought you stopped giving her the herbs like I asked."

"Um… well… we stopped the few weeks you were still here… But when she sent you away, I figured—"

"Wait? You said she was screaming for me last night?"

"Uh, yeah! Three times after she woke up from fainting. I stayed in here to watch her while Andry stayed with Ellie. Every time she'd start by mumbling something, then before I could get over to her, she'd start screaming for you. One time she thought I was you when I woke her up trying to get her to snap out of it. After that was when I had the doc come back in to give her something to help her sleep."

"What'd she say?"

"What, when she thought I was you?"

"Yeah…"

"Um… Well, not a whole lot… She just mumbled a bunch, kept saying she was sorry and wouldn't let me leave her. I kept telling her I wasn't you, but it didn't seem like she understood. Then she got kinda frantic, and I was worried she'd pass out again, so I had the doc come back in."

"Why would she be sorry? Did you believe her when she—"

"Just like I told you over the phone, she's not been with anyone, Miles… Yes, I believe her."

"How do you know? For three weeks, I couldn't get Hernandez to leave her alone. Then when I tried to get between them, it just made her more upset with me."

"Uh… I uh… I kissed her…"

"You did *what*? *When*?"

"Yesterday… I'm sorry, man… I just… Honestly, I was upset, and it was on impulse. I felt like it was the only way to prove I was right. I've kissed enough girls to know when they're experienced and when they're not… but… she's very *not*."

"Hernandez doesn't seem to agree… When he saw me come in this morning he already acted like—"

"He's a twat, Miles… Of course he's gonna act like they're together, 'cause that's what he wants… But believe me, after last night, it's clear she doesn't want anybody but you! The more of that stuff we give her, the more of you she's gonna want, too."

"Fine… I hate it… It's not what I wanted… but I can't stand to not be with her, either. The last four days have been a living hell not having her next to me. I thought I could handle it, but everything in your whole freakin' apartment reminds me of her."

"Good, I'm glad you finally approve 'cause I have Ellie making her a quiche this morning with more of the greens in it."

"Ugh… all right… but whatever you do, don't let Hernandez or any of his men find out. I'm still suspicious about how she was ever erased again in the first place."

"Sure thing, man! You gonna stay in here with her now so I can go back to Ellie?"

"Yeah, you don't think she'll be mad if she wakes up and sees I'm back, right?"

"Nope, not from the way she acted last night… I'd be surprised if she didn't sit up and beg you to stay."

"All right… Thanks for calling and staying with her… I'm good now, you can go back to Ellie. Just lock the door when you leave, please. I don't want Hernandez trying to come and check on her… Oh and Lane, later we need to discuss increasing her guard detail again. If her memories are gonna come back, so will the Sicari's signal."

"You got it, man… I'll have Ellie bring her breakfast here in a few."

"Jayde? Can you hear me? It's Jake, baby… I'm back now…"

"Kaleah… Baby? You gonna wake up? I'm back… It's Jake, sweetie…"

"Eva, it's me… It's Jake… I'm here, baby… Why don't you wake up now…"

"Jayde…"

I opened my eyes when I thought I heard Jacob saying my name. There he was, sitting in front of me, looking down at me. I knew it was a dream again though, just like all the others. I must have still been asleep.

"Hey…" He said with a sweet smile, "You're finally awake."

I didn't say anything back. I knew it wouldn't matter if I tried, since it was all just an illusion. I just lay there and stared at him. I missed seeing his face, hearing his voice, smelling his smell. I missed everything about him, but the more I thought about it, the more miserable I felt since I knew I wouldn't likely see him again, not without dreaming about it like I was, anyway. I was afraid to blink. I didn't want to wake myself up for real and look around again to see he wasn't really there.

"Are you all right?" He asked as he brought his hand up to my face.

I still didn't respond. I just wanted to lie there and watch him stare back at me, hoping he'd continue to talk.

"Are you still upset with me?" His face changed, like he wasn't sure why I wasn't answering him. "Do you want me to leave again, is that it? I know our last conversation didn't go well… I'm sorry I said what I did—"

"What?" I asked finally. I was confused if it was still a dream or if I really was awake. It was so realistic now.

"I shouldn't have accused you of cheating… I'm sorry, I was just upset and letting my mouth run."

"Jake?" I was lost. How could it really be him? Surely it wasn't. I looked around, then quickly sat up.

"Oh, hey… it's all right, baby… What's the matter?"

"This isn't real. I gotta wake up." I said, now ignoring him. I turned to sit on the edge of the bed.

"Kaleah… look at me… it is real, baby. I'm here now." He continued, but I knew it wasn't.

I looked down for my slippers, but they weren't there.

"Where are you going?"

"You're not real, stop talking… I'm going to wake up, that's where…" I said as I thought about what I could do to make myself break from the dream and snap back into reality. I still felt weak, but I figured that was an illusion as well. I leaned against the headboard to try to stand up. When I did, though, my feet weren't quite awake themselves and I felt myself beginning to fall.

"Oh my gosh… Kaleah!" Jake reached out and caught me just before I hit the floor. Then he slowly lowered me the rest of the way down.

"You're real." I said in disbelief, looking up at him.

"Yeah, baby… I'm real." He said softly as he hovered close to me.

I didn't say anything. I couldn't believe it. I looked from his eyes to his mouth, down to his chest, then back again. When suddenly it was like he thought the same thing I did and he leaned in to kiss me.

I reached up and held the back of his neck so he couldn't pull away. He kissed me hard, harder than before in the hall. I knew it had to be him though because his lips tasted the same as they had that day, and his beard hairs tickled me in the same spot as well.

He slowly ran his hand down along my side until he reached my hip, then stopped to let it rest there.

"I didn't cheat on you," I said finally when I got a chance to breathe right before he pushed in to kiss me again.

He didn't say anything back, but I felt his head move just slightly up and down in a nod as he mumbled, "umm-hmm."

"I swear I didn't…" I said again after I had another chance to pull my lips away from his for a second.

"I know… now stop talking…" He whispered, then continued to kiss me like he missed me as much as I did him. He laid his body down next to mine and wrapped his arm around my side. Then he rolled onto his back, pulling me to lie on top of him.

"I missed you…" I said between kisses. "I'm sorry I sent you away!"

He reached up and wrapped his hands around the back of my head. "I missed you more… don't talk, just kiss me." He said as he pulled me in to kiss me harder.

I didn't know what I was doing, but despite that, my hands seemed to have no problem knowing where to go. One held the side of his head as we kissed while the other reached down and untucked his shirt so it could slide up under it to feel his chest. I swirled my fingers around, catching his chest hair, then let it go again as I moved my hand across to feel how tight his chest muscles were.

"I don't know what I'm doing…" I whispered, then continued to kiss him.

"Do you want me to show you?" He asked, still speaking soft and low.

I didn't respond. I just continued to kiss him for a moment while I thought about it. So many things went through my mind when suddenly I felt like none of it mattered. The only thing that mattered was how I felt at that moment and what I wanted right then. I stopped kissing him for a second and pulled back to look at him. "Will you?"

He smiled, then bit his bottom lip, stopping himself from getting emotional. "Sure, baby…" He said as he lifted his hand to push the hair back from my face and tuck it behind my ear.

I nodded, "I'm scared…" I whispered.

He didn't say anything for a moment. He just looked up at my eyes, trying to read them. "It's all right, baby… I won't let anything hurt you…" He said softly as he moved his hand to rest on the back of my neck again.

I looked at his eyes, then his mouth, then his eyes again, before I nodded. "Okay… but—" I was starting to feel dizzy again.

"Yeah, baby?"

"I'm…"

"Jayde?" I head Ellie's voice like she was walking around the bed. "I brought you breakfast…"

I opened my eyes. When I saw I was in my bed still, and not on the floor next to Jake, I realized I must have been right, and it was all a dream. I looked up at her. She was smiling like she was proud of what she'd created. She set the platter down on the nightstand next to me, then pulled a plate and fork out from under her arm. "Ellie…" I said, wondering how to tell her I wasn't in the mood to eat.

"Jake… I'm sorry, I didn't make enough for you too, I didn't realize you'd be here," she said, prompting me to suddenly look around for who she was talking to.

"Jacob?" I said when I finally saw him sitting behind her in one of the chairs near the fireplace.

"It's all right, Ellie… I can eat later." He said as he quickly stood up and walked over to us. "Jayde, how are you feeling?"

"Jacob?" I couldn't believe my eyes.

"You look better…" He looked down at me and smiled. "You passed out again. I had to pick you up off the floor." He said, then winked at me.

"You're back?"

Ellie quickly turned to look at me after she had taken a large scoop of the quiche and set it on the plate. "It's my fault, Jayde… I asked him to come back when I saw you weren't feeling well again… Don't be upset with him."

I looked at her, confused. "Oh, okay…" I said, then looked back at him. "How long are you staying?"

"I don't have to leave again, unless you want me to."

"Don't make him leave again yet, Jayde." Ellie said suddenly, like she was desperate, "I mean… you might be sick like this for a while, and until we know what's wrong with you, he really should stay. He can watch you and make sure you don't fall again." She smiled, then turned to look at him.

"Okay, Ellie…" I said, picking up the plate and fork. "If you think he should stay… I guess that's fine." I said softly, then looked back at him as well.

She smiled, "Okay! Um… I'm gonna leave this in here with you, eat as much of it as you can… uh, you need your strength." Then she turned to walk back toward the door. "I'm gonna lock this… uh, you know… don't want any Sicari coming in." She said, then smiled again as she shut it behind her.

I quickly set the plate down at the same time Jake took two big steps over to me, then leaned down to kiss me. "I missed you so much, baby…"

I didn't respond. I just pulled him closer toward me.

"I can't lose you again, Jayde…" he whispered. "Please, never send me away again…" He said, squeezing me tight.

I didn't say anything back. I didn't know what to say. I didn't want to send him away again either, but at the same time I didn't know what I wanted, not really. I felt lost in a sea of men, all trying to set themselves apart, all vying for a chance to have me.

"I love you, baby… I freakin'… love… you…" He said as he continued to hold me tight.

I brought my arms up to tighten around him as well. But, as if it were all a dream yet again, I saw little brown clouds begin to blur my vision until I saw no more.

18

MOURN FOR HER

"Ellie's always been sweet like this. She used to be that way when we were little too," I smiled, talking to Xavier, thinking about how Ellie was when we were growing up. I wasn't sure if I was in the mood for herb roasted chicken, but it didn't look bad, so I figured I'd try to eat it.

"How do you remember that?" Xavier asked, as he sat down across the table from me.

I stared at him blankly for a second while I thought about it. "I don't know… huh, isn't that odd…" I smiled, then picked the chicken leg up to take a bite of it.

He got a strange look on his face, but didn't get a chance to say anything else before Jake returned from using the restroom. The two of them still didn't like to speak to each other, but they both acted way more amiable than they had been previously.

"I've got her now, you can go." Jake said as he pulled out the chair at the end of the table between us.

Xavier gave him a dirty look, but didn't say anything to him. He just stood up slowly, then looked back at me. "Jayde, do you mind if we speak later… privately?"

I stopped chewing for a moment then glanced over at Jake. "Um… uh, o… okay…" I said, looking back at Xavier.

"Good… I'll come see you in your room here in a little bit after you've had lunch."

I didn't say anything. I just nodded, trying not to look at Jake again. Xavier smiled, then shot Jake another dirty look before turning to walk out.

"What do you think that's about?" Jake asked when he saw he'd left.

I set the chicken down for a second and looked up at him. "I don't know… I need to ask you something, though."

He furrowed his brow suddenly, looking surprised. "Okay, what?"

"In the past have we, like… you know, made an agreement that we'd be honest with each other? Like I mean… you'll tell me the truth and be completely honest with me when I ask you about something, right?"

"Of course."

"Okay…" I licked my fingers off, then wiped them with my napkin. "You haven't been giving me that medicine that you lied to my dad about that Henry said you had, have you?"

As soon as I asked, he suddenly looked around and made a shh gesture with his hand. "Jayde… no one knows about that… you can't say it out loud out here like that…" He whispered. "You'll get me in trouble."

"Okay, I'm sorry…" I whispered back, "But you haven't been giving it to me, right?"

"No, I haven't…" He said then paused before he let his eyes trail off quickly. "Why are you asking?"

"Because I'm remembering things… and I don't know how… A lot of them are things I don't really want to remember either."

"Things like what?"

I swallowed. "Well, for one, there's this man. I think it's who I've heard you and Henry talk about, you know… Miller? The night I hit my head, I started to remember some things he did to me, and it really bothered me. Now, here in the last few days, I'm remembering even more…" I stopped to lean back in my chair. "I don't want to remember him."

Jake didn't respond for a moment. He just nodded slowly like he was listening then leaned back in his chair as well. "What about the good things? Don't you want to remember the good things, like about us? Like, how we met and how we fell in love… the night I proposed to you… that kinda stuff?"

I didn't know how to respond to where it wouldn't hurt his feelings. "Jake… I do… but I don't… I think it'd be better if we just started fresh and fell in love again, and then after that you can propose again… We can just do everything all over again."

He looked at me perplexed, unsure if I was serious. "Jayde… we already tried that, remember?"

"I don't want the medicine," I said suddenly, not in the mood to argue with him. "I don't want to remember Miller, or remember being a Sicari, or any of the other awful things that have happened to me."

"Shh… baby, calm down…"

"I'm not your baby. Stop calling me that." I snapped then instantly felt bad.

He looked at me like that hurt him.

"Jacob… I'm sorry, I didn't mean to say it like that… I just—"

"How much of me do you remember?"

"What?" I was confused.

"You said you're starting to remember Miller. What about me? How much do you remember about me and us and when we were first together?"

I looked away and relaxed again as I thought about it. "Not a lot… The dreams I had with you in them were just small clips… the most I remember is you laying next to me telling me something won't happen again, but I don't know what that something was."

"If you don't remember me, we'll never be able to make this work between us." He said it like it pained him to do so.

"That's not true. What about everything that's happened between us the last few days?"

"That's not the same, Jayde… The last few days has been mostly physical. If thats all I wanted then I'd go—" He paused and took a deep breath, stopping himself before he said something he regretted. "That's not what I want our relationship built on."

"But it's been good. I like it. I thought you did too."

"Sleeping together isn't enough… I wanna marry you, dammit!" He said low like he was getting upset, but knew he had to keep whispering.

I didn't respond; I didn't know how to. I just picked up the chicken again and took another bite while I stared at my plate.

"You used to be happy, Jayde… Really, I know you're scared to remember things again, but it doesn't have to be a bad thing… There is so much good mixed in with all the other, don't you want all that good again?"

"If you're not lying to me, then how are my memories coming back?"

He didn't say anything, he just looked at me, then after a few seconds looked away before he pushed his chair back and stood up.

"Are you leaving again?" I asked, not sure what he was doing.

"This isn't you, Jayde… The person you think you are right now isn't you. It's not Eva or Kaleah either… Your memories make you who you are… without the hardships, the trials… there's no character, no life. You're just a shell of empty emotions, fighting a world that doesn't understand you. If you never get your memories back of me, then the Jayde I know and love has died." He said, then swallowed like he was struggling to think about it. "I need to know if I should mourn for her."

"I wanna be with someone who won't lie to me, Jacob… If you're giving me the medicine and I find out, then it won't matter if I remember you."

He stood there quiet for a moment then nodded, "I'll be with Lane if you need me." He said solemnly, then turned to walk out.

"Jayde? It took you a while, you all right?" Xavier asked when he saw me coming up the stairs to go back to my room.

"Yeah…" I said as I ascended them slowly so I didn't have another fainting spell. "I stopped to talk to Pierce. He found me in the hall."

"What'd he want?" Xavier asked as he walked to the top of the steps and reached down with his hand, ready to help me up the last one.

"The same thing everyone wants," I said, trying to catch my breath as I looked up at him.

"Which is?"

"To be my knight in shining armor." I said sarcastically as I dismissed his hand and walked past him.

"Jayde? You must have misunderstood."

"No… I'm pretty sure I didn't."

"Please," he quickly moved past and around me, then turned to face me so I couldn't continue. "You have me all wrong."

I looked at him, then at my door only a few feet behind him. "I'm tired, Xavier. I need to lie down." I said, hoping he'd move before I fell again.

He nodded, then stepped to the side to let me pass. "Do you mind?" He stepped inside my room behind me and gestured like he wanted to shut the door.

"Fine." I said, walking over to the bed to climb in.

"What did the doctor say was happening to you?" He asked as he shut it, then walked over to sit on the bed at my feet.

"He didn't know… He thought maybe it was a reaction to having two tags, each with different frequencies sending different signals. You know, since the Sicari and Coldiers' tags aren't the same." I laid my head against the pillow, then turned my body so I could still see him as we talked.

"Oh, I guess that makes sense…" He shrugged as he looked away. "So what about you having memories again? Did you mention that to him?"

"No, it just started happening. I don't know why."

He smiled, then reached down for my foot. "What all can you remember?" He asked as he picked it up and started to rub it.

"Not a lot. Why?" I asked, intentionally being vague.

"No reason. I was just curious. I know you and Miles had a thing, and I didn't know if him being back was like you guys getting back together or just what."

"He doesn't like who I am now," I said as I thought about the conversation I just had with him over lunch.

"Oh yeah? So—"

"That doesn't change what I heard you say about me the other night, Xavier." I said, then pulled my foot away.

He rested his hands in his lap, not looking surprised. "I'm sorry about whatever you think you heard, Jayde." He said as he scooted up higher to sit closer to me. "All I meant by it was you're special and I hope I get to be the one you want to be your knight... I know you and Miles haven't been seeing eye to eye lately and... well, I guess the thought that I had a chance with you got me a little excited."

"Why? Because I'm the princess?" I figured I knew why he was interested and it wasn't exactly me he wanted.

He looked disturbed that I would even suggest it. "Of course not! It has nothing to do with who your father is, Jayde... I was interested the first time I laid eyes on you. You're beautiful and smart, not to mention when you weren't around Miles is when I really saw your true personality blossom. You were fierce that day in the interrogation room. Remember, I told you what you said..."

I didn't respond. I just stared at him. He was so convincing, just like Jacob and Henry both were. "I don't know who to believe..." I said suddenly, unable to contain the secret inside myself anymore. "How do I know who I'm supposed to be with when you all say the same things?"

His face relaxed. "Oh, Jayde, I didn't know that's how you felt... I'm sorry, I didn't mean to confuse you more." He said as he reached up to stroke my face. "You should be with whoever makes you happy... even if it's not me."

"How do I know who that is?"

He smiled, "Tell me how this makes you feel?" He whispered as he leaned down to kiss me.

I didn't want to kiss him back at first when I thought about Jake, but I didn't stop him when I thought about what he'd said. How was I supposed to know who made me happy if I never let anyone else in?

He didn't have a beard, so there was nothing on his face that tickled my lips. He didn't taste sweet like Jake either, but more salty, like he had just had chips for lunch. I didn't let it go on long before I reached up to push him away.

"Jayde?" He said as he lifted his face from mine to look down at me.

At that moment, I realized something wasn't right. I didn't care what he was saying or what anyone else said; I didn't want him. All I wanted was Jake.

"Xavier, I can't."

He shook his head slightly, like he didn't agree, then leaned in to kiss me again.

"No!" I tried to push him away, but it wasn't working. I didn't have enough strength. Then suddenly, a series of images flooded my mind. I saw the man with the mustache again, followed by another man, then another, all trying to do the same thing Xavier now was. "No!" I turned my face and tried to push him away again, but before I got a chance to, he was gone, like he was lifted from the bed.

When I opened my eyes, I saw Jake holding Xavier in a headlock, pulling him away from the bed. "She said no!" Jake growled as Xavier pulled at his arms, silently asking to be released. "You hear me?" Jake shook him, like he was expecting a response.

Xavier moved his head, trying to nod, then tapped Jake's arm.

Jake looked at me, then quickly let him go. Xavier fell to the floor and wheezed, trying to catch his breath.

"Jayde?" Jake said, looking at me like he was asking what I wanted him to do with him.

I looked down at Xavier, who was now beginning to stand up. "It was… just… a kiss…" He said, defending himself.

I shook my head as I started to cry when I thought about all the memories I saw. I didn't say anything. I just reached down for the covers to pull up over my head.

"If I see you touch her again, you'll wish it was Prescott that saw what you just did, 'cause I won't demote you, I'll freakin' beat your ass!" Jake growled menacingly then after a moment I heard the door slam like Xavier had left.

"Jayde?" Jake said softly, having come around to check on me.

"Go away… you're all the same…" I didn't mean it, but I didn't know what else to say or how to feel. I just didn't want *anyone's* attention anymore.

I didn't hear him for a second when I felt like I was about to pass out again, so I uncovered myself so it was easier to breathe.

"What the hell?" He said, looking down at me from beside the bed. "Jayde, your nose is bleeding. What did he do to you?" He quickly reached down, probably checking to make sure he wasn't seeing things.

I didn't respond. I just wiped under my nose with my fingers, then looked at them and saw that he was right.

"Jake…" I said quickly as I felt myself getting dizzy again. "I'm sorry, baby…"

"Jayde?"

"What happened? Did she fall again?"

"No, she was just laying there this time when her nose started bleeding. This one doesn't make sense, doc… She's never had that happen before."

"Well… I'm not really sure how to help her… I can take her in and have some testing done, but that might not tell us anything."

"Why would her nose bleed?"

"Where did you say her Sicari tracker was located again?"

"I don't know… somewhere in her head. She never knew either."

"Interesting…"

"What, you think it has to do with that?"

"I do, actually… Has she ever had an X-ray to locate it?"

"No… before she was erased last time, she was too scared of doctors to ever let one get near her, let alone let them get close enough to x-ray her head."

"But she's not like that now?"

"Um… Well, no, I don't guess so."

"All right, well then, that's what I think we should do. If I can see on an x-ray where their tracker is, then maybe we can take her into surgery and remove it."

"Surgery? Wait… Like brain surgery?"

"I'll need Mr. Prescott's approval first, but with as long as I've known him, I'm sure he'll approve."

"How safe is that?"

"Dear boy, nothing is guaranteed… but at this rate, if she continues to have both signals interfering with each other, I'm afraid she's just going to keep getting sicker and sicker."

"Wait… give me a second to think. How do you know—"

"I'm afraid the time for waiting is over… If she's getting nose bleeds today, tomorrow it might be something worse. If we wait too long, I'm concerned it could lead to actual brain damage."

"Uh… Okay…"

"I'll go inform Mr. Prescott."

"Jayde, baby… wake up… I need to talk to you… Please… I'm sorry. I hate it when we fight. Lane and Ellie have been the ones giving you the medicine, baby. I didn't lie to you, but I didn't tell you the truth either, and I'm sorry. I didn't want them to, but then I thought you were cheating on me and I just missed you so much. I didn't know what else to do. I don't want you to have to remember all the bad things that have happened to you either, but… I just didn't know what to do. I wanted you to remember me. I thought if you did, then we could get back together like we were…"

. . .

"Please, wake up, baby… You have to remember me. I can't live without you. I don't wanna live without you. If that makes me weak, then okay… I'm weak. But this life isn't the same when you're not with me, if you're not mine."

"Jayde… Please, open your eyes, sweetie… Just one more time before the doctor takes you away. I need you to look at me. I need you to answer me… forgive me. Tell me it's all gonna be okay. I can't do this… I act like I've got my shit together, but I don't, not when stuff isn't right between us."

"Jake?" I thought I heard him.

"Jayde? Good, baby… Wake up… look at me." I felt him clutching my hand.

I blinked a few more times until my vision cleared. Then I looked around until I saw him sitting next to me, looking down.

"Baby… I'm so sorry," He said when he saw me look at him. "I don't care what you need, I'll do it. If you don't want the medicine, you don't have to have it. If you want time to just be friends again first, okay, we can do that. If you need to just talk, then we can talk through it. I won't hover over you anymore. If you need your space, I can give it to you and still guard you. If you—"

"Jake…" I said, stopping him as I lifted my hand to touch his face. "Shhh."

He stopped but looked at me, confused by my reaction.

"I remember, baby… I remember you now."

"What?" He acted like he didn't know if he should smile or cry.

I nodded, but I was starting to feel like my brain wanted to shut itself down again. "I love you…" I said, trying not to blink. "You're gonna be okay…"

He nodded while making a face like he couldn't talk without

bursting into tears, then reached down to pull me up to hug him. "I love you more, baby… more than you'll ever know."

19

EMOTIONAL AWAKENING

"How's she doing, Miles? The surgery took a while. Were they able to get the tracker out?"

"Yeah… she's not woken up yet so I'm not sure how she feels but it's out now so…"

"You all right, man?"

"Yeah… I'm fine. It's been a long week. I'm just a bit emotional, that's all."

"I've never really seen you like this, man."

"I'm fine… How's Ellie?"

"Oh… umm… She seems to be doing all right. She knows it's a big surgery, but she's excited that the tracker won't be a problem anymore."

"Good…"

"I think I'm gonna ask Ellie to marry me…"

"What?"

"I love her, Miles… It's crazy 'cause I know we've not been together all that long, I mean nowhere near as long as you and Kaleah have been together but… I don't know, it's just, I feel like she's the one. I've never felt that before, and I mean, you know… I've been with a lot of women."

"Oh wow, okay… I'll be honest, it seems a little rushed… Is she pregnant?"

"What? No! No, man… she's a virgin… We've not been together yet."

"Really?"

"Yeah… I mean, we've kissed and made out and stuff but… she said she wanted to wait until marriage, so… I'm waitin'."

"You've never waited on anything in your whole damn life, Lane."

"Exactly, see? I thought the same thing. That's how I know she's the one, its not just about sleeping with her. It's everything else. I just can't get enough of everything else."

"Wow… okay… well, that's awesome… I'm happy for ya, man."

"You say that, but by the look on your face, I'm not sure."

"I mean it, I really am, its just… me and Kaleah were supposed to be married by now… I was only waiting for her to get her tag but then all this happened and now I'm not sure what we're doing."

"You said she remembered everything again, though. Why can't you just go ahead and plan the wedding now, then? You don't gotta worry about the Sicari anymore, I mean… no more than I do with Ellie."

"It doesn't seem that simple, man. Not to mention, I still got Mom and Dad that don't know who she really is yet and that complicates things."

"Oh, yeah… about that…"

"What?"

"You know how I told you about Eva dragging Kat into the interrogation room and letting her have it?"

"Yeah?"

"Ok, well… first, don't ever tell her I told you. She asked that I keep it a secret, and I fully intended to until I thought she went and did things with Xavier behind your back, then—"

"Get to the point, Lane."

"Sorry, okay… Umm… I didn't tell you because Kaleah was just erased and I didn't want to upset you more, but while she had Kat in there asking her questions, Kat told her about who filed for Kaleah's papers…"

"Okay?"

"Uhh… I uhh…"

"It's okay, Lane, just tell me."

"It was your mom… She knew they were counterfeit too, and she was the one who told Kat to report you."

"Are you serious?"

"I'm afraid so, man… I'm sorry. This is why I hadn't told you yet. I knew it'd bother you."

"Holy shit… hell yeah, it bothers me… Oh my gosh…"

"What're you gonna do?"

"I don't know… It's my freakin' mom. What the hell can I do?"

"Umm… well… you could tell uncle Duke. He married her ass. Let him deal with her."

"All right… that's probably my best bet."

"Sorry, man… I just thought you should know."

"No, it's all right. I appreciate you telling me."

"Hey, Jake… I brought Jayde some food. Is she still not awake?"

"No… the doctor said she could be out like this for quite a while so this is normal. I don't want you worrying about her, Ellie… She'll be fine."

"Here… why don't you just eat it then? I don't know how you're not hungry. You've barely left her side since the surgery."

"Okay, thanks… Wait… does this have the herbs in it from the recipe?"

"Yeah?"

"Oh… sweetie, that's… She shouldn't have those anymore… Did Lane not tell you?"

"Well… umm… he told me she got her memory back, but he didn't say anything about me needing to stop using the herbs… He's been a bit busy the last couple of days. Yesterday, he left Andry to guard me. He said he had to run a few errands in the city."

"Oh, right… okay… Well, now that she has her memory back, the herbs won't help her anymore. They'll just keep making her sick, like you know, dizzy and stuff."

"Ok, I didn't know that… I'm sorry, I was just trying to help."

"I know, Ellie, you're fine. I'm sure Jayde appreciates it."

"If I'm not supposed to worry about her, why do you still?"

"Hmm… Umm… Well… she's gonna be my wife. It's what a husband is supposed to do… So we can just look at this like I'm practicing."

"Okay… Do you think Henry ever worries about me?"

"Oh, I'm sure he does… That's why he'll only let Andry guard you when he can't… Andry won't let anything happen to you."

"Wasn't Andry there when Miller took Jayde?"

"Yeah, but no… it's complicated… He's a good guy though. You don't need to worry about him."

"Miller's not… he's bad."

"He is… Ellie… Are you all right?"

"No… I'm scared… If Miller can get Jayde, I'm scared he'll get me again."

"What? Ellie, what do you mean by again?"

"Nothing, I gotta go…"

"Ellie?"

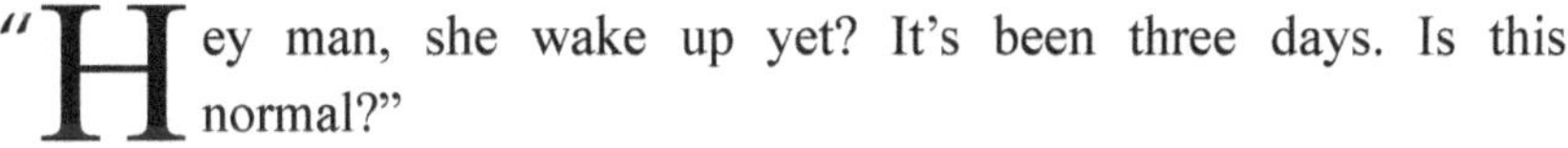

"Hey man, she wake up yet? It's been three days. Is this normal?"

"I don't know what's normal anymore, Lane… All I can do is just sit here and watch her. Hopefully that way I can be the first one she sees when she wakes up. The nurses keep coming in to check on her.

The doc came in again this morning, too. He said all her vitals are good. She just might still be too tired to wake up yet."

"Oh, okay… I went back to my house yesterday for a little bit to get some things and when I went into my guest room, I found this. It's the first time I'd really been in there since she was taken, so I never saw it before now. I know you thought she lost it, but it was just sitting right there under the mirror. I figured you'd like to have it back. It'd save you buying her a new one."

"Wow, man… It was just setting there this whole time?"

"Yeah! I mean, I assume so. She probably took it off that morning to brush her hair or something, I don't know."

"This is great… wow… I think I'll slip it back on her finger so it's a nice surprise for her when she wakes up."

"Yeah, I mean… it's so pretty, and you got enough money to buy her ten more. I thought about just keeping it to give to Ellie, like… you know… finder's keepers!"

"Ha, yeah funny… Hey, speaking of Ellie…"

"What? What's wrong?"

"Has she ever mentioned to you Miller doing something to her before?"

"Who… what? Ellie? Who are you talking about? Kaleah?"

"No, Lane… Ellie… Has Ellie ever mentioned Miller to you before, like referencing him doing something to her?"

"No! Why? She's never been around him… right? I mean… She hasn't, right?"

"Umm…"

"Dude, what the hell are you talking about?"

"Lane, just calm down… I'll explain."

"Yeah, explain, 'cause this is the first I've heard of anything like this."

"Don't be a hothead, just help me figure this out. Then we'll go from there."

"Ok, ok… I'm calm. Now tell me why you're asking?"

"Yesterday when I talked to Ellie, she came in to bring Jayde some food. We talked for a minute until Miller came up. She instantly acted like she was really upset. I thought maybe it was just 'cause, well you know… maybe she was thinking about everything he'd done to Jayde and that bothered her. But then when I asked her about it, she said she was scared, and that she was afraid he'd get her again… I tried to ask what she meant by it, but she said she didn't want to talk anymore and left… That's all I know. I thought I'd mention it to you so, I mean… I don't know if she's opened up to you about her past or not but… now you know."

"Holy shit… I'm gonna kill that bastard!"

"Get in line, Lane."

"Ugh, I can't believe this… Do you think Eva knows?"

"No… and you're not gonna tell her either, hear me? The last thing she needs when she wakes up is another reason to go try to find him and kill him. She's in enough danger as it is… I figure he'll turn up eventually, and when he does, I plan to go deal with him myself."

"Were you not planning on letting her in on it? 'Cause I'm pretty sure if she finds out you killed him and didn't let her in on the action, then you'll be next. Not to mention now I'd like a piece of it myself."

"Honestly, I hadn't thought that far ahead, man. I've just been so consumed with getting her back the last three months, what I planned on doing to Miller when he's caught hasn't been in the forefront of my mind again until now."

"So hearing that he did something to Ellie bothers you, too?"

"Hell yeah, it bothers me too! Jayde was right; I've never met anyone as innocent and sweet as Ellie. Not even Kaleah, which says a lot… So to think he… ugh… Yes, now I wanna kill him even more!"

"Okay, well… we find him then, me and you, Miles… I know Prescott has men out looking, but that doesn't mean anything. Those men don't care. Besides, you think if his men find Miller first, Prescott would let either of us around him? Not likely… He would just put him on trial before The Council, then all they'd do is hang him."

"You're right… that's not enough. That's not justice."

"K, so how do you wanna play this then? You want me to get our own men together to search?"

"Yeah… we can't let Prescott or anyone else know what we're doing, though, if that's possible. I don't want Eva knowing either."

"Prescott I get, but why not Eva?"

"I know she wants him dead, and I know she wants to do it herself… but you weren't there in Nashville. You didn't see what I saw. She was willing to let herself bleed to death just so she could strangle him. Taking his life means more to her than keeping her own… I can't let that happen again."

"All right? I don't know how you'll ever explain it to her… '*Oh yeah honey, by the way the man you've waited your whole life to murder… um yeah, I just did it without you, sorry… not sorry…*' But hey man, it's your funeral, you plan it how you want it to go."

"Shut up, Lane… Just think about how you'd feel if Ellie wanted to go anywhere near him again, even if she was capable of maybe getting him pinned… and maybe, just maybe he didn't have multiple men with him to turn it back around and take her again—"

"Yeah, okay, I won't say anything to Eva. I'll let you handle the aftermath of whatever you decide to do. That's between you two. Think about which of your men you wanna ask to search and let me know. I'll get our teams together. Right now I'm gonna go talk to Ellie. Maybe she'll tell me what happened."

"All right… hey Lane, just remember… you gotta be easy with her. If she doesn't want to talk about it, don't try to make her. It'll just make her want to push away from you."

"Okay, that's excellent advice. Thanks, man!"

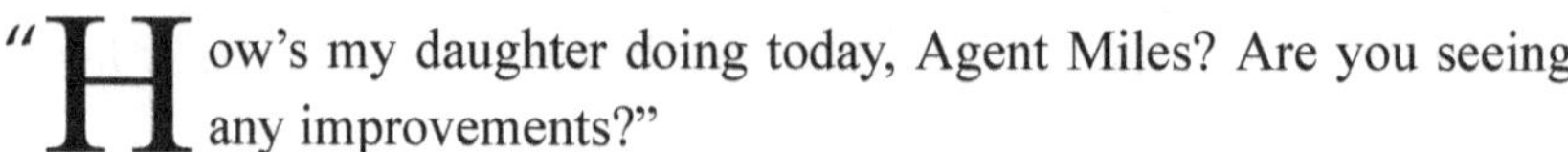

"How's my daughter doing today, Agent Miles? Are you seeing any improvements?"

"Yes, Sir… She's not quite woken up yet, but she's stirring around a little now and then. The doctor said he expected she should wake up pretty soon, hopefully by tonight."

"Good… You're a good man, Miles… I know we've had our disagreements but I can tell you love her, and that's what matters."

"Thank you, Sir."

"I see she's got a ring on her finger again… I assume the two of you have worked things out?"

"Yes, Sir… Permission to speak freely, Sir?"

"Yes?"

"I want to apologize for the things I said to you in the past. I spoke when I shouldn't have and it was entirely out of character, Sir. I never intended to show you any disrespect. I do absolutely love your daughter. I have from before I ever knew who she was. To be honest, I loved her even when I knew she was a Gypsyin and it was forbidden. I asked her to marry me when she didn't know who her family was, but… Sir… I… I wanted to ask for your blessing."

"It would be my honor, Miles… I trust you will take care of her better than I ever could. Love her with the passion I saw in your eyes when you found out she was erased again, and I believe she'll make you a happy man."

"Thank you, Sir!"

"You will make a fine son-in-law, Agent, both you and Agent Lane!"

"Sir?"

"He asked for Ellie's hand this morning."

"Oh…"

"Miles, as soon as Jayde is awake and feeling well enough to get up and walk around, bring her by my office. I'm sure she'd be proud to see you accept your second rank pin."

"My pin?"

"I know you didn't know about it, or if you did, you haven't asked… and that in and of itself merits that you're the right man to receive it. You brought my daughter back to me… There's no way to show you how much that means, so upping your rank is the least I can do."

"Um… yes… Sir… Thank you, Sir!"

"No, Agent… Thank you. You brought my baby back and you've kept her safe. I couldn't ask for any more than that!"

"J ake?" My head hurt, my mouth was dry, and it was difficult to talk, but I knew he'd be close enough to hear me even if I whispered his name.

"Jayde, baby?" I heard him at the same time I felt him clutch my hand. "I'm here, baby… right here."

I opened my eyes slowly to a bright blue light flooding the room.

"How are you feeling?"

"Like shit…" I said, trying to blink the haziness out of my eyes.

He chuckled slightly, "Welcome back, Eva."

"How long have I been… um… what's today's uh…" It was difficult collecting my thoughts enough to speak them.

"You had your surgery a few days ago, baby… But don't worry, it's not Christmas yet," He smiled, thinking he was funny. "You always have enjoyed your naps, haven't you?"

"Did they… my head…"

"Yeah, baby… they got the tracker out." He said it sounding relieved. "You're no longer a Sicari in a Coldier's body… I'm sure that's liberating, right?"

"Where… umm…" I was beginning to feel frustrated as I tried to sit up. "It was… where?"

"Hey… hey… just relax, don't get too far ahead of yourself, honey." He said as he gently pushed my shoulder back. "The doctor didn't say where exactly but you don't have any incisions that I can see, so I'm guessing it was high up in your nose."

"Ooh," I nodded as I let my head relax back against the pillow.

"Are you hungry?" He asked as he gently rubbed the back of my hand.

I shook my head, "Please… no more of her soup… I can't…"

He laughed, "Oh, baby, I really have missed you and your honesty… It tastes like shit, doesn't it? Lane didn't really do a good job of teaching her, poor thing. But you just ate it anyway… You probably didn't have a clue what food was supposed to taste like, or maybe you were just being sweet. Either way, don't worry, you never have to have the soup or anything with those herbs in it ever again, okay?"

I nodded as I let my eyes slowly close to rest again while I continued to listen to his voice.

"Hey… I got a surprise for you… wanna see?"

I didn't want to open them again, not yet, so I just shook my head.

"Ok… how about you just feel it then?" He said as he picked up my right hand and moved it over to where it was sitting on my left.

Initially, I had no idea what he was doing, but then when I felt it I forced my eyes to cooperate so I could look. "My ring!"

He nodded and smiled, happy to see that I was happy. "Lane found it!"

"Aww…" my eyes began to tear up as I looked at it.

"You still want to marry me, right?"

I smiled at him and nodded, then blinked, releasing the tears to roll down my cheeks.

"Good, 'cause I already asked your dad… and he already said yes… so I'm sorry but you're stuck with me now, because I think he also said no refunds… I not sure, but that's what it sounded like." He smiled.

"I love you…" I said as I leaned back again.

"Do you think it's too soon to start planning the wedding? Because I wanna marry you before you go getting yourself erased again."

I didn't respond. I lost my smile as I thought about why he'd say that and what I had done and said when I didn't remember who I was.

"Did that bother you, baby? I'm sorry… I didn't mean for it to upset you."

"Lane hates me…"

"What? No, no, baby… Don't think that. Nobody hates you, okay?

If you'll forgive him for giving you the medicine against your will, I'm sure he'll forgive you for not being yourself."

"You promise?"

He smiled again as he reached up to stroke my hair before stopping to rub my temple with his thumb. "Yes, baby, I promise!"

"Okay… how's my face?"

"Uh… what do you mean?"

"It hurts. I don't know what they did to me, but… am I ugly now?" I wasn't sure what medicine I was getting through my IV, but I felt a cool sensation in my arm where it was attached. At the same time, I heard a machine next to me make a pumping sound.

"What?" He laughed, "No! Honey, they couldn't make you ugly if they tried… you'll always be beautiful."

I didn't say anything. I just nodded, then looked down to stare at the IV again.

"Is that bothering you? Do you want them to take it out now? I can go get a nurse—"

"No," I clutched his arm. "Don't leave me again. Never… okay?"

He smiled even bigger than before. "All right…" He said as he leaned in to hug me. "Never might be tough but I'll do my best!"

"Jake?" I knew he was already asleep, but I wanted to talk to him. I rolled over and rested my arm across his chest just in case he didn't wake up with me saying his name.

"Yeah, baby? What do you need?" He asked as he started to rub my arm slowly.

"Everything that's happened over the last few months… well… It's been bothering me and I can't get to sleep."

"Okay, you wanna talk about it?"

"Yeah… I just don't know if you ever understood where I was coming from." I said as I started to play with his chest hair.

"I didn't at first… but then I did, right before your surgery. I had a lot of time to think about it and what it must have been like for you. I didn't realize that you felt so much pressure from other men on top of the pressure I was giving you. Lane told me about your talk with him in the library. He said you explained it to him and how you didn't know who to believe."

"Lane kissed me…"

Jake rolled over so he could look at me. "He told me about that too, baby."

"Were you upset?" He didn't sound like he was but I was curious.

"Nah… Well, okay, maybe a little at first until he explained himself." Jake said, then smiled, but it was hard for me to see it all that well in the dark.

"Why'd he say he did it?"

"Well… he said it was so he'd know if you were lying about being with other men. Which is fair, and apparently, it was helpful. But I think it was also a little so he could have a taste of the forbidden fruit. I can't fault him for trying… you are pretty tantalizing." He grinned.

"Oh, ok… I wasn't with anyone else. I told you that already, right?" I thought I had but between the surgery and dreams and everything else it was kind of fuzzy.

"Yeah, baby… I know, you told me already and I believe you… It helped when I saw you refuse Xavier's advances, too. Was that the first time he's tried to kiss you?"

"Yeah… unless that one time in the hall wasn't you…"

Jake chuckled like he was guilty. "Yeah… that was me. I'm not sorry about it either, not one bit." He said, then leaned forward to kiss me since we were on the subject.

"I'm sorry for what I did to you, and all I put you through." I started to cry when I thought about how hard the last few months had probably been on him.

"Oh, baby… don't cry." He reached up and wiped the tears from under my eye. "I forgive you. I never held it against you, but even if I did, I forgive you, okay?"

"I wanted to love you. I was just so confused. It wasn't ever about you… I just… I…"

"Shhh," he stopped me when he saw I was crying harder. "None of that matters anymore, honey… I have you back now and you have me back—that's what matters. We have each other back. And I'm not going anywhere!"

"Do you promise?" I asked, trying to curtail my tears.

"I promise." He whispered, then leaned forward to kiss me on the tip of my nose.

20
QUID PRO QUO

"You think I'm gonna be easy on you?"

"Jayde… Please, you don't understand… You don't have to do this!" Watching Miller sit there begging me for mercy was one thing, but thinking about how it would feel to see him scream in anguish was what I really wanted. "God, woman, you're insane! Put the freakin' pliers down!" His eyes widened as I walked closer to him.

"Oh, so you don't think I should use these?" I asked softly as I held them up to his face while I fiddled with them, trying to get them open.

"No!" He screamed, then gave me a look like he was about to piss his pants. "I freakin' swear, touch me with those and you're gonna die!"

"I'm not the one tied to the chair this time, now am I, Miller?" I smiled while I watched as he continued to squirm in anticipation.

"You gotta quit this… you've done enough, all right? I'll stop, I'll leave… You never have to see me again!"

I didn't reply. I just continued to clamp his right hand to the chair.

"What the hell! Stop… Just stop already!" He screamed out again when he saw me pick up the Exacto knife.

"Why? Did you stop when I begged you to?" I asked nicely.

"What the fu… I'm sorry, okay, I'm sorry! What I did was awful.

I'm a bad person, but I've repented, really, I'm not like that anymo… AHHH, stop… no… stop, you freakin' psycho!"

"Stop what, Miller? Stop doing this?" I continued to draw with it on the back of his hand like it was a crayon. His skin parted so neatly at the touch of the razor.

"Please!" He screamed again.

"You just can't handle your fun, can you? I haven't even got to the good bits." I said with a smile as I used the knife to point to his crotch.

"Uhhhh," he began to moan and cry like the big ass baby he was.

"You know… if you can't take it, you really shouldn't have dished it…" I set the knife back down and looked at what other tools I had to work with. "Oh… this looks fun…" I picked up a mallet.

"Jayde!"

"Oh, sorry… what's up?"

"You daydreaming again?" Ellie asked as she walked around to sit in front of me on the window seat.

"It's more like planning, but yeah… something like that." I smiled. "What do ya need?"

"Look!" she said, holding up her hand in front of my face.

At first I wasn't sure what I was looking for, but then, after my eyes had a chance to adjust, I saw it. There was a big, beautiful, shiny diamond ring on her finger. "What?" I looked from her hand to her face. She was smiling from ear to ear, bigger than I'd ever seen before.

"I know! Can you believe it? Henry asked me last night! Eekkk!" she squealed with excitement, then leaned in to give me a hug.

"Oh my gosh, wow…" I hugged her back as I looked over her shoulder at Lane standing beside the door watching us. He gave me a look like he was curious about how I was taking it.

"Where's Jake?" She asked, leaning away again to look around. "I wanted to show him too!"

"Oh, he's been busy the last couple of weeks. You know, agent stuff…" I shrugged.

"Oh, okay… Well, I think I'll go tell Cynthia and Annie. They'll be excited too."

"Uh… All right," I smiled. "But hey, do you mind if I speak with Lane for a minute? I'll send him to come find you as soon as I'm done."

"Sure!" she said as she got up and started to walk out. "I'll just have Andry follow me." She turned and gave Lane a kiss, then left.

The room was silent for a moment as I turned to stare back out the window.

"I'm sorry…" He said, assuming that was what I was waiting on.

"That's not what I need from you, Lane…" I didn't look at him yet. I couldn't, not when I thought about all the things that had happened between us. I knew if I looked at him I'd start to cry.

"I don't like it still being awkward between us like this, Kaleah."

"I've already forgiven you. Does that help?"

"For the medicine, telling Miles you cheated on him or… what, the kiss?"

"Everything…" I said, finally turning to look at him.

He'd walked in closer and was now standing just a few feet away. "Ok… that's good… so you're not upset about Ellie and me?"

"No," I was shocked he'd even suggest it. "That's great… You two are perfect together." I said, trying to smile.

"Then what's wrong?" He asked, then made a motion, asking my permission to sit.

I nodded, then looked back out the window to think about how to answer him. "I'm the one who should be sorry."

"For what?"

"Everything I said to you…" I swallowed, "I know I wasn't nice… and… um…"

"I forgive you." He said suddenly, not even having to think about it.

I looked back at him. "So, you don't hate me?"

He furrowed his brow. "What? Of course not!" He said like the assumption was ridiculous.

I smiled, then pulled my legs up to my chest to lean on. "Good…" I said softly, then looked back out the window. "Now that that's out of the way… you wanna tell me about the secret you and Jake are keeping from me?"

"What?" He asked suddenly, like he knew of one but hadn't expected me to know it existed. "We're not keeping any secrets from you." He said, trying to cover his initial surprised tone with a lie.

I turned to look at him again, then smiled like I knew better. "Lane, Kaleah can't see when you lie, honestly it's a fatal flaw of being naïve, but Eva…" I sighed, "Oh, Lane… you really aren't that good at it… not when I'm watching for it, anyway."

"What do you know?" He asked, probably knowing he was caught and figuring he had no choice but to discuss it with me.

"When Jake left *again* this morning, he said he still had some more work to do at the agency. I didn't ask what he was doing… Honestly, I knew he wouldn't want to tell me the truth, so I figured I'd spare him having to lie to me. He's been leaving to go there the last five mornings. So why don't *you* tell me… What's he doing?" I held my gaze to discourage him from lying again.

He quickly blinked a few times, then looked away. "I really can't tell you."

"Can't or won't?"

"He's a second rank now, Kaleah…" He said looking back at me. "You know, he's just probably involved with stuff that's over both of our heads."

I tightened my jaw as I nodded, then looked away again. "All right… Dad probably doesn't know what you're both up to then either, does he?"

"Kaleah…" Lane started, about to deny it again, then stopped probably when he realized I could see right through it. "Okay, fine… No, your dad doesn't know. No one else does either… Miles wants it that way."

"What took you so long to propose to Ellie? Was it the same thing that's been keeping Jake so busy? Because he told me like two weeks ago that you bought her a ring."

He rolled his eyes up a little, then turned to look out the window himself. "You really should talk to him about this stuff… not me."

"I should, you're right… It's just… Jake's been too busy to even ask me how I got erased last, let alone talk to me about what random things he's been up to when he leaves at the crack of dawn every day."

He turned to look at me again suddenly. "What? You know how you got erased?" He asked, surprised.

"Yeah," I said matter-of-factly.

"Okay? Well… how?"

I was about to tell him when I stopped. "Hmm… you know… it really is a wonderful story."

"Kaleah?" He tilted his head toward me, his eyes looking unamused.

"Do you know what a quid pro quo is, Lane?"

He stared at me for a moment, probably hoping I was joking. "Really?"

I tried not to grin as I nodded.

"Fine. What do you want?" He said as he rolled his eyes up and leaned his head against the window behind him.

"What's Jake up to?"

"Ugh…" He huffed. "I told you already; I can't tell you that."

"Why? Because you're more scared of him than you are of me?" I asked, reaching over to playfully slap his chest.

"As a matter of fact, I am." He said unashamedly as he sat forward to look at me again.

"Well, you shouldn't be… Believe me, I'm much scarier." I looked at him with my best scary face like I meant it.

"If I tell you, then not only do I have to hear him bitch at me later, but then I'll have to hear you bitch at me now for what it is that I'd be telling you."

I smiled, then shook my head. "I won't bitch at you," I said sweetly.

He hesitated, not sure if he wanted to go through with it or not. "Fine… but you tell me first," he said finally.

"Okay," I smiled, knowing I'd won. "It was Xavier's man, Stevens."

He furrowed his brow. "That's it? What happened?"

"Oh, I told you who. That's enough until you tell me Jake's secret." I knew I couldn't give him everything or he might take it and run.

"No, no, no… I'll tell you, don't worry about that. Now finish the story." He said, not willing to compromise again.

"Hmm," I moaned a little as I relaxed back against the wall like that wasn't how I wanted it to go. "Fine…" I said, pushing my foot over to playfully kick him so he knew I wasn't pleased. "It was my fault. I was upset that Dad was gonna make me get my tag when Jake hadn't gotten back yet and Xavier was trying to enforce it… So I, uh…" I shrugged. "I kinda pulled his gun on him."

"You what?" Lane looked at me like he didn't think I had it in me, then he quickly changed the look like after he'd thought about it he realized I probably would do something like that. "So… what then? He wasn't trying to force himself on you or anything?"

"What? No…" I said nonchalantly. "He was just pushing me about the surgery and I was pretty upset. I would have shot him… and I think Stevens knew it, so…" I shrugged again. "He stuck me before I had a chance to turn around… Xavier was pretty mad though, ticked actually —so there's that."

"That doesn't make sense. If it wasn't his fault and it was just an accident… I don't get it. Why wouldn't he have said something?"

"Well, would you? I mean… he kinda had a good thing goin' for him before we all got here. He was the lead guard of the First Rank and his daughter… Even if it wasn't technically his fault, it kinda still was because he's over Stevens… If your men do stupid shit, it's still on you, right?"

"Well… yeah, I guess so." Lane shrugged.

"Right… okay, now it's your turn." I smiled.

He lifted his eyes to stare at me, not even saying anything.

"Lane? You said…" I thought I would remind him of our deal.

He swallowed, then leaned forward to rest his elbows on his knees.

"Oh, come on, buddy… you'll be all right… I promise, I won't let Jake kill ya, okay?"

"And no bitchin' from you?" He asked, looking at me from the top of his eyes.

"Right… no bitching," I smiled again.

"Our men found Miller." He said hesitantly, probably afraid of how I would react.

"What? That's great!" I said suddenly as I got up. "I'll go get ready. You can take me to him."

"Kaleah!" He didn't move. "You can't go!"

I turned to look at him still sitting there, "Of course I can."

"I'm not taking you." He said as he finally stood up.

I furrowed my brows, not sure what his problem was. "Lane? Why not?"

"You said no bitching…"

"I'm not bitching. I'm excited! You're the one with the attitude. Now, come on!" I said, as I turned to walk away again.

"I'm serious, Jayde!" I stopped when I heard him. As far as I knew, he'd never used that tone with me before, not even when he was mad about me not remembering Jake.

"Is that what he said?" I turned back around to look at him. "Did Jake tell you I couldn't come?"

He didn't say anything else, he just hesitantly nodded.

"Oh… okay… Well, in that case, I'll just be in my room then." I said softly as I turned back around to walk away again.

"Please?" He groaned, sounding like he was trying to plead to my good nature, probably to Kaleah. "For the love of God, will you just listen to me for once?"

I stopped but didn't turn back; I didn't want to see his face when I answered him. "No…"

"Dammit, Eva, I wouldn't have even told you if I thought you were going to do this!"

"You're lying…" I said when I heard it in his voice. I turned around again to see if his face told me the same.

He threw up his hands exaggeratedly, giving up, then rested them on his hips.

"It's Jake that doesn't want me to be around Miller again… Not you, you know what killing him means to me."

He made a face like he couldn't deny it. "Okay… fine. You're right, I felt like you should know… but then the moment you got up and… and… I realized what you wanted to do… I get it now. I know why Miles said what he did. We can't let you be around that man again, Kaleah! I don't care if you think you'll be all right… Just seeing him again will warp you, let alone if you try to kill him. I mean it! It's not even about if you'll be safe physically or not, it won't be good for you mentally!"

"You're wrong!" I was so sick of people telling me what was and wasn't good for me. "But even if you weren't, I don't care, Lane. I'm going to go down there whether you like it or not." I said, then turned back around to continue walking away.

"No, you're not!" He yelled. As he caught up to me, I felt him grab a hold of my upper arm, ready to stop me.

"Lane… you know what I'm capable of… Let go of me right now before I break your fingers." I said as I turned to look back at him sternly, so he knew I meant it. "I'd hate to maim you before you get a chance to marry my sister."

He stiffened his expression and tightened his grip. "Try me," he growled, stepping closer so his face was right above mine. There was so much intensity in his eyes, I couldn't help but be stilled by the silent tension I suddenly felt between us. "I care about you too much to let you get hurt again. You—"

"Ellie?" a man's deep voice suddenly interrupted us.

Lane stared at me for a second like he was telling me we weren't done yet when he let go so we could both turn to see who was coming.

"Oh, I thought I lost you there for a minute," Andry said as he slowly walked toward us.

"Andry? Where's Ellie?" Lane asked, seeing he was alone.

"El—" Andry looked at me and started to point, then realized as he got closer that I wasn't her. "Uh…"

"Where is she?" Lane's voice deepened.

"It's fine, Lane... She's probably just in her room." I said, hoping to help him stay calm.

"I just looked there... I'm sorry, Chief. She was talking to one of the maids in the great room and I fell asleep."

"Holy shit!" Lane's eyes widened.

Oh no... What if she's been taken? "She's gotta be around here somewhere, Lane. She never leaves the house. I'm sure someone's seen her." I said, trying to reassure him again even though deep down I could tell I was beginning to freak out myself.

"Ugh!" Lane reached up to roughly run his hand through his hair as he started to pace. "Shit!" He yelled in frustration.

"Could she have been taken?" I gave in and went ahead and said it. If that's what had happened, the sooner we figured it out the more likely we'd be to find her.

"No, dammit, I know where she is." Lane said suddenly. "Andry, call Miles! Hopefully, he's still there. Tell him we're coming!"

"What?" I asked, confused.

"She probably went to the freakin' agency," Lane said as he grabbed a hold of my arm again. "Let's go, you might as well come too."

I wasn't going to fight him, considering that's precisely what I wanted, but I was still perplexed. "How do you know that's where she is?" I asked, trying to keep up with his faster pace.

"Because she knew we had Miller... She said she wanted to see him locked up, like for closure, I guess. I just didn't think she'd... Ugh... never mind." He said, now in a hurry.

"How long have you had him?"

"We knew his location the last few days. The plan was for Miles to take a team this morning to go and capture him."

"Wait... I thought you said you *had* him... Have you talked to Jake since he left? Did he get him?"

"Well, I assumed we had him. I mean, that's what Miles does... he captures people."

"Does Ellie know you assumed, or did she think what I did, that he was really '*had*' like… '*had, had*'… like secured—*had*… not leaving, tied to a chair—*had*?"

He turned to look at me as he continued to pull me along. "I don't know."

"What the hell, Lane?" I said when I realized how much danger she was probably in now.

"That's why I didn't want either of you to go!" He said as we passed several agents when we entered the parking garage.

"What? She acted like she wanted to go?" I asked as we rounded one of the vehicles. I still couldn't believe it.

"Yeah, now get in!" He said quickly as he opened the back door.

"Then why didn't you stop her?"

"Because she's just like you!" His voice was thick with irritation as he motioned something to the other agents. "She manipulated me with her good looks and her pouty lips…" He said as he quickly got in and slid over next to me. "I told her *no*, and she said *fine*… So I thought we were good."

"And you believed her?"

"She said *fine*!" He threw up his hands.

"Yeah, Lane… but fine doesn't mean fine when you're speaking to a woman."

He gave me a dirty look then turned to tap the driver's shoulder, "Phillips, take us to the agency."

21

SMOKE AND MIRRORS

I couldn't believe my eyes. He was there, really there. I had complete tunnel vision when I saw him, like no one else was in the room. Everything was silent until it wasn't…

"Jayde? What are you doing here? Lane, explain this!"

"I'm sorry, Miles, it's a long story, is Ellie… Oh my gosh, Ellie! Come here, baby… Are you all right?"

"Henry, I'm so sorry. Please don't be mad at me."

"Jayde? Look at me! Shit! Ugh, Lane, she shouldn't be here."

"It's okay, Ellie, I know why you did it."

"Eva! Look at me, dammit!"

I blinked a couple of times, then turned to look at Jake, unsure why he was yelling. "Can I kill him now?" I asked nicely.

He didn't say anything for a moment. He just looked at me blankly, clearly lost. "No, baby…" He said like he hated to deny me. "He's in my custody. I need to do things right… He'll be punished. You don't need to worry about that. I just gotta figure out how to—"

"I can do it for you." I interrupted him.

"Eva! Look at me." Jake said suddenly, trying to pry my eyes away from Miller and back to him. "This isn't good for you, baby. You shouldn't even be here."

"Please?" I asked calmly as I looked back at Miller. He was in an interrogation room, ripe and ready for me. It looked like Jake already had a chance to get in a few blows to his face too.

Jake was silent for a moment, then slowly shook his head like he wanted to but didn't know how he could allow it. "I can't let you kill him, Eva… We have laws. I'm a second rank now. If I just did whatever I wanted because of my rank, I'd be no better than him."

I nodded like I understood as I looked away again. "I figured you'd say that."

"Please, Jayde… don't be upset with me. He'll get what he deser—"

"Can I just talk to him, then?" I interrupted again.

He furrowed his brow, then looked over my shoulder, probably seeing what Lane thought. "I… uh…" He started as he looked back down at me. "That's… Wait… Why?"

I smiled, "You know… closure." I said, trying not to sound sadistic, though that's exactly how I felt.

He furrowed his brow again as though he thought there was something off and he didn't believe me. "Eva… I'm sorry… but no… If I thought you seriously would just try to talk to him, okay, that's different. But do you honestly think I believe you're just gonna walk in there and do nothing but talk to him?"

"Yeah…" I said like I was clueless why he would assume I had any other plans.

He narrowed his eyes at me like he knew I was lying. "No, for one, you're not being honest. And for two, I don't really ever want you in the same room with that bastard ever again."

"Please?" I asked again nicely. I wasn't going to argue with him. I wanted him to give in just because he wanted to, not because I persuaded him to.

"No!" His stance was firm, clearly done talking about it. "Lane, take them both back home." He said as he looked over my shoulder again.

"You're making a mistake." I said calmly, giving him a look like I meant it.

"Are you threatening me?" Jake asked softly under his breath, squinting his eyes at me.

"Lane, take Ellie and step out into the hall for a moment. I need to speak to Jake alone, please." I said, still focusing on Jake.

I didn't hear Lane agree, but I saw Jake look back at him and nod like that's what he wanted as well. Then, after a few seconds, I heard the door shut.

"Look, Eva… I know what you want. I know what you've been after from the moment you first got your memories back at the cabin over a year ago. And I'm not trying to deny you that, but you have to understand, I can't just let you waltz in there and murder the man. Even though that's what I would love to see and frankly what he deserves… I just can't allow it!" He said raising his voice a little, upset with the situation we were in.

"Then just let me talk to him. I won't murder him…" I said calmly again.

"Look at you, this isn't normal. There's something off about you already and you haven't done anything but look at him so far, let alone speak to him. It wouldn't be good for you, baby." He said, trying to plead with me to understand.

"I won't beg you, Jake."

"Ugh, dammit!" He reached over and hit the wall. "You weren't even supposed to be here!"

"But I am!" I said, raising my voice before I stopped myself. "I am…" I said again, but softly.

He didn't reply for a moment, he just looked at me as he thought. "Baby, I want to, I do… I just—"

"I won't kill him… I promise."

He stopped and looked at me, surprised. "Sweetie, *I* can't even be around him without wanting to strangle him myself. I really don't see how you'd be able to restrain yourself enou—"

"I promise!" I said again when I saw that was the magic word to get him to reconsider.

He didn't say anything, he just looked at me, then looked over through the glass at Miller sitting there, chained to the table.

"He can't hurt me, baby… The only weapon he has is his mouth… and he can't do any more to me with that than what he's already done."

Jake still didn't say anything, he just kept staring at him, deep in thought.

"And you're right here… nothing will happen… I'll be fine!"

"Fine," Jake said finally, then looked back at me. "Eva… don't lie to me… A promise is a promise."

I knew better than to smile when I realized I'd won. "I know."

"I love you… don't make me regret this." He said, leaning in to wrap his arms around me and kiss me on the forehead.

"I love you too, baby."

I wasn't sure what the look on Miller's face would be when he saw me walk in, but the one I saw didn't disappoint. He didn't say anything. He just watched as I walked over and sat down across from him.

"Do you know how long I've been waiting for this day?" I asked, trying not to sound excited even though deep down I really was.

He didn't respond, he just stared at me, so I stared back at him while I thought about what exactly I wanted to say next.

"You know it must really suck to see Miles is a second rank now…" I said as I leaned back in the chair, putting my legs up on the table, then crossing them.

He still didn't reply. He just made a face like he wasn't sure what I was up to, then looked at my legs like he wanted to touch them.

"You know I don't always get to interrogate someone that's been trained in the art as well as you have. I mean… It's kinda like Sicari versus Coldier, you know… technique wise… So, this should be fun." I said as I watched him sit there stone faced, knowing what I wanted and refusing to give it to me.

"I betcha I'm better than you, though… You know since Coldiers suck… The Sicari always were so much better at… well, pretty much everything… especially getting intel."

The look in his eyes changed. Finally, he realized I was playing a game and now he wanted even more to win.

"Hey! I got an idea… How about if you crack, I get to kill you, and if you don't…" I shrugged, "then I let you go? Whatcha say to that?" I smiled.

He finally did something other than stare at me. For a split second, I could see the corner of his mouth twitch, indicating he liked that idea.

"Oh, good… it's a deal then!" I smiled again, then leaned forward to take my jacket off. "You know… I don't know how the Coldiers taught you how to do this, but with the way the Sicari taught me, you not talking actually tells me more than when you speak." I said, then reached up to untie my shoes. "You see… it's all in your eyes. They scream at me everything you're thinking. So it's actually pretty helpful when you keep your mouth shut, 'cause it's honestly just distracting when you run it." I stopped looking at him for a moment to pull my shoes off and drop them on the floor.

"Like, for example… right here your eyes are screaming 'what the hell is she doing?' What, Miller? You afraid I'm gonna use the laces to strangle you again? I mean, it doesn't appear that I walked in here with any weapons, but you'd be surprised what all can kill a man." I said, then leaned back in my seat again. "How's your neck from the last time I strangled you? It looks like you've recovered well… or well, maybe not… maybe that's why you're not talking. Maybe I broke your vocal cords."

"No, Princess… I can talk." He said, lowering his face to look at me menacingly from the top of his eyes.

I smiled. "You know, it used to bother me when you called me that. But honestly now, I don't mind it so much. After all, that is kinda what I am… You know what isn't nice though, Miller? That freakin' mustache! Who the hell still cuts their facial hair like that? I mean… wow, man… it's bad. Like fugly, for real!"

He squinted his eyes slightly. I could tell that bothered him, but nowhere near where I was trying to go.

"I realized something…" I said as I leaned forward again to pull each of my socks off one at a time. "I know why you wanted to keep erasing me, it's obvious… You have a baby tiny weannie," I pointed to his crotch, "and you were embarrassed… So I guess the best way for me to not make fun of you each time I saw it was if I didn't remember what a real man's looked like." I said it matter-of-factly as I leaned back again.

"You know what I said I'd do if you didn't give me all the intel?" He asked suddenly. I must have touched a nerve with that last one, prompting him to change the subject.

"Yeah… something about killing me, or Miles, yada yada yada… babble, babble. Honestly, I don't remember. Since you're so full of shit, whatever you say doesn't ever really matter." I knew what he was trying to do. He was trying to gain control of the conversation. He was trying to make me scared however he could so he could be in the lead, rather than me.

"You didn't give me all the intel, Princess… Now Miles is gonna pay for that." He said like he had a plan, but I wasn't going to let his attempt to bluff distract me.

"You know who always wins this game, Miller?" I asked as I let my eyes slowly work their way down him.

He didn't reply.

"Whoever's more psychotic…" I said calmly, then smiled like I was claiming the title.

"I told my men to kill him… but only after they make sure you're watching." He tried that angle again.

I smiled, thinking his attempt was cute, then stood up out of my chair. "You think you know what I care about most… That way if you threaten it, I'll just cow down." I said as I started to remove my pants and kick them off to lie beside my shoes.

"What are you doing?" He asked, forgetting he wasn't supposed to speak in this game. Then I heard a knocking on the glass behind me, probably Jake telling me to stop undressing. I ignored it and continued what I was doing.

"You know when a person is the most vulnerable, Miller? It's when they're naked… So, my thought is, I'll enjoy beating you even more when I do it while I'm at my weakest." I smiled again. "But dammit if that isn't also my best weapon against you," I said as I watched him continue to stare at my bare legs. "Knowing your opponent's biggest weakness is kinda helpful, too."

His eyes suddenly shot up to mine, having finally realized what I was doing.

"So really, how bad did it bother you that I didn't give you all the intel? Who would have thought missing one tiny little digit would have caused so much of a fuss? Were you crying over it? I wanna know, when you got to the vault and saw you missed the mark, yet again... did that hurt your ego?" I didn't really care if he answered me, I just wanted to see the pain in his face when he knew I had beat him at something else.

"You tell me, did it hurt when I forced you to stab your partner to death?"

"Hmmm," I smiled like that didn't bother me, then leaned down to pick up one of my shoes to remove its laces when I heard another strong tapping sound on the glass.

"Doesn't look like you're allowed to kill me, Princess..." Miller said, then smiled, thinking that would bother me.

I continued to remove the shoe's lace as I leaned forward to whisper, "This is just a distraction," I said, grinning, then winked as I leaned back.

He squinted his eyes slightly, then stopped suddenly, knowing I was watching them.

"Every day I think about how I wanna kill you... torture you, I mean. I've done it in my head at least a hundred times, a thousand different ways..." I stopped to watch him again. "But then I realized something..." I paused to see if he'd ask what.

"What?" He said finally after a moment like even he couldn't resist.

"That's not good enough..."

He furrowed his brow like something I was saying finally started to bother him.

"Killing you won't satisfy me. I mean, don't get me wrong, the idea of watching you beg for mercy and scream in pain... yeah, that's... well, that'd be great. But it's just not enough... 'Cause life is so fragile, and you're so pathetic... I wouldn't get anything done before you wimped out on me... you know, just like how you were in bed... And that's not satisfying, now is it?" I made a pouty face, then quickly threw up my hands as I continued. "I wanna be satisfied. And to be satisfied, you have to suffer for *way* longer than just a few minutes..."

"You're too weak to kill me. You already tried that and couldn't do it." He said, obviously challenging me. Instantly, I saw right through him. *Game over!*

"Oh, there ya go, you just showed your cards!" I smiled again, really big. "I win!"

"What?" He acted like he wasn't following me.

I didn't say anything at first. I just reached up to unbutton my blouse. "You're not scared to die, Miller. Just like I wasn't... and that's all I wanted. I begged you, just kill me, but noooo... that wasn't good enough. So when I was thinking about how I planned on killing you, I realized something. You already figured it out. You already thought of the perfect way to make someone suffer for *way* longer than just a few minutes of torture. What you did caused suffering that, if I allowed it, could last me a lifetime. You planted a seed... a cancer... so then even when you're not there, it'll still do the work for you."

"What are you talking about?" Something I was saying must have started to bother him by how he asked.

"When I was erased, I realized something... Nothing matters in life like your memories, not even life itself. You can take everything from a person, but if they have their memories, they can rebuild again. In contrast, you can take nothing from someone except their memory and, well... that's everything. Essentially, it's like taking someone's soul while still keeping their body alive. Mentally, that's the worst anguish of them all... Not having any freakin' clue who you are or where you came from." I said calmly as I continued to stare at him.

He still didn't respond, but I could tell he was scared now by the way his eyes began to dart randomly from one thing to another like he was secretly freaking out inside.

"You're not afraid to die, Miller… Just like I wasn't… So what makes you think I'd be so merciful to you to give you that, when you wouldn't give it to me?" I asked as I rested my hand in front of me and opened it.

His face suddenly showed the fear that I was hoping for the entire time when he saw what I was holding. He didn't have a chance to do any more than look up at the glass and begin to cry out when I quickly stood up.

*"**CHECKMATE, BITCH!**"* I screamed, leaning across the table and grabbing a fist full of his hair, then I stabbed him in the eye with the needle and injected the serum as I heard the door open.

"Eva!"

I let go and left the needle in Miller's eye as I turned around.

"Dammit, woman!" Jake scolded as he wrapped his arm around me to pull me backward.

"I didn't kill him!" I said as I let myself fall to sit back down in the chair. "Don't you remember? He crossed his heart and hoped to die asking me to stick a needle in his eye… or something like that. I was just giving him what he asked for!"

Jake gave me a dirty look, then leaned over and pulled the needle out to look at the syringe while Miller continued to tussle about, still screaming.

I smiled while looking up at Jake, hoping he was happy that I kept my promise.

"Get dressed!" He said as he turned to motion for agents to come in to shut Miller up. "Where the hell did you get this?"

I leaned forward to pick up my pants and slip them back on. "Xavier owed me a favor."

"What?" Jake asked, confused, then reached down to take me by the arm to remove me from the room after he saw I had my pants back on.

"Wait… my shoes?" I said, turning back, but really I just wanted another chance to watch Miller slowly fade into a pile of nobody.

"You promised, Eva!" Jake said, then pulled me again.

"He's not dead!" I smiled, "I mean… he might lose an eye, but I didn't kill him… Promise kept!"

He shut the door behind us as soon as he got me back into the adjacent room. I didn't give him a chance to say anything else though, before I leaned forward and kissed him. Apparently, he wasn't too upset with me because he didn't pull away or say anything. He just let me continue as he reached down to pull me in tighter.

"I'm good now," I said quickly as I reached up to run my fingers through his hair and continue to kiss him.

"You knew what we were doing this whole time, didn't you?" He asked between kisses.

"Umm hmm…"

"So, you planned this?"

"Umm hmm…"

"Okay, then. Now what?"

"Kiss me first," I said, pulling him toward me as I leaned against the wall. "Then we'll talk about what to do with him next!"

"Ahh, you wanna put all that adrenaline you're feeling now to good use?" He snickered.

I didn't say anything, I just grinned.

"You got it, baby…" He said, taking my hand in his then leaned down to kiss me.

22

PILLAGE THE THIEF

"Hang him!" Dad gave Jake the order, clearly upset something had been done to Miller before he got the chance to speak with him.

"What? That's it?" I threw my hands in the air. "You can't just hang him… What if you threw him in prison so all the other inmates can do to him what he did to me… or throw him naked out in the wild so he can get eaten by wild animals or whatever, I know the grotto lands got a few! You can't just hang him… that's not enough!"

Dad initially gave me a look like I didn't have a choice in the matter since I already had my chance at revenge, then his look quickly changed like he thought my suggestions seemed off. "We don't have prisons anymore, Jayde… Three years in, it wasn't conducive to keep them active, so we hung all the inmates with severe enough crimes and erased the rest to use as Gypsyins. Which is precisely what is going to happen to him. I don't want to lie awake at night thinking about what he could still be capable of if I let him live."

I looked over at Jake to see if he would speak up to agree with me, but he didn't say anything. He just stood there, wanting left out of it.

"That's not good enough! You can't just simply kill him, he needs to suffer!"

"Jayde…" Dad got quiet suddenly, looking concerned. "Nothing we can do to him will ever take away the things he's done to you… I'm sorry."

I didn't say anything. I just looked at him, feeling myself deflate. I knew he was right even though I didn't like it. "Fine," I said softly under my breath. "You could at least push him off a building or something…" I turned to open the door to leave. I was done with the conversation.

"You're dismissed, Agent Miles." I heard Dad behind me as I stepped out, then after a moment I felt Jake's hand on my waist as he caught up to walk beside me down the hall.

"I'm all messed up, aren't I?" I asked.

He chuckled softly, then leaned over to kiss me on the head. "Yeah…" He said unapologetically, without reservation.

"Why don't I feel better?"

"Time heals wounds, baby, not revenge." He said softly, seeing I felt vulnerable. "I don't know how much time… It could be months or maybe years, but it'll happen. One day you'll wake up and have so many good memories to think about that it'll crowd out the bad ones."

I didn't say anything, I just nodded.

"Everything will be better now, baby…" He stopped, then turned to look at me, stopping me as well. "I never thought this day would come." He said as his eyes turned glossy. "Everything has been so hard. It's been one thing after another. But all I ever wanted was for it to be just us, you know… together, safe and happy. And I can finally see that happening now. It's like sitting, watching a sunrise… You know it's gonna get better… brighter… It has to, that's the law of nature. It's always darkest before the dawn." He smiled. "And the sun never fails to rise."

I closed my eyes and leaned forward to hug him. "Okay… help me make more happy memories then, baby."

He pulled my head in tighter, then kissed the top of it. "Every day, Jayde… We can make more every day!"

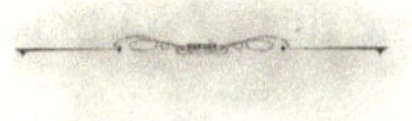

"Is this good for us?" Ellie asked as she walked away from Lane to come take a seat beside me.

"This should give us closure, hopefully…" I said as I took off my jacket to wrap around her when I noticed she had begun to shiver even with hers on.

"Thank you…" she said, staring at Miller. "Will it take a while?"

I looked over to see what she was asking about. It wasn't anything like I pictured it'd be. The process seemed more straightforward. Almost too simple and clean, really. "Do you mean will he suffer?"

She slowly looked over at me and nodded slightly before looking away again like she felt guilty for whatever reason.

"Do you want him to suffer?" I asked as I reached up to rub her back.

"I don't know," she said softly. "I just don't want to be scared of him anymore."

I smiled wryly, then pulled her toward me to hug her. "He'll never hurt anyone ever again… I promise!"

She nodded, then jerked when she saw him fall after Jake released the lever.

"It's okay…" I said as I looked for Lane over her shoulder. "It's all over now, sweetie."

"How many men have you seen die, Jayde?" She asked as she began to shiver harder. She must have noticed how calm I was and thought that was why.

Lane finally caught my eye and started to quickly walk over.

"Too many," I sighed, resting my head on her shoulder.

"Ellie?" Lane asked, reaching down for her, "Do you need to leave now, baby?"

"Take her home, Lane… She's seen enough." I said before she had a chance to act like she was fine when I knew she wasn't.

"Okay…" He pulled her up to stand next to him. "Are *you* all right, Kaleah?" He asked before he turned with her to walk away.

"Couldn't be better," I said with a forced smile, so he would take her away before she got more upset.

"Good…" He said, believing me, then turned to walk away with Ellie.

I wanted to sit there and stare at Miller's dead body dangling from the rope, while telling myself this would make it better, but I knew it wouldn't. Sitting there thinking about all the things he'd done to me and how this was supposed to help, when it actually didn't, was exactly what he would have wanted. He took my power, and it was time for me to get it back.

"Screw this!" I stood up and brushed myself off, literally and metaphorically. "Miles!" I yelled out as I walked up the steps of the hangman's platform and over to him. "Give me your knife."

He gave me a curious look, but didn't ask. He just nodded, then reached around and pulled it from its sheath at his back. "Here, baby…" He said, handing it to me.

I smiled, then stepped away to stand over the opening where Miller's body was hanging. His body was still twitching, but I knew he was dead. I reached out and cut the rope that was still holding him up, then watched as he fell to the ground like a limp bag of shit.

"Eva?" Jake said suddenly, unable to stop himself from asking any longer.

I didn't respond. I just walked back past him, down the steps, and under the platform to stand over Miller's lifeless body. Then I squatted down close to him just in case he was still in there and could hear what I was about to say to him.

"You've taken enough. You don't get to take anything else from me. Not another second, not another hour or another day… no more, you hear me…" I whispered. "Everything you've stolen, it's mine… It's all mine, you stupid, sick bastard!" I said, beginning to cry. "I'm taking it all back… you don't get to keep it. They're my memories… it's my life, it's my happiness you took… but not anymore, you piece of shit!" I whispered again, then reached up and plunged the knife into his chest where I knew it would hit his heart. "They're mine! You have no right to them. They're freakin' mine!" I screamed, then pulled the knife back out before stabbing him again. "I'm. Taking. Them. Back!" I yelled with each plunge of the knife.

"Eva, baby?" Jake was behind me now.

"He can't have me anymore, Jake…" I said, crying harder, "I'm mine!"

Jake's hand quickly slide down my arm to take the knife before I could plunge it in again. "I know, baby…" He said as he got on his knees behind me, wrapped his arms around me, pulling me back to rest against him. "I know…" he murmured into my hair.

"I'm mine…" I sobbed. Feeling broken, I turned to bury my face into his chest.

"Shhh… baby… it's okay… It's over now…" He said softly as he ran his hand down my hair then kissed my head. "It's all over now."

"Jayde, you in here, baby?"

I didn't even attempt to hide what I was doing; I needed a drink or four, and I hoped this once he'd understand. "Over here," I said as I set the bottle down on the coffee table next to where I was sitting.

Jake looked at it but didn't say anything. He just sat down directly in front of me on the floor. "Are you all right?"

"Never… better…" I said solemnly.

"How many glasses have you had?" Jake asked finally, looking down at the near empty bottle.

"Fi… um, I don't know." I reached for the bottle to pour another.

"No, baby…" Jake said, reaching up to motion for me to stop. "Please!"

"What? I'm celebrating," I leaned back.

He looked doubtful, knowing me better than that. "If you're having issues, then let's talk about it. Drinking doesn't solve problems, it just creates more."

"I need to get out of here… being around agents all the time… I can't breathe."

He furrowed his brow slightly; either confused or curious, I wasn't sure which.

"I don't wanna be this. I don't wanna be the princess, I just wanna be with you… I wanna be a mommy."

"Okay?" He said, wanting me to go on.

"Can we get a house now? Or you can take me to yours in Nashville?"

He smiled, "Baby—"

"I just wanna be normal, Jake… I don't wanna be this anymore."

"Then marry me." He said suddenly. "Jayde… Marry me and I'll take you wherever you want. We don't have to live here. We can get our own house like what Lane has."

"Then we'll make babies too?" I asked, looking away from him over at the bottle again.

"Jayde…" He sat up on his knees closer to me then reached up and turned my face to look at him again. "You want babies, we'll have babies! You want a house, honey… I'll get you a house! Whatever you want, so do I."

I didn't say anything for a moment. I just sat there and stared into his rich hazel eyes before I started to cry when I realized there was still a problem.

"Baby, what's the matter?" He asked, looking confused as he reached up to wipe the tears away. "There's nothing stopping us now. You have your tag. Miller's gone. The Sica—"

"Your mom wants me dead…" I moaned through my tears, crying harder. "I didn't tell you, but it was her… the papers were her."

"Oh, okay… Shh… Come here, sweetie…" He leaned in to wrap his arms around me. "It's okay… I know, Lane already told me."

"How's that okay?" I asked as I rested my forehead on his shoulder. "She's evil!"

"Try to calm down, baby… you're gonna make yourself sick if you get too worked up. Just breathe!" He said as he stood up, then leaned down and picked me up. "I already handled it," he said as he turned around then sat back down with me in his lap. "She's not gonna hurt you, okay?"

"She won't?" I asked, trying to pull myself back together and stop crying.

"No," He pulled me to rest against him. "She won't." He said definitively, with conviction lacing the words.

"What did you do?"

"I didn't do anything. My Father's the one that's going to deal with her… and my sister."

"Your sister?"

"It was Chelsey too. Mom got the papers and Chelsey let her use her prints… They knew what they were doing…" He said it like it hurt him to think about them that way. "After Lane told me, I crossed the original papers through the Coldier database and saw who the prints belonged to."

"Really?" I sat back to look at him. I felt more upset now, thinking it was multiple people who didn't like me.

"It's okay, baby." He said, seeing I was about to cry again. "Dad still won't divorce her, but…" He stopped to push my hair back and make sure he was looking me in the eye. "He's going to strip her of everything. He's going to take away all her Gypsyins and all the money…" He stopped again, trying not to grimace. "Neither of them will get any of it, baby…" He paused to inhale sharply. "That's another reason we gotta get married… Dad's gonna put all of their portion aside for our kids."

"What?"

He nodded, "Yeah… it's a lot for me to process, too."

"But what about Bethany? What'll happen to her?"

He smiled, "All the Gypsyins still get to stay at the house and be there for when Dad needs them—the once a month that he goes home. So it'll work out for them… I don't guess having free rein of that place is really all that bad, you know? Mom won't be there anymore, he's going to make her move to one of his investment properties outside the city."

"Oh, okay…" I said, still thinking. "How did your mom take it?"

"He's not told her yet," Jake said, looking away, clearly uncomfortable. "Dad wanted to do it after they come here to meet you and your father first."

I felt my eyes widen at the thought of that conversation. "Oh…"

"Yeah…" Jake signed, likely thinking the same thing. "Will that bother you?"

I sat there for a moment to think about it. I was trying my best to stay with it but the alcohol was beginning to make me drowsy. "No…" I said finally. "I don't really want to see her again, but I'll do what I gotta do."

He smiled, then leaned in to kiss me. "That's my girl!"

"Hey Miles, you guys coming down for supper or… uh… oh sorry…"

"She's asleep, Lane. Don't worry about it, we're good to talk. I found her drinking in the library after we got back. She'll probably be out the rest of the night."

"Oh… ok… if you're staying, you want me to bring you back something to eat then?"

"Yeah, if you don't mind. I don't wanna leave her. She's not been doing well."

"Oh no? What do you mean, like is it that time of the month or uh…"

"No, man, not that… It's just the whole Miller thing. It's harder on her than she probably expected it'd be. How's Ellie doing? She didn't look well earlier, either. I saw she was shaking pretty bad before you left with her."

"Oh, uh… Ellie… uh… Yeah, she's good now… She's actually doing way better than I expected."

"Really?"

"Yeah… I don't know exactly how it works or whatever, but yeah, she's like a whole new woman now."

"What do you mean?"

"Uh yeah, Miles… you know… like… we uh… we finally uh… you know!"

"Really?"

"Yeah, man. I didn't expect it either, you know, since I was waiting and all. But when we got back, she was just really emotional, and we started kissing and well, it pretty quickly turned into everything else."

"Okay… Well… I'm happy the thing with Miller didn't bother her too much."

"Yeah… I knew I loved her, man, but now we're like on a whole other level… She's seriously my everything!"

"You used protection, right?"

"Ugh… yeaughnoo… Shit!"

"Lane? You serious?"

"Shit, shit, shit! Ugh… Well, no… no, no, it's okay… it was just once, no big deal. I mean, what're the odds?"

"Uh… she's young, she's healthy… They're good, the odds are really freakin' good."

"Crap… okay, well…"

"When's the wedding? If you didn't already have a date picked out, now's the time… Better sooner than later."

"Shit… Miles, you're not funny. Stop laughing."

"Whatever you do, Lane… don't let her drink, it's not good for the baby… She'll need to eat more now too, so if she wants something just get it for her. Don't ask questions."

"She's not pregnant, dude… Stop!"

"Hey, if you wanna use your big boy toy, you gotta take responsibility for where your bullets land."

"Ugh… Seriously, man? I will, you know that! I want kids, all right… I just wasn't planning on them so soon."

"Ahh, Bro, I'm just messing with ya, you'll be fine… Give me another month or so when Jayde's birth control wears off and we can make babies at the same time… Kinda like our moms did… Wouldn't that be cool?"

"Yeah, then they could be brothers like us… but this time mine'll be older!"

"Nah, Lane… now you're gonna make it a competition and I'm gonna have to win like I always do."

"I guess we better both get our wedding dates set then, 'cause I don't know of any woman that wants to walk down the aisle in a maternity dress."

"Well, Jayde's the older sister so it's only right that she has her wedding first."

"What? Miles… Nah, dude, that's not fair. That'll give you a head start."

"I asked my girl first. We've been waiting the longest… you can wait your turn."

"Well… I asked Mr. Prescott first!"

"Dude, I'm done with this conversation. Shut the hell up and get out… Oh, and when you come back, bring me some sugar for my tea too, will ya?"

23

POMP AND CONSEQUENCE

"I didn't know you knew how to bake," Jake commented as I took back the spatula that he was licking.

"Lane taught me," I grinned, expecting him to suddenly act like he didn't like the batter anymore.

"He did?" He asked as he leaned back against the counter, then pulled himself up to sit on it.

"Yeah, he actually taught me a lot. I mean, you practically had him babysitting me every weekend." I snickered, knowing I was exaggerating, then began to scrape the brownie batter out into a pan.

"Oh, really?" He grinned. "Too bad he didn't teach you to grease the pan first," he said, poking back.

"Oh, dammit… I knew I missed a step. You're distracting me." I stopped, then tried to pour the batter from the pan back into the bowl.

"What else did he teach you?" He seemed stuck on that for whatever reason.

"Oh, well… um, how to cook grilled cheese, pancakes, cookies, um…"

"All the carb loaded crap?"

"Yeah," I laughed.

"Ok, so he taught you some cooking... what else?" He asked, reaching over to dip his finger into the bowl to take another taste.

"Oh, I don't know," I stopped scraping to think about it. "Uh, how to tie my shoes, I mean, like how to tie a proper bow, you know? When they kept coming apart, he said it was 'cause I was doing it wrong... Um... He taught me how to brush my teeth the right way t—"

"What?" Jake interrupted, looking surprised.

"Yeah... It seems easy, but it's kinda technical, you know? You need to do the inside, then the outside, then the upside, then the down and you can't rush it... You gotta give each section its due attention." I smiled. "I figured this was all stuff normal people that hadn't been erased already knew. Maybe not..." I shrugged.

He didn't say anything, he just stared at me, taking it all in.

"Oh, and then there was how to blow my nose—"

"You're joking, right?"

"No... It was from after I had that cold that one time. I was complaining to him about how my nose was raw, so he showed me how he blows his. Like how he holds the tissue when he blows and avoids actually wiping the outside of his nose so he's not rubbing all the skin off, making it raw."

"That's incredible," He said, grinning. I wasn't sure if he was being sarcastic or not, though.

When I finished pouring the batter back into the bowl, I lifted the pan and started licking it out while I looked at him through the glass bottom.

"Baby, you gotta stop doing that..." He said after he watched me for a minute, then cleared his throat. "It's not sanitary at all, amongst other things. " He winked, then looked over his shoulder, unsure who all was around.

"Oh, sorry..." I sat it back down, wiped the corners of my mouth with my thumb then slowly licked it off with a grin.

Intensity flashed through his eyes. "He didn't teach you that too, did he?"

I smiled. "No, he wouldn't ever let me lick out anything, the big meanie!"

Jake laughed. "Good!"

I turned around and got some butter from the fridge, then opened it to spread it on the pan. "Your family likes brownies, right? I guess I should have asked first."

"My dad does and I do… it doesn't matter what anyone else likes." He said, hopping off the counter.

"Yeah, I hadn't thought of it like that but I guess that's true."

"I'm surprised your wanting to make something. Since you know that Mom and Chelsey will be here too. I need to know, where are you hiding the poison?" He asked as he stuck his finger in the batter again. "I better get all my tasting in before you add it."

"I want to show them I'll be a good wife." I said as I bopped his hand, intentionally dabbing the batter onto his nose.

He groaned, wiping it off."Ok, I won't tell them you licked the pan then." He grinned as he stepped behind me so he could wrap his arms around my waist and rest his chin on my shoulder. "Don't worry about what they think, baby… You're gonna be the best wife any man could ever hope for."

"You're just saying that to earn brownie points." I laughed, then turned to give him a kiss.

"Oh, I meant it. But don't tempt me. I might just sweep you off your feet, take you back to our room and leave this batter sitting here for the random buzzard agent that walks by."

I giggled, trying to imagine what he described.

"Actually, better yet…" He bent down suddenly and picked me up, making me gasp in surprise. "I say, I take both you *and* the batter back!"

I giggled again as I rested the bowl in my lap and licked the spatula while he carried me away.

"Jacob?" I heard his mom's voice. "Oh hey, honey… This place is amazing. Why haven't you invited us to dinner before now? Where's your new girlfriend?"

I couldn't move. After hearing her, I was frozen, standing in a shadow in the hall where they couldn't see me.

"She's coming, Mom. She's just finishing getting herself ready for supper."

"What did you say her name was again? Jayde, right? Oh dear, this is exciting. It's such an upgrade from that last one. I knew she wasn't good for you, honey."

"Mom, please… I know we haven't had a chance to sit down and really talk in months, but there's a lot I need to explain to you."

"She's the First Rank's daughter, isn't she, Jake?" Another woman's voice spoke that wasn't his mom, probably his sister.

I heard him take in a deep breath, likely knowing he was in for a special night. It was only before we were getting ready for dinner when he told me neither of them had any idea that he was still with me. My stomach felt twisted when I thought about stepping out and going into the great room to see them again.

"Hey Uncle Duke, it's good to see you, it's been a minute…" I heard Lane's voice now, apparently having entered the room from another direction.

"Henry, my boy, it has."

"Jacob… We get to meet Mr. Prescott, right?" His mom asked. She sounded like she'd been planning for this night her whole life.

"Yes, mom… and both his daughters."

"Oh, this is so exciting!" It sounded like his sister again. "Does he have a son?"

"You're married, Chelsey," Jake said, disapproving.

"I know… I'm just joking." She replied, but I doubt she was joking. She sounded like she very much meant it.

"Hey…" Ellie's voice spoke suddenly, soft and faint, like she'd entered the room and felt overwhelmed seeing all the new people.

"Jacob?" Jake's mom sounded confused.

"This is Ellie, Aunt Liz, my fiancée. She's Jayde's sister."

"Um… she looks…"

I turned to step out from the corridor into the room. "We look alike, don't we?" I said as I walked into the room, making everyone's face turn suddenly to look at me.

"Uh… Jacob?" Liz said softly, staring at me in shock.

"Hi!" Chelsey said like she was blissfully unaware of who I really was as she walked over to me like she wanted to give me a hug. "I'm Jake's sister, Chelsey."

Seeing it was obvious she had no clue, I followed along and hugged her back while keeping an eye on Liz and how she was reacting.

"Mom, Dad…" Jake raised his arm, motioning for me to come stand by him. "I believe you've already met my fiancée before, just by a different name. This is Jayde Prescott, or as you knew her, Kaleah Eva."

It looked like Chelsey was about to crap her pants as she stared at me with her mouth still half ajar.

"Jacob…" Liz said suddenly, clearly indignant. "What is this?"

"It's what you think it is, Elizabeth," I said before Jake got a chance to say anything.

She quickly looked down from my face to my arm, checking to see if I had a tag. "No… but… you…" She started to stammer, like she wasn't sure what to say or what she was even seeing. "Kaleah was a Gypsyin…" she said finally, finding her words.

"I was a Gypsyin, you're right."

"But this makes no sense. How were you a Gypsyin if you're the First Rank's daughter? I mean, you have a tag, I can see it." Chelsey piped up, probably feeling guilty.

Jake turned and looked down, allowing me to continue. Apparently, he was approving of how I was handling the situation thus far.

"Not everyone is who you think they ar—"

"This is absurd!" Liz interrupted me, "Jacob, come! We need to speak in private." She said, turning to walk out.

"Elizabeth," Duke raised his voice to stop her. "No… Jacob doesn't owe you or anyone else an explanation."

She stopped and turned back like she knew she wasn't about to get her way.

"I love her, Mom." Jake finally spoke up. "I loved her when she was a Gypsyin. I still loved her when I found out she was a Sicari and I love her now… It's not my fault that you can't see past your own prejudices."

"A Sicari? What? Jacob… I can't with this!" she said, beginning to turn around again. "Come!"

"No, you're gonna stand there and listen to me!" Jake demanded. "You're my mom and I love you, but the things you did… Kat confessed, Mom, she told us it was you and Chelsey…" He stopped to take in a deep breath. "You knew I loved Kaleah, you knew I asked her to marry me… but none of that mattered to you! You hate Gypsyins so much, you couldn't see past what you thought she was to see that I was happy… Finally, in my whole damn life, I was happy! But you hated her more than you loved me… She didn't do anything to you, and you still tried to get her taken from me! They would have killed her, Mom!"

"What?" Dad suddenly walked into the room. Apparently, he'd been listening. Everyone quickly hushed and turned to look at him. "Agent Miles?" He said, suggesting Jake fill him in on what he'd missed.

"I forgive her!" I said suddenly as I looked from Dad over to Liz. I had no clue what Dad would do to punish her if he found out exactly what had happened. Even though she was an awful person, she was still Jake's mother. And I hated the thought of him hurting because of something she'd done. So I hoped to defuse the situation before it got out of hand. "I honestly don't like you and I really hope to never see you again, but I forgive you."

Her face changed like she suddenly wasn't as angry and evil as she'd been portraying.

"Dad…" I swallowed, "Don't do anything, please… Let Duke, Jake's father, deal with her."

"Sir?" Duke spoke up, "She'll be punished accordingly… you have my word."

Dad looked from Duke over to Jake, who was now holding me tight to him. "Agent… Second rank comes with its own responsibilities… I defer this decision over to you. I trust she'll be dealt with."

"Yes, Sir!" Jake said as he let go of me to stand more at attention.

Dad nodded as he turned toward Lane and Ellie and motioned for them to exit toward the dining room. Then he turned back toward Duke, "Please… come, have supper with us." He said before turning again to walk out with him, leaving just Jake, me, his sister and his mother standing there.

"Jake…" Chelsey said suddenly, "I'm so sorry."

"I'm not…" Liz's face changed back to look like it had previously, just like I'd always seen it—mean and foul. "You tricked me, Jacob! And now you've embarrassed me beyond belief. I can't believe you'd say those things about me when you knew the First Rank was able to hear you. If I have prejudices, it's only because I'm a good Coldier and I care about my people—*our* people!"

"Mom…" Jake said, done listening to her.

"No! This isn't fair! If you would have been honest with me and told me from day one that she was the First Rank's daughter, then none of this would have ever happened. I could have accepted her and loved her just like I did Kat. But no, instead you go behind my back, trying to trip me up since you know I don't like those people. You trapped me, and now look, you've made me an outcast."

"An outcast? *Really*?" I couldn't stop myself from yelling at her. "You think any of this is worse than the things you said to me? *I* was the outcast! I was gonna make myself jump off of a freakin' roof because of you. You made me believe that I was *nothing*… that I was worthless! All because I was different than you…"

"You weren't good for him!" She shouted back. "I love my son, and I'd do anything for him, even if he thought he loved you. If I had to get rid of a Gypsyin that he was having illegal relations with, for his own good, then I was gonna do it, and I would do it again!"

"Get out of my house, Liz…" I said, lowering my voice. "I won't stop you from seeing your son, but I never want to see your face again. You're not invited to the wedding and you'll never meet your grand children…" I said softly as I turned toward Jacob, giving him a look so he knew he could finish, then I turned back around to walk out.

"What? You can't do that… Jacob, she can't do that!"

"Mom, she can do whatever she wants… That was her being lenient."

"What? What are you doing? I'm not leaving… let go of me, Jacob!"

"Come on, Chelsey, let's go, you too…"

"I'm sorry…" I said, breaking the silence as I rolled over and leaned my head against Jake's arm.

"You don't have to be sorry, baby." He pulled his arm up and wrapped it behind my back, pulling me in closer to him. "It was a hard situation, but you handled it well. I'm really proud of you."

"You are?" I asked, looking up at his face.

"Of course I am…" He leaned over to kiss me. "She deserved everything you gave her."

"So you're okay with her not coming to the wedding?"

He hesitated like that was a hard one to answer, "Yeah…" He said finally.

"Jake… I just—"

"I don't wanna talk about my mom anymore, baby…" He stopped me, then leaned down to kiss me again.

"Okay?" I asked before he pulled me back in to kiss me harder.

"Just you and me and our future… that's all I wanna talk about." He said between kisses.

"Oh, okay," I murmured as he went from my lips to my neck. "It looks like you'd rather do more than talk, though."

He stopped and rested his forehead against my chest. "Do you wanna go look for houses tomorrow?"

"What?" I asked, ecstatic about the idea. "Yes!"

He raised his head and smiled like he knew that was something I'd like. "We can do that then… We just can't move in until after the wedding."

I quickly lost my smile when I remembered there were steps that had to happen before we could leave and be on our own. "Oh…"

"What's wrong?"

"Well… I wanna be married, but I…" I stopped to think about what I was trying to say. "I don't know anything about how to have a wedding, let alone an Elite Coldier wedding." All I could think about was the one we had gone to, how elaborate it was and how much time and effort it would take me to plan one like it, especially since I had no clue what I was doing.

"Oh, is that it?" He asked with a warm smile.

"Yeah… It's just, I don't know… like a ton of work."

He smiled bigger. "Sweetie, that's not your job. That's what a planner is for. We'll hire someone to do all that stuff."

"Really?"

"Yes, really!" He relaxed suddenly, looking relieved. "Is that the reason every time I've asked you to set a date the last few weeks, you don't want to?"

"Yeah…" I mumbled, not sure I wanted to admit it.

"Aww, baby… what the heck!" He said playfully as he rolled toward me a little, then tightened his arms around me and rolled back, pulling me on top of him. "If I'd have known that, then we'd have been married already!"

"Sorry…" I said, making a whoops face.

He didn't say anything. He just smiled, pulled me down, wrapped both his hands around my head, and pulled me in for another kiss.

"You sure do seem to be in a hurry to get me hitched." I said, teasing him as I slid my hands down to rub his chest.

"I have to be… that way next time you go and get yourself erased, when you wake up there's no way out." He said, then bit down on my lip gently.

"Oh, that's how it is, is it?" I asked as I lowered myself now to kiss his chest.

"Can't '*I love you*' be enough of a reason?"

"Sure…" I said, moving my hands lower, to get his attention. "So it doesn't have anything to do with Lane?"

"What?" He mumbled..

I leaned up and and gave him a stern look.

"No…" He said finally, "It has nothing to do with Lane."

"Oh, okay…" I said, kissing his chest again. "'Cause I thought I heard you guys say something about a competition…"

"Ugh… Shit…" He groaned, having forgotten I could hear people talk in my sleep. "Can we maybe talk about this later? Right now I have other things on my mind." He winked.

"Don't worry about it, baby…" I said moving up to kiss him on the lips. "I like competitions… I'm in… let's win this thing."

24

SEIZING SHATTERED PROMISES

What are memories? They're not just snapshots. They're emotions, feelings, things we've seen, heard… *experienced*—**all fused together and preserved. They're the complete construct of who we are. Everything that I am is because of what I remember, the people, the pain, the joy… the love…**

"Jayde? You up here?… Hey, honey, what're you doing? The baby's crying. I'm pretty sure he wants you."

"I'm writing…"

"Oh, yeah? About what?"

"Everything, Jake… Everything I can remember."

"Oh, okay… You afraid you're gonna forget or uh…"

"Just in case… you know, if something happens again, this way I can look back."

"Oh… well, okay, that's probably a good idea."

"I started where we met. That's as far back as I needed."

"Ok, well don't worry about us then, just come down when you're ready. I'll watch EJ. Take your time."

"Thanks, baby…"

"Your mother wanted you to have this." Dad said softly as he walked into the room, shutting the door quietly behind him. He reached out his hand and held up a gold necklace with a single pearl pendant. "You look beautiful, sweetie. Next to your mother, the most gorgeous bride I've ever seen." He smiled, trying to hold back tears.

"*It's* beautiful," I said, taking the necklace from him to inspect it closer.

"It was your grandmother's. She wore it on her wedding day and your mother wore it on our wedding day…" I could tell he wanted to go on but stopped himself again. His eyes were now red and glossy.

"I miss her…" I said, standing up and handing the necklace back. "Will you put it on me?"

He nodded.

I smiled, then turned around and held up my hair.

"She never lost faith that we'd find you." He said now choking up. "She kept pushing, telling me she knew you were still alive, out there somewhere… She was so stubborn… that's where you get it from." I turned back around to see his smile through tear-streaked cheeks. He nodded proudly, looking down at the pendant. "So beautiful…" He murmured before pulling a hankie from his pocket to wipe his tears away.

"You never stopped looking?" I was trying to hold back my own tears so it wouldn't mess up my makeup but it was hard.

"Never, Jayde…" He said as he began to cry again. "Every night I'd pray, begging God to bring you back to us, safe and sound… I love you so much, honey. I just want you to know how proud I am of you."

In that moment, I realized it felt like my whole life I'd been holding my breath, waiting to hear those words come from my father's mouth. And now, finally hearing them felt like the largest burden had been lifted from me. *He's proud of me… He does want me… I am loved…*

The large iron-gilded doors swung open. The musical melody of the bridal march played softly on a single violin and everyone in the room stood and turned to cast their gaze upon me, but… nothing mattered once I saw Jake's face. Not how sleek or elegant my dress was, how many people were there, how elaborately they'd decorated everything, nothing… just his face. He was glowing, like the joy he'd been holding back this whole time from fear of losing me was no longer able to be contained.

"I, Jayde Kaleah Eva Prescott, vow this day to take you, Jacob Adrian Miles, as my lawfully wedded husband. I promise to love you like no woman has ever loved a man. You're my heart and soul and I promise to hold you, keep you, and treasure you.

In sickness and in health, I promise to honor you. From the second the sun rises to dawn the next day and every day, I will show you nothing but love and gratitude for the person you are and the person you've helped me to be.

I promise to cherish your person and your life like it is my own. Let every breath I take stand as a symbol of my undying affection for you, because without you there would be no more breaths in me, nor would there be any more I would want to take.

Whether we're rich or poor, I promise to protect the bond that we have and forsake all others. You and you alone have my heart. From this day to the end of time, there is no one, nor will there ever be anyone except you.

Jacob, I love you with everything that I am. You are my world and the light that sustains it. You are my blessing, my joy, my peace, and I would have nothing and be nothing without you."

"Jayde..." he whispered when I was done saying the vows I'd written. I'd made him cry. It was one of the rare times I'd seen him without his usual strong, held together expression. He paused as he brought the back of his hand up to gently wipe under his eyes then cleared his throat before going on to say his own.

"I, Jacob Adrian Miles, take you Jayde Prescott to be my lawfully wedded wife. I promise to have and to hold you from this day forward. Just like the moment we met, once I had you and held you, I knew it was you and only you that I wanted to spend the rest of my life with.

I promise to cherish you and honor you, both in sickness and in health. Just like the moment I held you in the cave while you lay there dying in my arms, I promise to be with you, side by side, until the end.

For richer or for poorer, I promise to be there, no matter what life throws at us. When I found you wondering around the woods, alone with nothing of your own, I loved you. And now, as I stand here marrying the First Rank's daughter, with all that we have, I still love you.

I promise to protect you. Anywhere we are or intend to go, you have me, Jayde... My body is your protection. I give my life as a sacrifice, and my body as a shield, to keep you safe. Just as I have from the moment we met.

From this moment on, I promise I am yours and only yours for the rest of our lives. I only have eyes for you, a heart for you, and love for you. You are mine, and I am yours until the moment we take our last breath. Kaleah, Eva... Jayde... I love you more than I've ever loved anyone, and I promise you, baby, you are my life and that's how it will forever be."

I stared at him, enchanted by his words. At that moment, it didn't feel real. How was this my life? I never felt like I ever deserved anyone like him, yet here I was, standing before this gorgeous man that truly loved me more than life itself.

I was so lost in his eyes that I didn't hear the words 'you may now kiss the bride.' I just saw him lean down like he knew what to do. If any moment I'd ever experienced truly felt magical, it was that one. *His kiss was like the seal of a thousand promises.* It was gentle, sweet and sincere, marked with a sense of relief on his face, like he finally had everything he'd ever wanted—me!

"You've been to the beach before, right? I can't remember." Jake asked, pulling me closer to him. He must have noticed I was still chilly, even though the sun was bright and high and we'd been playing in the sand for over an hour.

"Yeah, I mean, not this one obviously… When you said we could go to Florida I thought you were joking."

He smiled. "I wouldn't have taken you anywhere else. I still remember the moment I mentioned it to you at Lane's… the way you lit up. After that, I figured I'd find a way to get you down here somehow, even if we had to bring the whole agency with us." He smiled again then glanced over his shoulder at the three agents on guard behind us.

"Yeah… I'm just not sure how romantic of a honeymoon this is gonna be if we're constantly being watched."

He didn't respond, he just leaned in to kiss me. He pushed until I was laying down in the sand, then finally let up and looked down at me with an enormous grin. "We'll make it what we want it to be, baby… You want romance?"

I smiled and nodded.

"Then you got it." He leaned down and kissed me again. Then reached down and picked me up to carry me.

"Where're we going?"

"Back to the house. I have something planned already."

"You do, like what?"

He grinned again, reluctant to give up the surprise. "Well," he said finally, like he couldn't stop himself even if he wanted. "Since we both have sand all over us and it's chilly, I thought you'd enjoy a warm bath, then I have a nice supper planned and after that... well... I thought you might enjoy practicing for when we're gonna beat Lane and Ellie."

I laughed, "Just practice?"

"Yeah, just practice..." He smiled. "We'll really get working on it when we get back home."

———

"Hey, guys! How was Florida?" Lane greeted us as soon as he saw we'd gotten back.

"I'm tired..." I said the first thing that came to mind, not even thinking how a man would take it.

"Oh, I bet you are." Lane laughed, then slapped Jake on the back. "Sounds like you had a blast, man!" He laughed again.

"Oh, don't worry, you'll have your turn soon..." Jake pulled Lane in for a hug, then looked around. "Where's your soon-to-be wife?"

"Ahh dude, it feels so surreal you calling her that." Lane said like the reality of it all hadn't quite hit him yet. "She's in our room, taking a nap. She was up pretty late last night getting our bags packed. Then with the wedding this weekend, I mean... well, you know, she's a bit stressed, and a little nervous."

"A nap sounds good right now." I said, looking around, ready to lie on the first thing that was flat and comfy.

"Man, Miles, you must have put her though the wringer... poor thing." Lane hit him on the shoulder again. "Kaleah, you gonna be recovered by Saturday? Ellie needs you, you're all she's got."

I turned around and smiled at him, then walked over to give him a big hug. "Lane, I missed you. Yes, tell your brother no more practicing for a couple of days and I'll be just fine."

Jake burst out laughing but didn't say anything. He just shrugged when Lane looked at him, confused.

"The rings?"

Ellie turned around and opened her hand, waiting for me to hand her Lane's. I opened my palm, then gently placed it into hers. Just like Lane had said, it felt surreal to see them together. I stood there watching as they pledged their lives to each other, hand in hand, then leaned in to kiss. I couldn't help but let my eyes slowly drift over to Jake's though, instead of watching them, he was contentedly gazing at me.

"May I be the first to present to you Mr. and Mrs. Henry Lane!" The words were loud, but I was still stuck, almost dazed, staring at Jake. His eyes and the way he looked at me were mesmerizing, truly like I was the only girl in the room.

"Jayde?" Lane's mother came over to speak with me after the cake had been cut. I had never met her before, so I didn't know what to expect, but I hoped she wasn't anything like her sister, Liz.

"Yes?" I said softly as I set my fork full of cake back down on my plate.

"I'm Henry's mother, Jacob's auntie… It's a pleasure to meet you! Henry has told me so many good things. You and your sister are both so precious to our family."

I didn't respond right away; I think I was awe-struck, probably with my mouth hanging half open. As far as I could tell, she was absolutely nothing like Liz, except maybe for some facial similarities. "Oh… well, um… thank you." I stumbled with my words, wondering what to say. "Your son really is an amazing man. I wouldn't have been happy with my sister marrying anyone else!" The exact words I wanted finally flowed out without resistance.

She smiled and nodded, then stared at me for a moment. "You're glowing," she said suddenly, like she wanted me to know she noticed, though it was off topic. "I'm happy my nephew finally found someone who will treat him like he deserves." She said, then reached down to hold my hands as she patted the top one. "You must be a very special woman, my dear, a true diamond... you know, because those boys never liked the same girl before." She said, then smiled like she couldn't clarify, but hoped I would know what she meant.

"Uh... Thank you..."

She didn't say anything else. She just smiled again, patted my hand once more, and turned to walk away.

"Are you excited?" I asked. I was. I knew what the layout of the apartment looked like, but in many ways still didn't know what to expect. Had Jake had it decorated, and if so, what style? Had the movers moved all of our things in, or just certain things? Was anything unpacked or would it just be bare with all of our things still in a stack of boxes? Jake had been taking care of the details so I could be surprised but now the suspense was almost more than I could handle.

"Of course," Jake said, hesitant to push the button just yet.

"I'm ready, go ahead," I was trying to contain my excitement when I felt the elevator stop.

"This first," he bent down to pick me up, then spun me around. "Now, I'm ready." He said, then raised his knee to hit the open-door button at the bottom.

As soon as it opened, a flood of light filled the elevator. "We're home, baby!" Jake announced as he stepped out, then leaned in to kiss me before he set me back down on my feet.

"It's beautiful..." I stood there, letting my eyes jump from one thing to another before the view of the skyline through our windows stole my gaze. All the questions I had wondered about in the elevator didn't seem to matter anymore.

"It's home…" He sounded like it meant more to him than he was letting on by the way he said it.

"It's ours…" I said softly as the realization that I could call this place mine suddenly filled my heart with happiness.

He smiled, "It is, baby… You wanna go see the bedroom now?"

I nodded, then took his hand for him to lead me.

"**E**llie?" I thought I heard her voice. I rounded the corner to see her and Lane in the entryway talking to Jake. "Hey, what are you guys doing here?"

Lane looked up suddenly, "Kaleah!"

"Jake, you didn't tell me they were back already?"

"Yeah, we got in last night." Ellie said with a big smile, not looking nearly as tired as I'm sure I had looked when we returned.

"That's great!" I said, walking over to stand next to Jake.

"They have some news too…" Jake pulled me in to wrap his arm around my waist.

"What? Are you pregnant?" I blurted out, looking at Ellie. I was excited at the thought, but also not, since I thought it would be fun to be first.

"No… no, not yet," Lane laughed as Ellie sheepishly shook her head. "We're moving in…"

"What?" I asked confused, then looked over at Jake.

"Just kidding," Lane said suddenly. "Well, kinda…" He smiled, teasing me.

"They got an apartment a few floors below us," Jake apparently already knew.

"Really?" I was ecstatic. I walked over to hug Ellie. "That's awesome!"

"Yeah, Dad insisted…" Ellie said like she was excited too. "I mean,

I wouldn't have minded anyway, but he said this way it'd be easier for the agents to keep their guard detail."

"Yeah, I figured you'd gotten used to my cooking and wouldn't know what to do with the crap he makes for you." Lane smiled then elbowed Jake, teasing him.

"Oh, I've been the one cooking." I said, grinning ear to ear, hoping they'd be proud.

"What? Kaleah? No…" Lane looked surprised. Probably considering the first time we met, I had absolutely no clue what I was doing.

"Yep, she makes me grilled cheese, pancakes, cookies and that's about it… thanks a lot, man." Jake said sarcastically, then laughed as he elbowed Lane back.

"My pleasure! I figured if I'm ever gonna be the better looking one of the two of us, I should figure out how to sabotage you." Lane grinned as he reached up to put his hand on Jake's shoulder, "Looking at this gut, it was easier than I thought." He said, then laughed again.

Jake chuckled, then pushed Lane's hand off of him. "You wish! You just wait, buddy. Your newlywed pounds just haven't shown up yet… Either way, I'm glad you guys had a good time and you're back."

⁂

"Jayde… wake up baby, you're having a nightmare."

I opened my eyes and looked around. Normally that would break me from the sickening feeling that always accompanied them, but it didn't this time. For whatever reason, it lingered. "Jake?"

"I'm right here, sweetie." He pulled me over to rest against him, then used his other hand to rub my back. "You're all right."

"No…" I felt frantic, and I didn't know why. "I'm not."

He moved away for a second, then I heard him pull the chain to turn the lamp on. "What's wrong?" He looked down at me, then moved back over to pull me close to him again.

"I don't know, I just feel so sick." I said, moving my head to rest against him.

"Hmm… okay…" He rubbed my back again. "What do you think will help? You want a drink or something to eat?"

"No," I tried to shut my eyes again since I felt really lethargic but was afraid if I fell asleep I'd start the cycle again and have another bad dream.

"Okay, I think I know what will help. Just rest for a minute and I'll be right back."

"Okay…"

I had no clue what he was doing, but after a few minutes, he came back into the room again. "Here, baby," He said, then threw the comforter off of me and picked me up.

"What are you doing?" I moaned, resting my face against his chest.

"I drew you a warm bath," He said as he carried me into the bathroom then set me down in it. "Here, this'll help." He got down on his knees next to the tub, then leaned to sit with his back to the wall. "Just relax, baby. I'm not going anywhere."

"Jayde… Are you not hungry, honey? You've been in bed almost all day."

I could barely open my eyes; I was so tired. "No…" I moaned, then tried to roll over and get comfy again.

"You gotta eat, baby…"

"I can't… I need to sleep."

"This isn't normal… you shouldn't need this much sleep. This is the third day in a row you've been sleeping all day." He sounded concerned.

"I don't know." I mumbled against my pillow. I didn't really feel like talking. All I wanted to do was rest.

"I'm gonna call the doctor. I know you don't like them but…" he hesitated, not wanting me upset with him. "You need to be seen."

"Okay…" I didn't want a doctor to see me, but I felt too tired to argue with him, so I agreed.

"What are you doing?" I was trying not to freak out when I saw the needle.

"I'm just giving you an IV, sweetheart. Since you haven't been eating or drinking much, you've gotten quite dehydrated. This will help. I'm going to take a small amount of your blood too and have it tested, but that's all, I promise." The woman seemed nice, but I was still leery.

I looked over at Jake, scared. Then I closed my eyes and looked away. After a moment, I felt him take a hold of my hand and sit down in the bed next to me on the other side of where the doctor was sitting. "It's okay, baby…" He whispered, "I'm here… no one's gonna hurt you, I promise."

I didn't open my eyes. I just nodded, then I felt him kiss me on the forehead.

"Jayde?" Jake's voice broke.

I opened my eyes to see he looked like he'd been crying or at least teary because his eyes were red. "Oh, baby, what's the matter?"

He smiled, then crawled into the bed to lie down beside me. "Guess what?" He said, pushing my hair out of my face.

"What? Are you okay?"

He nodded silently, about to talk, but had to wait to let his emotions die back down. "I'm great, baby…" He said, his voice cracking, stopping him again.

"Then what?" I felt so confused.

"You're pregnant!" He said suddenly, his voice catching again, making him clench his teeth to try to stop himself from crying.

"What?" I gasped. "Holy shit…" I couldn't believe it.

"I know!" He reached down to take my hand. "I was so worried. I didn't know what was wrong with you… but then the doctor told me that's all it was, and I lost it… I'm so excited and relieved…" He stopped, then smiled again. "I love you, baby… you're gonna make the best mommy, I know it."

I didn't reply. I just leaned in to kiss him.

"See, all that practice was good for something," he laughed as he leaned back again.

I smiled, then pulled him toward me. "Cuddle with me, baby… mommy needs you."

"Wow, you're both so beautiful… with your matching bellies," Lane smiled.

"I blame you two and your stupid competition," I said, looking at him then over to Jake.

Lane made a face, knowing what I was saying, but hoping I wouldn't mention it again.

"What?" Ellie asked with a smile, like she was just realizing she wasn't aware of something.

"You never told her?" I looked back at Lane like I couldn't believe him.

"Told me what?" Ellie still looked clueless, but not upset.

"Nothing, honey, Kaleah just likes to stir shit up." Lane laughed, I'm sure hoping that'd end it.

"It won't work if they're not both boys, but hey, I did my part, man..." Jake added, intentionally fueling the fire and now trying to get Lane in trouble.

"Oh, come on, man! It was your idea." Lane fired back.

"Bull shit, it was..." Jake said then paused like he wasn't actually sure if that was right or not since he couldn't remember.

"What?" Ellie said again, raising her voice, wanting them to cut it out and just answer her.

"They planned on getting us both pregnant at the same time, hoping we'd both have boys so then they could be brothers like these two knuckle heads!" I said finally, so she'd know.

"Oh," she smiled. "Is that it?"

"Wow, Ellie... You are way too easy... You really should learn how to give Lane more crap than you do." I laughed.

"Hey, now!" Lane interjected. "Don't be telling her that. She's perfect just like she is." He smiled, then leaned down to kiss her belly. "And so are you, mini-me."

I couldn't help but roll my eyes. "I hope we have two girls! That'll teach you both!" I smiled again, then winked at Jake.

"Lie back down, baby. You need to rest." Jake crawled over to where I was sitting on the edge of the bed and rested his hands on my very pregnant belly.

"I can't. I have too much to do." I said, looking down where his head was lowered now. It didn't look like he was listening, though. His eyes were gazing intently at his hands as he used them to gently push against wherever the baby was currently resting his knees, making that area of my belly protrude slightly.

"Does it hurt?" He asked, flattening his hands to rub my belly now as he looked up at me.

"What? Him kicking, or you pushing him back down?" I smiled.

"Any of it?" He asked, lowering his head to rest in my lap so he could put his ear against my belly to listen.

"No, it's just uncomfortable more than anything." I answered him, but again he looked distracted.

"I can hear him…" He whispered, then looked back up at me with a giant smile.

"You're gonna be a great daddy, baby…" I smiled back as I began to rub the side he wasn't leaning against.

He turned his head back toward my belly to kiss it, "I love you, already…" He said, speaking to the baby. "Now be a good boy and don't hurt mommy."

I smiled, then reached down to run my hands through Jake's hair. "I hope he looks and acts like you… The world needs more of you."

Jake pushed against the bed to sit up. "Baby, I'm sure he's gonna be beautiful, just like you." He said, then leaned in to give me a kiss.

"Jayde, baby, breath!" Jake said softly as he rubbed my back.

"I can't do this!" I clinched my teeth, trying to ride the next wave of contractions.

"Yes, you can… you can do anything, honey… If you can kill a man, you can have a baby… remember, take one, give one."

"Please stop…" I moaned, trying to breathe deep again. I knew he was trying to be funny, but I was in too much pain to listen to him.

"I'm sorry… okay, just breath!"

"Jake! Jake!" I screamed before clenching my teeth again.

"It's coming… I see the head."

"One more push, baby… just one more…" Jake's hand rubbed my back harder.

I don't remember if I pushed or anything else. As soon as I heard my baby's cry, I was lost to the world and everything in it. A rush of emotions shot through me, numbing the pain and muffling my senses to everything except that baby.

"It's a boy!"

"Hand him to me!" I said as I leaned back and rested.

"Oh, baby…" Jake came back around to lean in and kiss me. "He's so beautiful!"

"More than Lane and Ellie's boy?"

Jake smiled, with tears now in his eyes, then nodded.

"Here, mama…" The doctor gently rested him against my bare chest.

I looked down at him. He *was* beautiful, just like Jake had said. "He's mine?" I asked softly, like I couldn't believe something so amazing and precious was actually mine.

"Yes, baby! He's all yours!" Jake leaned in to kiss me, then rested his face against mine. "And you're both all mine…"

I didn't want to do anything except lie there and stare at him. "Elis Jacob…" I said softly as I leaned down to kiss his head. "I love you…"

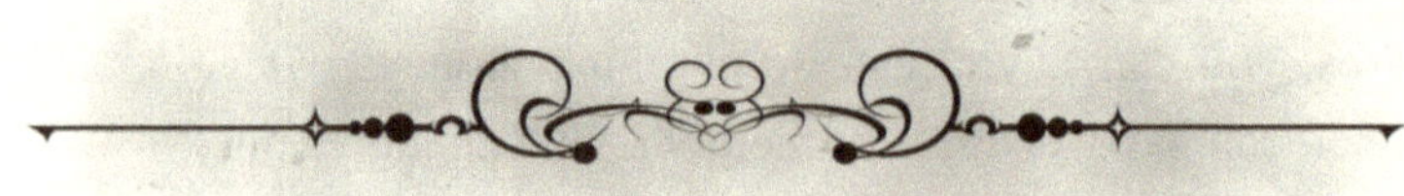

ABOUT THE AUTHOR

SARA NICHOL QUINCY is a website designer and novelist born and raised in Indiana. She's a mother, wife, and entrepreneur. The ERASEHER Series reflects her passion for writing romances that are sexy, twisty and edgy. Add in a little dystopian suspense and a touch of crazy and you have yourself an epic love story that only she can tell.

To read more of her personal story and see what other books are in the works, you can visit her website at:

SaraNicholQuincy.com

There you can subscribe to get new release updates and exclusive offers!

Plus… only subscribers get:
- Launch date perks (1st week sales get 20% off!)
- Cover reveals before launch date!
- Exclusive Bonus Chapters that aren't available anywhere else!
- FREE books! (When available)

- ARC Reader offers for new book series and much more…

Got a question or comment about her work? She'd love to hear from you. Reach her anytime at **Sara@SaraNicholQuincy.Com**

Thank you again for taking your time to read Seizing Shattered Promises. Please consider leaving an honest review. It would help immensely!

facebook.com/saranicholquincy

twitter.com/SaraNQuincy

instagram.com/saranicholquincy

tiktok.com/@saranicholquincy